Gabe cau

He had a clear view to her bra, Felicity realized, glad she'd worn the black one.

She looked up at him, close enough for a kiss. She was vividly aware of his strength, the muscles beneath his brown skin, his intense eyes. He was all man and he had her in his power. He could crush her, snap her bones, but she knew he would never let her come to harm.

Her dress had ridden up on her thigh, but she had no urge to pull it down. She wanted him to see, wanted him to hike it higher.

He was staring at her mouth now. He leaned down and kissed her.

A charge shot through her, waking up every cell. She felt Gabe fighting to be gentle, holding back. He shifted his mouth, sliding his tongue to graze hers, the contact so thrilling she made a needy sound that should have embarrassed her, but didn't.

He groaned, sounding as desperate as she felt. Felicity couldn't believe this was happening to her. This amazing man was as hot for her as she was for him.

Dear Reader,

This is a story about redemption and forgiveness, about seeing beyond differences to the deeper connections between two people falling in love. Gabe Cassidy and Felicity Spencer seem the unlikeliest of couples. He's a half Chicano martial arts coach with a gang-leader father and she's white, wealthy and, worse, the new principal who wants to kick his gym out of her school.

On top of that, they have a painful history. Gabe's brother Robert was Felicity's boyfriend when she was fourteen. Gabe blames Felicity for the arrest that put Robert in jail and later led to his death at age sixteen.

Forced to work together to save her school and his program, Gabe and Felicity peel away the layers of blame, guilt and the differences between them to find their deeper connections and a love more intense than either has experienced.

The story is built around an inner-city school—familiar ground for me as a former teacher in a low-income school. Felicity is the best kind of principal—clear-headed, compassionate, dedicated and savvy as hell. Our schools need thousands more like her.

I hope you are warmed by the emotional journey Felicity and Gabe take to their happy ending. As I wrote, I found myself wishing I could give them both a hug and my best wishes for their future together. I hope you feel the same.

All my best,

Dawn Atkins

P.S. I love to hear from readers! Please contact me through my website at www.dawnatkins.com.

His Brother's Keeper

Dawn Atkins

TORONTO NEW YORK LONDON
AMSTERDAM PARIS SYDNEY HAMBURG
STOCKHOLM ATHENS TOKYO MILAN MADRID
PRAGUE WARSAW BUDAPEST AUCKLAND

Recycling programs
for this product may
not exist in your area.

ISBN-13: 978-0-373-71753-8

HIS BROTHER'S KEEPER

This edition published by arrangement with Harlequin Books S.A.

For questions and comments about the quality of this book please contact us at Customer_eCare@Harlequin.ca.

www.Harlequin.com

Printed in U.S.A.

ABOUT THE AUTHOR

Award-winning author Dawn Atkins has written twenty-five novels for Harlequin Books. Known for her funny, poignant romance stories, she's won a Golden Quill Award and has been a several-times *RT Book Reviews* Reviewers' Choice Award finalist. Dawn lives in Arizona with her husband and son.

Books by Dawn Atkins

HARLEQUIN SUPERROMANCE

1671—A LOT LIKE CHRISTMAS
1683—HOME TO HARMONY
1729—THE BABY CONNECTION

HARLEQUIN BLAZE

253—DON'T TEMPT ME...
294—WITH HIS TOUCH
306—AT HER BECK AND CALL
318—AT HIS FINGERTIPS
348—SWEPT AWAY
391—NO STOPPING NOW
432—HER SEXIEST SURPRISE
456—STILL IRRESISTIBLE

Other titles by this author available in ebook

To Calle 16, the real Phoenix mural project that inspired elements of this story...

¡Muy bien hecho!

Acknowledgments

Total thanks to Detective Tim Lantz from the Gang Enforcement Unit,
who gave me vital background.
Thanks also to juvenile public defender
Mara Siegel, who steered me straight on juvenile justice issues. Any errors are strictly my own.
Eternal gratitude to Carolyn Greene,
Lynn Greener and Laurie Schnebly Campbell,
who pulled me from deep weeds at crucial points in the writing of this book.
Thanks always to my intrepid critique partner,
Amy Dominy.

CHAPTER ONE

"YOU FIGHT IN THE GYM, not the street, Alex," Gabe Cassidy said, easily blocking the fourteen-year-old's jabs. "You know the rules." The kid was so much like Gabe's little brother it almost hurt to look at him.

"Li'l B disrespected Carmen," Alex said, extending his leg in a side kick that Gabe blocked. "I couldn't let that pass." The boy's eyes were on fire and he practically trembled with fury. Just like Robert, he had a lot of anger packed into his small body.

"You let him rile you." Gabe led with his right fist in order to work Alex's weaker left. "Stance," he reminded quietly. "Elbows." Alex forgot the basics when he got upset, so this was good practice for the upcoming meet. "Li'l B figures if you get kicked out of STRIKE, you'll join the gang."

Gabe's fighters stayed in school and out of trouble or they didn't train.

"Carmen's my girl. I had no choice."

"You always have a choice. You want STRIKE shut down? It's bad enough the window out front got broken." He worked Alex into the center of the ring, waiting for him to control his footwork.

"Li'l B's crew threw Carmen's bike at the window."

"What about the tags on the plywood? Any of them yours?"

Alex was an artist—also like Robert. He exercised

his talent too often as graffiti, risking fines and jail time, which worried the hell out of Gabe.

"That's all toys," Alex said. *Toys* were wannabe taggers.

"Tagged-up plywood over a broken window is no way to impress the new principal." Last week, Charlie Hopkins, the principal who had let Gabe set up his gym in the charter school, had been fired over some political B.S. Now STRIKE's fate lay in the hands of his replacement, due any day.

"They won't do that," Alex grumbled, guiltily ducking his face into the padded sparring helmet.

Good. Gabe could use guilt. He used whatever worked to get through to his kids and keep getting through, day by day, as the pressure to drop out, screw up and go gangster mounted in their lives.

"Alex didn't throw a single punch, Coach." Victor had abandoned the bags to defend his friend, though they all knew Gabe would be fair. That was the promise of STRIKE.

He'd named his program after the offensive moves in Muay Thai and because his kids had to hit hard to break the barriers they faced in life. This part of Phoenix was a tough place to grow up if you were poor, brown and male.

"Only because the cops stopped the fight," Gabe said. His buddy on the gang squad had filled him in on the incident. The news hit Gabe hard. The idea of STRIKE was to give his boys the physical and mental confidence to stay clear of street fights, damn it.

He cared about all of his boys, but Alex got to him. The kid was a tough case, but he had so much potential.

"And he got the crew to step off," Victor insisted. A strong fighter, Victor ran nearly a mile from North Central High after his last class so he didn't miss a minute of STRIKE.

"You don't know how Double Deuce rolls," Alex said.

The 22nd Street gang—*El Doble* in Spanish—ran the neighborhood, and Gabe knew more than he wanted to know about how they rolled.

"Whoa, homes, Coach's old man was Ochoa," Victor said, awe in his voice.

Gabe's father, a lieutenant in Phoenix's oldest home-grown gang, the Baseline Kings, had been murdered when Gabe was thirteen, Robert ten, the twins newborns. Gabe hated gangs and always had. He did all he could to erase the lingering respect his boys had for the criminal thugs.

"Back on the bags, boys," his assistant coach hollered at the kids hovering around to hear Alex's fate. "The meet's coming up."

Reluctantly, they obeyed Conrad's order.

"Shadow my moves," Gabe said to Alex, delaying the verdict to sweat him a little more. Shadowing built a sense of rhythm and timing—finesse skills that trumped technique every time and two of Gabe's specialties.

Alex bobbed and shifted, matching Gabe's every move. The kid had focus and fire and heart. He could be a real champion if he could just keep his head on straight. Gabe swore a silent vow. *I will not lose you.*

Not like he'd lost Robert at age sixteen. His brother had been headed to his first Muay Thai bout when he was killed in a gang brawl. Gabe, on his way to watch the match, had found his brother bleeding on the sidewalk and held him as he died. That was fifteen years ago this week, and the old ache and regret shadowed Gabe as relentlessly as Alex now shadowed his fight moves.

Gabe sped up, working Alex until he was about to drop.

"Done," Gabe said, tapping Alex's fists. "Here's your punishment. A hundred words on ways you could have beat Li'l B without using your fists. Also, you're on your own this week. No clinic with me or Conrad."

"No!"

"No?"

Alex blanched. Back talk was not allowed. "Sorry. What about the meet?" He was pushing hard to take a trophy this time around.

"You're lucky you're still here. Train up the newer fighters. You want to coach one day, right? You'll learn, too."

Clearly crestfallen, Alex set off to take his punishment.

With Robert's death so fresh in his head, doubts darkened Gabe's thoughts. Had he gotten through to the kid? Sometimes it seemed hopeless. No one escaped the fight he got dropped into, try as he might. The match was rigged, the outcome set, the winners and losers known in advance.

Dead-end thinking. Useless. He leaned on the padded bar of the ring and surveyed the place. STRIKE was a tough gym, known for training winners, and Gabe was damned proud of it.

He'd equipped it frugally with secondhand gear, donated items and punching bags he'd made himself by filling military duffels with sand.

His pride and joy was the ring—a regulation MMA Octagon he'd inherited from Kurt Cost, the coach he'd found for Robert, who had later trained Gabe.

He even loved how it smelled—of sweat, rubber, dust and a hint of laundry soap left from when the gym had been a Laundromat, since the school was located in a failed strip mall.

Now the music of the place washed over him—the shouts, grunts, thuds and clunks of his fighters building their bodies, beating their weaknesses, boosting their strengths, learning self-control and discipline.

He watched them work, sweat pouring down their bodies, muscles straining past all endurance, pushing themselves and each other with all their might. Each boy had a story. Each boy needed STRIKE.

Every month they scraped together the fifty bucks Gabe charged in addition to the "scholarships" he provided from the cash he'd also inherited from Kurt.

Damn it, STRIKE was worth it. It made a difference. He had to believe that. His boys' lives hung in the balance. If the new principal had a heart in his chest, he'd see that, too.

FELICITY SPENCER'S HEART raced. She hadn't expected a line at the bakery counter and time was tight if she was going to set up her meet-the-new-principal breakfast before the teachers began to arrive. This was her first day and she wanted to greet each person when they entered.

She'd called ahead with her order of *pañuelos*—Mexican sweet rolls topped with flavored sugar—from the market near the school, but there were four people ahead of her and service was slow at Feliz Mercado, which had tables in the bakery area for diners to enjoy their purchases.

She shifted the sack she carried from one arm to the other. She'd spent too much of her paltry savings—*come on, first paycheck!*—on the freshly ground Italian coffee, real cream and three kinds of juices she'd bought. But she wanted to show her staff she valued them even in this subtle way.

First impressions were crucial.

She wiped the trickle of sweat from her temple. Her walk from the light-rail stop had been short, but the early March sun was warm even at 7:00 a.m. She'd selected her apartment because it was only a few stops from Discovery Middle School, since she had no car.

Now the bakery smells reminded her she'd had to skip breakfast, since she hadn't had time to unpack her kitchen boxes. She'd moved into the tiny studio apartment only two days before.

The job offer had come abruptly, contingent on an immediate start, since her predecessor had been fired.

She was excited…and scared. This was her first principalship and it was at a middle school. Her experience as an assistant principal had been at two elementaries. On top of that, Discovery was a charter, also new to her.

She faced challenges, for sure, but she would meet them head-on, as always.

If she could just get to the darn school in time. She glanced at her watch. *Hurry up!*

She caught snatches of conversation from the nearby tables in both English and Spanish. She hoped her high-school Spanish would be enough to communicate with the non-English-speaking students and parents.

"I still can't believe they fired Charlie," someone at a table slightly behind her said. Felicity's ears perked up. The man she'd replaced was Charlie Hopkins.

"The district got tired of him complaining about money," someone else answered.

They were definitely talking about her school. Felicity listened hard.

"What did your friend in personnel say about the new one?"

"Not much. She's cute. A cheerleader who looks all of twelve."

Hey. Felicity was thirty-one, damn it. Sure, she was petite and bubbly with a high voice that might make her seem younger, but she had experience and she'd proved herself over and over. She would prove herself here, too.

"From California, right?" the other woman said.

"Yeah. She was pedaling some New Age self-esteem program as a consultant, but had to get a *real* job."

"Funding has dried up everywhere," the other woman said.

Exactly. Felicity wanted to hug her.

"If I had a dollar for every touchy-feely California pipe dream they foisted on us, I'd buy an island in the Pacific and retire."

"You and me both, April."

April... Felicity recognized the name. An English teacher? Felicity had pored over the school's website and asked the assistant superintendent for as much background as possible so she could hit the ground running. They were partway into the spring semester already.

She wasn't surprised by the cynicism, but Enriched Learning System was research-based and had earned awards. Teachers loved it once they heard the details. She was sure they would love it at Discovery, too.

"Maybe she'll be good. We can always hope," the nice one said.

"How good can she be? They're paying her a first-year teacher's salary."

Felicity cringed, embarrassed this fact was known. The pay was low, but there were few midyear openings anywhere. Plus, this was a chance to test her system with older students in an at-risk school, which would earn her the credibility she needed. Her goal was to score a curriculum-director spot in a large district so she could bring her system to thousands of kids. Eventually she would reopen her business in California and reach thousands more.

The bakery line moved, but Felicity held back to listen.

"It's all part of the plot, Marion. The district wants us to self-destruct, so they can say they tried to reach at-risk kids, but it couldn't be done."

"I don't buy that. The alternative schools are Tom Brown's pet projects." Tom Brown was the man who had hired Felicity.

"He's an idealist. He ignores what he doesn't want to see." This made Felicity's stomach tighten. Tom had promised district resources. Would he come through?

"With regular schools hurting, boutique schools are a luxury we can't afford. That's the hard truth."

"We can't abandon these kids," Marion said.

"They mess up the district's No Child Left Behind scores."

"Screw the scores. What about the kids? These kids washed out of regular schools. The alternative schools are their last chance."

"You're preaching to the choir, Marion."

"If we're on the chopping block like you say, we need a powerhouse principal. Why did Tom hire a lightweight, for God's sake?"

Felicity's cheeks burned.

"Don't you know? Phil Evers is a relative. She's his niece or stepdaughter or something. Tom *had* to hire her."

So. People knew she was related to the superintendent. That was unfair. Jefferson district was so big her uncle had no involvement in personnel decisions. She'd confirmed that with Tom before she'd accepted the job. Besides that, her mother had been estranged from Phil since before Felicity was born.

"I help you?" the round-faced Latina behind the counter asked Felicity.

Not likely. Even if she greeted her staff with a seven-layer flaming tiramisu, they would still think she was an unqualified phony. Turned out her first impression had already been made for her.

She paid for the rolls, then turned, thinking maybe she could clear the air with April and Marion. But they were gone, leaving only lipstick-stained mugs, wadded napkins and *pañuelo* crumbs—pretty much what remained of Felicity's hopes for the day.

She set off down the block, lugging the food, the bag of rolls fragrant and warm against her arms, with just enough time to spare. When she reached the school, she saw one window had been boarded up and was covered with ugly gang tags.

So much for the cheerful breakfast greeting she'd planned. This was what the teachers would see when they got to school. She'd be lucky if they didn't throw her precious *pañuelos* right back in her face.

AT FOUR THAT AFTERNOON, Felicity lifted her head from the budget printout she'd been struggling over and took a deep breath. One thing she liked about her tiny office was how it smelled—like shoe leather and polish, since it used to be a shoe-repair place. She'd loved to help her daddy shine his shoes when she was a child—and he was in a good mood.

The teachers had eaten her rolls and drunk her coffee and made polite chitchat with her. Each time she'd introduced herself she'd wondered if the person knew about her uncle, her puny salary or believed her to be a useless cheerleader. Maybe she'd bring pom-poms to the first staff meeting to show she could take a joke.

After the meet and greet, her first official act as principal had been to insist the landlord replace the window ASAP. Leonard Lancaster had hemmed and hawed over the phone, but finally agreed it would be replaced today.

She'd set up her office as best she could and had begun making her way through the mess Charlie had left. Bills and reports were stashed willy-nilly, and the man didn't seem to have ever used his computer.

Right now, what annoyed her almost more than the snarled budget was the gym that still took up some of the school's much-needed space. Charlie was supposed to have had it cleared out before she got here.

She would have to talk to the coach herself; she needed the room for her After-School Institute, a crucial part of her program. And, since she'd had enough of numbers that didn't add up, she left her office and started down the hall.

The school was arranged in a U around a grassy courtyard with picnic tables where the three hundred students ate trucked-in lunches. With space at a premium, why would Charlie give away a thousand square feet to a boxing gym? And a controversial one at that. There were parent complaints that the coach was a gangbanger, of all things.

No way would Charlie Hopkins permit that. For all his organizational flaws, he'd been an advocate for the school and protective of his students. That was obvious from what she'd read in the few files she'd found. He'd refused to put in a metal detector, saying it was a breach of faith in his kids. She liked that attitude.

He'd probably sacrificed the space for the rent money,

since the school was strapped. The landlord had grumbled over replacing the window, and she'd found a receipt that showed Charlie had bought a small AC unit for the library out of his own pocket.

As she reached the gym door, she heard yells and thuds and punches hitting home in there. So ugly. So violent. She hated violence. *Fight with words, not fists.* That was her mantra with students. The gym had to go.

Inside was pure chaos. She smelled gym stink and, oddly enough, laundry detergent. Two boys flipped giant tires along one wall. Another dragged a boy on a metal cart by chains around his waist. Some older teens beat on crude-looking punching bags made of green canvas. Another wailed on an older man wearing pads on his arms and legs, both of them yelling at the tops of their lungs.

The place looked as beat-up as the punching bags. The beige paint was cracked and peeling. Water stains formed continents and island chains all over the ceiling. Half the fluorescent lights were dead, few had covers. The walls had fist-size holes punched in them. *Punched.*

In a menacing-looking ring rimmed by chain-link, not ropes, a Latino as big as a linebacker fought a short boy in a padded helmet. The man had to be the coach, Gabriel Cassidy.

She walked closer and saw the guy was all muscle. He was dressed like a professional fighter in black nylon shorts and a tank top. His skin, the color of mocha, was shiny with sweat. Add to that black, shaggy hair, a large tattoo on his forearm and a menacing expression on what she could make out of his face, and she could maybe see how parents might be intimidated by him.

No excuse to call the man a gangster, but prejudice was insidious.

She got close enough to see details—the gold cross

around his neck, the twining muscles on his shoulders. And that tattoo. It was an image of a young fighter with his fists up. The face looked so familiar....

It was Robert. Electricity jolted her. Her gaze shot to the man's face. She recognized him, too. "G?" she blurted, totally stunned.

Startled, he let down his guard. The boy landed a punch to his jaw. G didn't react to that, only stared at her in shock. "Cici?"

Robert had started calling her that. *Fe-li-ci-ty is too damn white and too damn long.*

Gabriel Cassidy was Robert's brother? "But your last name is Ochoa..." she said, her mind slowing to sludge.

"I changed it to my mother's," he replied flatly, giving her the same hateful glare he had at Robert's funeral when she'd mumbled her sympathy to his mother and little sisters. Why had he hated her so much?

He still seemed to. Felicity's cheeks burned. The air practically buzzed with tension.

"Coach?" the boy spoke from behind.

"Hit the bag, Victor," G said, keeping his eyes on Felicity. He didn't speak until the boy was gone. "What are you doing here?"

His tone made her want to apologize, even though he was the one who didn't belong. "I'm the new principal."

"The what?" His head shifted back in surprise. "*You're* replacing Charlie?"

She bristled. Yet another person who doubted her. "Yes. Is that a problem for you?"

"No." He seemed to realize how rude he'd been and softened his tone. "Charlie's a friend and he didn't deserve to get fired." He stared at her, clearly sorting a dozen thoughts at once. "Congratulations on the job, I guess."

That was supposed to make her feel better?

"Thank you, I guess." Despite her irritation and shock, she couldn't help comparing the man before her with the one she'd last seen fifteen years ago. His square jaw, straight nose, strong mouth and storm-dark eyes seemed more striking, as if he'd grown into his features. He'd been big before, and confident, but now he was all muscle and totally in charge.

And very, very hot. She couldn't help but notice *that.*

He took his own quick survey of her. Interest flared, then got put out, as if by a bucket of water. "What can I do for you?" He didn't even try to smile.

"For starters, I couldn't find a copy of our lease with you."

"That's because there isn't one. Charlie wasn't using the space so he offered it to me."

"Okay.... Then how much rent do you pay?"

He shifted his weight, foot to foot, now looking uneasy. "Since I train some Discovery students, there's no charge."

"How many from Discovery?" She looked around the gym. Plenty of the twenty-some boys pounding the crap out of each other looked high-school age.

"Maybe ten. The rest come from North Central High."

A short boy with fierce eyes approached them. "Can I fight Brian? I know I can beat him."

"Then you know what you need to know. Fight above yourself, not below. And you're supposed to be coaching." G glanced around, his gaze landing on a boy huddled over a textbook. "Devin! Get your ass over here."

The boy looked up. "But I've got math."

"That's why they call it *home*work. Alex will train takedowns with you."

"Not him again," Alex mumbled.

"What did I tell you? The master—"

"Learns from the pupil. Yeah." He sighed.

Devin approached and G gripped his shoulder. "You lookin' to get tossed in another Dumpster, homes?" The boy shook his head. "Then work on your hapkido escapes with Alex." The two boys walked away.

G had made the boy quit his schoolwork to practice fighting? Unreal.

"So is that it?" G asked her. "Are we done?"

Almost. He had no lease and he paid no rent. All she had to do was tell him to leave. But that seemed too abrupt. "I can see you're busy. When you finish for the day, stop by my office."

"Can't. Sorry. Got another job to get to." His tone was dismissive, as though she was an annoyance, a fly buzzing over his sandwich.

"I won't keep you long," she said. "Stop by." She didn't wait for his response, simply left the gym for her office, but she felt his eyes on her all the way to the door.

It was so strange to see him now. Being back in Phoenix— especially in March—had brought Robert constantly to mind. The robbery had happened on March 4, three days away. And Robert's funeral had fallen on the same date two years later.

She remembered walking toward the church, aware of all the new life—swollen buds on the cacti, tender leaves on the mesquite trees, baby quail like puff balls, scurrying after their parents beneath the sage hedges, and everywhere the perfume of orange blossoms.

Meanwhile, inside the dim, incense-heavy chapel, all was lifeless and still. Even the flowers that surrounded Robert's casket, deceptively bright and vibrant, were dying. To this day, she regretted she'd let G intimidate her so much that she hadn't dared go to the cemetery for a final goodbye.

And now, fifteen years later, here he was again. It all came back. Her hurt and anger at his hatred. Her guilt and remorse over what had happened with Robert.

And something else she hadn't quite grasped until now.

She was still attracted to him.

The stupid truth was that she'd had a crush on G back then. He'd been seventeen to her fourteen, and tough and sexy and serious. Even though all he did was boss Robert around and give Felicity looks of disdain, she liked when he was there. He made her feel safe.

G was strong and smart and responsible. G did the right thing.

He'd helped her once. After a terrible fight with her mother, she'd swiped her mother's keys and driven to Robert's house, even though she'd been behind the wheel only twice and that had been sitting on Robert's lap.

Misjudging a turn, she'd hit a streetlight, denting her mother's Ford car. They were barely getting by. A car repair would have made her mother go ballistic. Already, they fought constantly.

"Are you hurt?"

She'd looked up from the steering wheel to find G leaning in her window. She shook her head, fought to hide her tears. He'd motioned her to the passenger side, then, without a word, drove her to a body shop and had a friend hammer out the dent. He'd even bought her a Slurpee while she waited and pretended he didn't see her crying.

When they got to the house, he'd turned to her. "Don't be stupid, *chica.*" His gaze had been as physical as a punch and it took her breath away. She saw that he wanted her.

They never said a word about it, but whenever their eyes met, he looked at her *that way.* With a jolt, she realized in that smelly gym, he'd done it again. And she was certain she'd looked at him exactly the same way.

CHAPTER TWO

"YOU LOOK LIKE YOU SAW a ghost," Conrad said to Gabe after Cici walked away.

"I guess I did. That was Robert's girlfriend—the one who got him arrested and sent to Adobe Mountain, while she skated free and clear." That had been the first domino in the terrible tumble that ended in Robert's death two years later. "She's the new principal, believe it or not."

"Damn. I hope you were pleasant."

"She caught me up short." He'd been terse, which wouldn't make her more inclined to cut him slack. "Now she wants to talk. About rent, I guess." Which he couldn't afford. With the twins' beauty-school fees to pay, he barely made ends meet driving cab and working landscaping jobs.

"What the hell. You got time for a coffee first?"

"Nah. I've got to drive a shift. Why? You struggling?" Conrad was two years clean and sober, but he sometimes needed company when the urge to drink got bad.

"I meant so you could blow off steam."

"And not step on my dick?"

"Pretty much. You've done the same for me." Conrad had been a professional wrestler until booze broke him. Gabe had hired him, no questions asked, reading his recovery in his determined eyes and proud stance.

"I'll behave. I have to. Close up for me, would you? I'd better allow some time to throw myself on her mercy."

"Only if you swear you'll count to ten before saying anything hard."

He raised his right hand. "I'll do my best."

Later, heading down the hall to see her, he noticed his pulse kick up. She'd been cute as a kid. Now she was beautiful—short and shapely, and sexy as hell. Her voice was still girlish, but it had heft to it—like a creek with a powerful current beneath its deceptively bubbling surface.

She dressed well. No surprise. Expensive and form-fitting, but classy. And it was still there—that vibration in his blood when he looked at her. Less than useless at the moment.

As he neared her office door, he saw she was bent over, dragging a cardboard box into the hall, the tight blue skirt riding high on a fine pair of legs—great muscle definition and a nicely balled calf. Runners' calves were leaner, so maybe dancing. Tennis? Some regular activity that also did great things for her glutes, now that he looked more closely.

Mm-mm-mm.

He realized he was staring like a teenager and jolted forward. "I'll get that." He bent for the box, but she held on, lifting with him, despite the fact the carton had about a hundred pounds of books and she was in heels.

She had color in her face from bending and her hair floated around her head like duck down. Her eyes were that same unusual color—big, bright and blue.

She gave off a familiar sweet smell.

Same as in her car the day she'd dented it. He'd figured the scent came from all the candy jewelry she wore back then. Except today she wore a gold locket and an expensive-looking watch, no candy beads to be seen.

She seemed to realize it was dumb to wrestle with him

and let go of the carton. "If you'd put it on the table in the hall, I'd appreciate it."

"Those, too?" He nodded at the boxes stacked in her doorway.

"Please. I'm going to set up a faculty library." She tucked her shirt into her waistband. It wasn't low-cut or lacy, but it hugged her shape like something a stripper might shimmy out of.

When he finished, she was sitting behind Charlie's battered steel desk, which had been spiffed up. She'd dusted the computer Charlie never touched and replaced his stacks with a neat rack of color-coded folders, a legal pad and pen at the ready, and some goofy desk toys—small magnetized pieces of metal that could be shaped into a sculpture, an acrylic box of blue water over white sand balanced on a pointed pedestal, tiny Tinkertoys, small cans of Play-Doh and a gel-and-glitter-filled wand. A magic wand? Really?

He stood across from her, hands on his hip. "You kept Charlie's poster." He nodded behind her at the shot of Marcus Moreno, MMA star, with the fighter's description of what made a champion.

"I haven't finished redecorating. Have a seat please."

He wanted to say, *Just say your piece,* but knew he had to seem friendly, so he sat, scooted closer to the desk and softened his expression. His sisters said he always looked too fierce.

He touched the water box, setting it rocking. "This is cool."

"Desk toys reduce anxiety, ease tension and boost creative problem-solving abilities."

"And cast spells?" He picked up the pink wand and waved it in the air.

"You're missing the point." She took it from him, her

fingers soft against his for an instant. He felt a small jolt. Her eyes shot to his, wide with surprise. Damn. It was mutual.

"Watch." She tilted the wand between her fingers so the pink beads and bits of glitter and stars slid slowly downward, then up again. It was kind of hypnotic, but he kept getting distracted by the sight of her breasts just past the wand. "See? Soothing, right?"

Depends where you look. He cleared his throat. "Like magic."

She set the wand on her desk and smiled uncertainly, her face now pink. He'd made her nervous, he could tell. "It was a shock to see you."

"Yeah. Me, too." *Let's get to the point so I can get out.*

"How have you been?"

She wanted to chitchat? "Good. You?"

"I've been good. And your mother? How is she?"

Now she cared? She hadn't given a crap while she was getting Robert to steal jewelry for her, keeping him out all night, scaring their mom to death. After Robert's murder, his mother had dissolved into painkillers, becoming a shadow for five long years, her eyes empty even when they were open. She'd gotten clean, but relapsed again. For the past five years, she'd been solid, thank God.

"She's fine," he said flatly.

Cici's smile faltered, but she rattled on. "Gosh, your sisters must be in college by now."

That's it. The twins were none of her business. "Look, let's skip the small talk and get to the point."

She recoiled as though he'd slapped her, her cheeks flaring red. Before he could apologize, she recovered. "The *point,*" she snapped, "is that I need your gym for my after-school program. Without a lease, I could make it effective today, but I'll give you two weeks to find another location and move."

This was worse than he'd expected. Much worse.

"In the meantime, I need to see the liability waivers for each student. Mr. Hopkins doesn't appear to have held on to our copies."

"You're kicking us out?"

"Yes. That is my *point.*" Her blue eyes lit with fire, her chin was up, her jaw firm, no give at all. "I'm sure you can find a more appropriate venue for a fight club than a middle school."

Anger flashed like a series of struck matches along his nerves. There were no *venues* he could afford, appropriate or otherwise. Not nearby, anyway. "What about the Discovery kids I train?"

"They'll join my program. We offer tutors, workshops, guest speakers and other enrichment activities."

"My guys aren't into any of that."

"That's no wonder, considering your attitude."

"What does that mean?"

"Isn't it obvious? You made Devin fight when he had homework to do. This is a school. Studying comes first."

"Are you kidding? Devin *lives* for homework. What he needs is the balls to defend himself from bullies."

"So you teach him to be a bigger one?"

"Bullying is a head game. To beat it, you need better game. Trust me, without STRIKE, Devin Muller's back to getting swirlies in the girls' john."

"These kids experience enough violence in their lives without you teaching them how to do it better."

He gave a half laugh. "What I teach them is self-discipline, self-control and physical confidence. They fight in my gym, not the streets."

She held his gaze. "A good principal's focus has to be on helping students perform better in school."

"A good principal knows kids need different approaches and trusts her staff to do what works for each kid."

"You're not on my staff, G."

"Don't call me that," he snapped. "It's Gabe or Coach Cassidy. No one calls me G." Robert had given Gabe the nickname to make him sound more gangster. Hearing it was like sandpaper on a sunburn. "Look, Charlie was a great principal. He got fired for defending the kids no matter what scores showed up in the newspaper."

"You assume I won't stand up for my students?" Clearly riled, she tapped her desk with a short wooden dowel from the Tinkertoys.

"All I know is that Charlie got done in by politics. You're clearly better connected than he was."

She sucked in a breath. "My uncle had nothing to do with me getting this job."

"Your uncle? Who's your uncle?" Where the hell had that come from?

She blinked, startled. "Phil Evers is my— But that's not the point—"

"Wait. The superintendent is your *uncle?* Oh, I get it. Phil Evers's niece needs a job, so Charlie gets the boot."

"That is not true." Her face went from milk-white to bright red. "Phil wouldn't know me on sight—not that it's any of your business. My program works. That's why I was hired. And I will implement it no matter what obstacles I have to jump, sidestep or knock to the ground." She was completely fired up, ready to fight—body tensed, jaw locked, eyes hot, lips a stubborn line.

Part of him—his caveman soul—enjoyed seeing her

this way, wanted to go chest to chest with her, hip to hip, thigh to thi— Uh, forget that.

He was chagrined to realize that this entire time the undercurrent of sexual attraction had been humming through him like a supercharged V-8 on idle, ready to blast to life, zero to sixty in four seconds flat.

Enough. He lifted his hands in surrender. “I get it. You’ve got something to prove. All I’m saying is that kicking out STRIKE won’t help.”

“It might. Parents have complained that you condone gang activity.”

“That is total bullshit. STRIKE is what keeps half my kids out of gangs. I don’t allow gang colors, signs or talk in my gym. And who complained? Beatrice Milton? The parent-group lady? She’s pissed because she wanted the space for her craft business.”

“It doesn’t matter. I don’t believe boxing is appropriate in a school.”

“I coach Muay Thai, which is a revered martial art, for your information. And you’re flat-out wrong. You don’t know this neighborhood or these kids, what their lives are like, what they need.”

“I’ve studied and worked with at-risk kids for several years. And I used to live near here, too, in case you’ve forgotten.”

“Oh, I remember, all right. You were slumming and when things went bad you beat it out of town in a hurry.”

“My mother got a job in Flagstaff, so we moved.” She was breathing hard, turning a glass paperweight over and over in her hand.

He considered telling her exactly what her spoiled selfishness had done to Robert and his family, but that wouldn’t help his cause. “Look, I’m sure you mean well, but a lot of these kids have messed-up lives. School is not a priority." Gabe softened his tone, fighting to stay calm. "STRIKE changes that. They have to go to school, get good grades and stay out of trouble. They gain physical and mental skills every day. At the very least, they forget for a few hours all the crap they endure trying to survive around here."

He stopped, breathing hard, blood pounding in his skull. He'd raised his voice at the end and was leaning across the desk glaring at her.

She didn't back down, he'd give her that. She had a muscle-bound, tatted-up *cholo* yelling in her face, and she hadn't called the police or even flinched.

"You're obviously very passionate about your gym," she said. "I respect that, but that doesn't change my decision."

He stared at her.

"Find a place that wants you, Gabe. You'll be better off and so will we."

Frustration boiled inside him. His stomach churned, his muscles tightened, ready to fight. *Count to ten before you say something hard.* He was too pissed to count. "Look, I need to get to work now," he said, pushing to his feet. "We'll have to talk later."

"I believe I made my point. Two weeks. Be sure I get those waivers."

Waivers? Charlie never gave him any waivers.

Gabe stalked off, fuming. Damn it all to hell. This was worse than getting let go from the South Mountain recreation-director job. They'd claimed the position suddenly required a college degree, but the real deal was that a scary-looking half-Mexican dude didn't present the right image for the yuppies the city wanted to attract from the pricey houses that had recently been built. He'd seen their point, but that didn't mean he'd liked it.

He'd been low until he got word about Kurt's bequest and Charlie had offered him the space for the gym. That had been the silver lining to losing the job. It was a way to honor Robert. Every kid he trained was Robert to him and that felt worthwhile. Corny as it sounded, that meant more than the ego stroke or cash from the city job.

And now he might lose it all. Talk about a kick in the teeth. And from Cici, of all people. She'd wrecked his brother and now she was going after him. If he weren't so pissed, he might laugh.

What would he do? Try to find another space? Scrape up rent somehow? That would take a while, and what would happen to Alex in the meantime? Or the boys from North Central? Or, hell, Devin?

Nothing good, that was certain. Gang life loomed always, ever ready to sink its claws into his boys, like a lion peeling off the weak from a herd.

He stopped walking and gathered himself together. He never backed down from a fight. He tended to butt his head against the wall until the wall gave or he passed out from blood loss. To win with Cici, he'd have to be smart, think outside the box.

Not easy for him. It was funny. He'd wanted to be a lawyer, work in civil rights, help the underdog, until he'd had to quit school to support his family. He knew now he would have made a lousy lawyer. Lawyers compromised, made deals, sold out, gave in. That was not Gabe's way. Not at all.

What would get through to Felicity Spencer? He had no idea, but he'd better figure it out before he and his boys ended up on the street.

FELICITY STABBED AT A Tinkertoy wheel with a red dowel, her hands still shaking, her breathing coming fast and hard. She was still angry. And hurt, if she were honest with herself.

She dropped her head to her desk. *You let him get to you.* He'd accused her of running away, of *slumming.*

As if she and her mother were living in that run-down, bug-infested apartment *for fun.* As if Felicity couldn't wait to attend that seriously scary middle school. They'd been utterly broke after her father's business failed and her parents' marriage fell apart. That apartment had been all they could afford.

After the case settled, she'd been relieved when a friend offered her mother a bookkeeping job in Flagstaff. Who wouldn't be happier living in a better neighborhood, going to a nicer school? And Felicity had been glad to leave the kids who knew what had happened to her and Robert.

That didn't mean she didn't understand what these kids faced. She knew to her bones what it was like to feel ashamed and afraid and trapped because you were poor. And she knew how to help them. She had piles of research and fieldwork to support her system. Gabe was wrong about her.

She tried to jam the dowel into the spoke opening, but it wouldn't go. What the hell? She threw the pieces across her office.

Settle down. Get control.

Anger was her enemy. Her father was an angry man, and Felicity refused to be like him in any way. She wouldn't define herself by her net worth or wallow in self-pity or lose her temper when things went wrong the way he did.

She made herself take a slow, deep breath and forced a smile, since the gesture automatically reduced tension.

She regretted what she'd blurted about her uncle. Now

Gabe had joined the crowd who thought she'd got the job because of who she knew, not what she'd achieved. So infuriating. So unfair.

Let it go. So what? Her work would prove her worth to the district doubters, to her staff, to the Discovery parents, even to Gabe Cassidy. She always worked hard, strove to be the best. That was the point, wasn't it? To be better every day.

Gabe's accusations stung all the same.

Of course, she realized teens would be more challenging than elementary kids. Peer pressure meant far more to them. On top of that, Discovery Charter was a last-chance school for last-chance kids. So it wouldn't be easy. She knew that. What if she failed? What if Gabe was right?

She swiveled back and forth in her chair and noticed the poster Gabe had commented on. It was of a fighter, for God's sake. That was the last thing she needed in here. She yanked it down and marched it to the tall trash can she'd been filling with Charlie's useless junk.

The quote at the bottom snagged her attention:

Champions are built, not born.

The drive comes from inside, fed by dreams, fueled by desire.

Champions fight harder, longer, faster than all the rest.

They have the moves, yeah, but what counts is the heart.

A champion's heart beats a rhythm only he hears.

El corazón es todo—the heart is all.

That was kind of touching, actually. Without thinking it through, she rolled the poster into a tube and set it in the corner to deal with later.

THE NEXT AFTERNOON, Gabe arrived at the gym an hour later than usual. He'd asked Conrad to start training because he'd had to pick up the engraved marble vase his family would add to Robert's grave when they visited on the anniversary of Robert's funeral in two days.

As he pulled up to the school, he noticed that his fighters were crowded onto the sidewalk, marching and carrying signs. *Picket* signs. What the hell?

He got out of the car, his eyes scanning the slogans, all drawn in Alex's fat-cap graffiti style. Jorge Largo's said Kids Need Gyms. Digger Jones carried Strike Back for STRIKE. Tony Lizardi jiggled On Strike for STRIKE.

The boys were chanting, responding to Victor's shouts from a mic hooked to a boom box. "What do we want?" he yelled.

"STRIKE back!"

"When do we want it?"

"Now!"

"What's going on?" Gabe asked Conrad, who was standing near the curb.

"Dave Scott chased us out for not having some forms. Then he tells us we're getting kicked out for good. What the hell did you say to the principal?"

"We're still talking," he said, angry that the vice principal had gotten involved prematurely. "Damn. He had no business saying that."

Alex noticed Gabe and came over. "We're gonna be on the news, Coach. I called that TV 6 *On Your Side* hotline." He looked so proud Gabe didn't have the heart to tell him that unless this turned into a drive-by or a drug bust, he doubted a reporter would show.

"So what's the story on this?" he asked Alex. Watching his boys march, their voices loud, strides firm, faces determined, he got a tight feeling in his chest. They were standing up for what they believed in. They weren't beaten down. If they could stay that way long enough to make good lives for themselves, Gabe would be happy.

"We have a right to the gym, so I got the idea to protest."

"It's the principal's call. We don't have a lease. But I'm impressed with what you got going here." He noticed Devin fidgeting near the door. "Devin! Get in there with a sign." Damn, that kid needed to nut up.

Victor started a new chant. "Strike back for STRIKE… On strike for STRIKE… Strike back for STRIKE…" The fading afternoon sun glinted off the windows, making the signs flash golden. Cars driving by honked their support, hip-hop blaring from open windows.

Smalls Griggs ran up to the group carrying a case of water bottles and bags of tortilla chips Feliz Mercado had donated to their cause.

The kids broke for snacks until a cop car pulled up. Then they picked up their protest signs and started marching again.

A female officer stepped out, face stern. "Who's in charge here?"

"Gabe Cassidy. I coach these boys. They're protesting the loss of their gym." He figured she was mentally skimming statutes for possible violations, so he jumped in. "This is legal, since they're not disrupting traffic or interfering with commerce. And a permit is not required." This kind of deal was why he'd wanted to become a lawyer—to defend people who got mowed down or tossed aside, work toward fair play and justice.

He'd been naive.

She stared at him, deciding if he was being a smart-ass.

He had to smooth that. "If it helps, I've got the number

to the principal's office." He wondered why Felicity wasn't already out here having a fit.

Seeing that he wasn't challenging her authority, the cop relaxed, took the number and went to her cruiser. When she returned, she told him the principal was on her way from the district office, and asked him to keep a lid on things until she returned from a dispatch call.

"Aren't we getting arrested?" Alex asked him as the cop drove off.

"You're already in the system, Alex. You don't want juvenile hall." Robert's stint there had sunk him. That and Cici abandoning him. That had broken him in two. And what was her excuse? She moved. *They don't write letters in Flagstaff? Use phones?*

"But it's publicity. We need publicity."

"Keep your nose clean. I'm not kidding, Alex."

A few minutes later, a white van with the district logo on the door pulled up and Felicity jumped down from the driver's seat. She headed over, her mouth an angry line. "I got pulled out of a district meeting to take a police call. You organized this?"

"Just got here myself. This is on your guy. Dave told the kids they were being evicted, so they got understandably upset."

"I did not authorize him to do that. I asked him to call the district to find out if the waivers you're having the kids sign would suffice."

"Hell, no, we won't go!" was the current chant.

Tyrell, from North Central, waved his sign: STRIKE a Blow for STRIKE. Beside him Devin waved a piece of notebook paper that said Defend Our Right to Fight. The kid had a way with words, at least.

"This is not good," Felicity said. She was maintaining

her cool, but was clearly flipped out. Maybe he had some leverage here.

"It's about to get worse. The TV 6 investigative team should be here any minute. I believe the police will be back, too."

Felicity's eyes went wide, but she kept her voice calm. "You need to stop this right now."

"I'm not sure I can."

"Come on. You can't control these boys?"

"Maybe I shouldn't. Aren't you impressed with their initiative? This is democracy in action. Don't you teach kids to stand up for their rights? Isn't that a lesson these poor barrio kids need to learn?"

"You think sarcasm helps?"

"Probably not," he said. "Couldn't resist."

Anger made her eyes flash in the fading light. He doubted she'd appreciate him telling her she looked pretty when she was pissed.

She glanced over his shoulder. "Damn it."

He turned to see a TV 6 van turning the corner. "Looks like the media circus is about to raise a tent."

"You're an ass, you know that?"

"No doubt." He fought a grin.

"What do you want, Gabe?"

"What the kids want. The gym back."

She glared at him, then glanced nervously past him.

"Getting closer?"

"All right. You can stay four weeks, but you'll have to split the space with my after-school program, fifty-fifty."

He considered that. They could condense the equipment, he supposed. Clear out a few mats. "Make it eight weeks and then we negotiate."

She glared at him. "This is not over." She went to the

gym entrance. "Attention, please," she said. The boys stopped marching and looked her way.

"I need to speak to your leader."

Silence. They glanced at each other, not sure who to name.

"Okay, who called the TV station?"

"I did," Alex said.

"Then it's you. The rest of you go in and take your signs with you. Alex and I will finalize an agreement on your behalf." She unlocked the door and pushed it open for them. The boys ran into the gym yelling in triumph.

Alex stared at Felicity, a look of mild awe on his face. Good God. He had a crush on her. Gabe hoped to hell the kid wouldn't fold at her first demand.

"Your coach and I agreed that we'll keep the gym open for eight weeks, Alex, but only if you and I can keep the protest out of the news."

"But the TV people are already here."

"That won't matter if you tell them we've worked out our differences."

"But I want to explain about our rights and fighting for them and all."

"If you want your gym back, you need to shut down the story. That's the deal. Take it or leave it."

"Shit." Alex cringed over the swearword. "Sorry."

They all watched as a guy in a golf shirt with the station's logo began unloading a camera from the back of the SUV.

"Do we have a deal?" Felicity held out her hand, looking at him steadily.

"I wanted to be on TV so bad."

"When you're a leader you have to look out for the group's interests, not just your own."

Alex nodded and squared his shoulders, as if taking on a heavy burden. He shook her hand.

"Great. Let's go straighten this out." She looked over her shoulder at Gabe. "After this, we need to talk."

He watched her walk away, her hand on Alex's shoulder. She wore another designer business suit, this one pale yellow, tailored to fit every dip and swell of her figure. She looked fresh for this late in the day. He could watch her hair float around her head for hours. Not to mention her hips, the way they swayed. And those legs, striding fast on swanky heels. For the first time, he saw why women got obsessed with shoes. The ones she had on made her legs look great. *Mm-mm-mm.*

She reminded him of an actress. Who? Cameron Diaz. Yeah, in her early films. No doubt men tried to take care of Felicity, though he'd bet she shut them down right quick. She was soft, but steely. The girl next door with a shotgun under her bed she could strip and clean blindfolded.

He'd bet she got underestimated a lot.

He'd be sure not to.

CHAPTER THREE

AT SIX O'CLOCK, Gabe headed for Felicity's office, hoping to talk her out of however pissy she still was from the afternoon's incident.

The media situation turned out fine. The guy had been sent only to get footage of the protest. With nothing to shoot, he got into his truck and drove off, no problem.

Fired up by the win, his boys had been maniacs in the gym, fighting with total focus, every strike dead center, every kick razor sharp, happily doing all the reps he demanded and then some.

They would wipe the mats with their opponents at the upcoming tournament. Damn, he loved these kids. He would do what he had to do to keep coaching them. Step one was talking this through with Felicity.

He'd changed into a fresh T-shirt—one with sleeves so he'd look more civilized. He ran his fingers through his hair to clear the tangles. He needed a cut, but he was resisting his sisters' offers to practice on him. He had no interest in having his initials shaved into his hair.

Through Felicity's open door, he saw she stood on a table against the back wall trying to push up a window. She'd taken off her jacket and was stretched up on tiptoes, poised and graceful as a dancer. He made himself stop staring and cleared his throat.

She turned at the sound. "The window's jammed."

He climbed onto the table beside her, inches away.

Her face was pink from the heat and there were dots of perspiration on her lips, which still held some gloss. She fanned her face, sending him waves of sweet-candy scent. "It gets stuffy in here."

He braced his shoulder under the frame and shoved. With a wrenching shriek, the wood broke free and shot upward.

"Thank you," she said, giving him a blast of those big blue eyes. Each one had a silver starburst in the middle. They held him in place, made him go so still he could hear his own heartbeat, possibly hers, too.

Now the window let in the smells of spring flowers and freshly mowed grass. Before Robert was killed, Gabe had loved this season. Now the new smells made him feel the old loss. He jumped off the table and offered Felicity a hand down.

She bent her knees to one side for modesty's sake, making him fleetingly curious about her underwear. Would she go sexy, like his ex-girlfriend Adelia, who'd loved elaborate beaded silk numbers?

Simple and sensible were more her style, he'd bet. Maybe a little lace as a tease. He preferred sheer and easy to rip off. Or naked. Naked was the best underwear of all.

"Gabe?" Felicity looked at him strangely.

"Yeah?" He let go of her hand, which he'd held too long, and backed up so she could get to her desk.

FELICITY'S PALM RETAINED the warmth of Gabe's grip even after he let go. He'd definitely been thinking about her *that way.* She'd felt a surge of unwelcome lust. There was no accounting for chemistry, she guessed.

On the other hand, Gabe was dead-on hot. Sexual confidence poured off him like body heat. With his dramatic features, long, tousled hair and that diamond stud in one ear, all he needed was a ruffled shirt to pass for a pirate.

Pirates were so sexy—dangerous and fierce, but also charming. When he smiled—and admittedly she'd only seen him do it when he'd thought he'd gotten the best of her at the protest—his features softened and his eyes lightened from espresso to dark caramel.

He was the classic bad boy. So not her thing. Though she wasn't sure she *had* a thing. She didn't seem to have much, well, passion, when it came to men. Or at least the men she'd dated so far.

Right now she had no time for a friction-means-fire moment. She had a major problem and she needed Gabe's cooperation to solve it.

The humiliation of the police call in the middle of the district meeting was not the worst news she'd had that afternoon. Not even close.

Tom Brown had pulled her aside to tell her that due to a budget shortfall, the bulk of the funds he'd promised for her Enriched Learning System had been "redirected" to more crucial district needs.

In short, she'd been screwed.

She'd begun to suspect April might be right about the conspiracy against Discovery. During the meeting Felicity had picked up hostility toward the alternative schools and caught definite eye rolls during her report. Some important people expected her to fail—maybe even *wanted* her to.

Now she was frustrated and outraged and scared. She'd known she had an uphill battle. But she hadn't expected to have someone dynamite the ground out from under her.

She'd held a faculty meeting as soon as school was dismissed that first day to lay out the tenets of her program. She'd watched their faces go from resistant to curious to wary to almost hopeful. When she'd told them Tom had promised district funds to implement it, their faces had plain lit up.

But that turned out to be a lie. When her staff found out, they would think her a blowhard, a liar, a fool or all three. Felicity would seem weak, maybe even her uncle's flunky, part of the plot to sink the school.

She had to turn this around. She saw a way through Gabe. All she had to do was get him to agree.

"So, are we good?" Gabe asked, bracing his hip against her desk, arms folded. He was acting casual, but he homed in, assessing her for weak spots, like an opponent in his boxing ring. "We ducked the news like you wanted."

She decided to emphasize her losses, make him feel guilty. "But not the police. Now my bosses think I had to quell a riot."

"The kids didn't call the cops."

"No. They just created the disturbance that drew them."

"Anyway, you handled that well. You took the boys seriously. You talked to Alex with respect. That was good for them."

"You think so? And what was the lesson? That blackmail works? Threaten media exposure and the principal will fold?" She felt angry all over again. "We both know what happened. You played me and hijacked half my Institute space for eight entire weeks."

"True." He had the decency to look sheepish.

"That said, I need to clarify some things." She'd start with the easy part. "First, I arranged with the district to use group liability coverage until you get the forms from each kid. But we do need the forms."

"Great. I appreciate that. You'll get them." He seemed startled by her concession.

"Also, I'll need my half of the room cleared out by next Wednesday, when I want to start the Institute."

"We can give you some space, but—"

"Fifty-fifty. We agreed. Also, you'll need to keep the noise down so we'll be able to hold discussions and run workshops."

"We're training. We hit bags and toss tires. It's loud." He frowned, shifting his weight, not happy about what she was saying.

"Make an effort."

He just looked at her. "Is that it?"

"There's one more thing." She took a deep breath before delivering the blow. "I'm going to need you to pay rent."

"Rent? What the hell?" He pushed to his feet, as if braced for battle.

"Don't loom over me, please. Sit down so we can discuss this."

He stalked around the desk and dropped into the chair. "Rent was not part of the deal."

"It is now. I lost my funding. Your rent will help cover it." It would get her through the end of the year, she hoped, if she was brutally frugal. After that, she had no idea what she'd do. Hope for a budget boost? A grant? A charity? A miracle?

"How much?" he said through gritted teeth.

"We can be reasonable. Five dollars a square foot is well below current rates. With you using five hundred square feet, that's $2,500 a month."

"You're crazy."

"You charge fees, don't you?"

"The kids pay fifty a month when they can. The full

rate is one hundred and fifty. I cover the rest as scholarships." He glared at her. "You're reneging on our deal."

She held his gaze. "You extorted that deal from me and you know it. Circumstances changed, so the deal has to change."

"I can't pay rent." He paused, staring at her. "But then, you knew that, didn't you?" Fury roiled in his eyes, like dark water in a storm. "You want us out. I get it."

"You can stay if you pay."

"You always get what you want, don't you? No matter what it takes or who it hurts. Well played, Cici."

"What does that mean?" But she knew. He meant Robert—that she'd used him, left him in jail and run for the hills. Her face burned. She'd been a scared, angry kid. She'd gone along with Robert, not dragged him into trouble. And when her mother got a job, she'd had to leave. And her mother—

She stopped her awful thoughts. "No matter what you think about me, Gabe, I'm doing what's best for the kids."

"Save your speeches for the PTO or the press or whatever politician you need to snow."

She could tell he wanted to let her have it, tell her exactly what he thought of her, then and now. His fists were clenched, his jaw was working and his breathing was ragged. But he only said, "You win. We'll be gone as soon as I find a place." He turned and left.

She stood, as if to call him back, but her throat was tight and she was breathing as though she'd run ten miles. Where did he get off acting so self-righteous? She'd made a reasonable offer. He was supposed to bargain with her, not give in and stalk out.

She sank into her chair, irate and hurt. He'd insulted her integrity and accused her of exploiting Robert in one vicious sentence. He was an angry man with a chip on his shoulder so broad you could balance a tray of drinks on it.

A drink was what she wanted right now, but that would be a mistake. She always stayed in control. That was the only way to get by. That and being flexible. She knew how to roll with the punches, adapt and move on.

Not Gabe. For Gabe, life was black or white, yes or no—make that yes or *hell* no. Gabe was a brick wall. Under pressure, he would crack and fall, while she bent and shifted and found another way. He was so wrong.

So wrong.

She had loved Robert. What happened had devastated her. She'd locked down emotionally after that, gone numb. She hadn't had a single boyfriend in high school. Only a few dates in college, for that matter. Truth be told, she still missed him. He showed up in dreams. She remembered him on his birthday, on the date they first kissed and on the day he died. Tomorrow, it would be fifteen years since he was buried.

She tipped the wave box, wanting the gentle waves to soothe her, but she was trembling, so the waves were as jerky and jagged as her nerves.

Underlying everything was her blasted attraction for Gabe. Anger and lust both fired the blood, she supposed.

When he stared at her, untapped feelings stirred and flared. He made her think about sex. He made her *long* for sex.

How would he be in bed? Rough and demanding? Tender and generous? Both, depending on what she needed? And he would know because he would read her like a book and—

Oh, for heaven's sake. Still shaking and upset, she opened the Play-Doh and began to knead and roll the bright green clay to calm down, to help her think, to do some creative problem solving.

No way did Gabe want to move, but he'd be too proud to come back. She'd have to make the first move—ask for less money, though the less she got, the less she could offer her students.

She looked at her hand and realized she'd squeezed so hard, the dough had squirted from between her fingers like the spikes of some martial-arts weapon. Not good. She needed to make peace, not war.

GABE STEPPED OUT OF HIS VAN in front of Discovery at noon the next day, muscle-sore from the landscaping job he'd left early to try to work out a deal with Felicity. His friend Carl was happy to hire him whenever Gabe could do it. He'd need more work to pay the rent she was extorting from him. He clenched his jaw.

Settle down. Be nice. This was for his boys.

He regretted bringing up the way she'd used Robert, but the rent she'd asked was insane and she'd known it. Clearly, she wanted him out.

But he needed to stay. Even on the west side, he'd have to pay at least a grand a month, and he'd lose half his kids for lack of transportation.

He could manage a thousand, he figured, if he scrimped, bought no equipment, worked more for Carl and took double shifts with the cab he shared. He hoped to hell he wouldn't have to tap into the scholarship cash.

Outrage surged in a hot wave. So she'd lost funds for her stupid homework club. That didn't justify breaking the deal she'd made with his boys. This was extortion, pure and simple.

Kind of like blackmailing her with a media threat for more time?

He shrugged, uneasy about his own behavior.

On the way over, he'd grabbed award-winning gyros from Giorgio's Grotto, the Greek restaurant owned by his mother's new husband, as a peace offering.

A shared meal cured a lot of ills. He liked cooking for people he loved. He wasn't much for hugs or flattery, but a loaf of herb bread hot from the oven, served with basil butter and gazpacho from farmer's market heirloom tomatoes said plenty about what was in his heart.

Part of his trouble with Cici was he kept mixing up anger at her with wanting to get her naked. He didn't understand her, didn't even like her, but she spiked his wiring somehow, blowing all the circuits with a look, a move, a twitch of her glossy lips.

He'd felt like this way back, when he'd watched her thump into the pole outside his house. She was so short that at first he thought the car was driverless. When he ran to see if she'd been hurt, she turned away to scrub off her tears, then acted tough as nails. He could see she was terrified to tell her mother. He had the idea her home life was grim, even if she was a Scottsdale snot.

Raul owed him a favor, so he'd fixed the bumper for free. When Gabe had brought her that drink, she'd looked at him with so much amazed gratitude, you'd have thought he'd found her long lost kitten.

A feeling had surged in him then—the urge to take care of her, be with her, figure out her quirky workings.

They never talked about it, but the vibe was always there, a constant low hum. And her candy smell hanging in Robert's room liked to kill him at times.

Her office door was half-open, so he tapped on it, then went in.

She looked up from a yellow pad, her eyes crackling,

her mouth tight, her movements jerky with anger. Not at him, though. Couldn't be.

Something more recent, he figured, noticing that she'd smashed the magnetic sculpture flat and set the wave box rocking wildly.

He picked up some Tinkertoy pieces on the floor. Had she tossed them there? Damn. He hoped to hell Giorgio's gyros had the power to soothe a savage principal.

The smile she managed looked almost painful.

He stopped the thrashing wave box with one finger and put the Tinkertoys on her desk. "Bad day?" he asked gently, braced for her to throw something at him.

"You could say that," she said through gritted teeth.

"Lunch should help." He set the sack on her desk. She simply looked at him. "From Giorgio's Grotto," he added, to get the conversation going.

Crickets.

"Best gyros in town."

Still nothing.

"And I'm not just saying that because my mom married Giorgio."

This time she broke. "She did? That's…great."

FELICITY TRIED TO SMILE past her pain. Gabe had returned, which meant he wanted to negotiate. He'd brought food and was offering personal news, clearly trying to be friendly.

"Yeah. He's a good guy. He makes her happy."

Thank goodness. Robert's mother was okay. That relieved her, especially after Gabe had bristled the first day at the mere mention of his family.

"So…you hungry?" he asked.

"Not really. Bad day and all."

"Want to talk about it?"

He *was* trying hard, inviting her to vent. "It's complicated." The less he knew about her troubles, the better her negotiating position.

The incident that had churned her stomach and made her wreak havoc with her desk toys was hearing from her teachers the rumor that she was about to be fired.

Word about the lost funds had beaten her to school, too.

Her teachers' reactions had troubled her. There was no outrage, no anger. Just shrugs and resignation. *Typical. That's how they treat us.*

They didn't think less of her for it, but only because they hadn't thought much of her in the first place. That stung. And she was determined to come through for them. That meant making a deal with Gabe.

"I've got time," he said, but she knew better.

"You've got work. Please eat while we talk."

"You keep it for when your day gets better."

"Thanks. My cupboard's pretty bare. New apartment."

"Sure. Takes a while to settle in." They were outdoing each other being nice. It was getting sickening.

He seemed to realize that, too, and his expression went intent. "Look, I was out of line yesterday…what I said at the end."

"We were both upset."

He nodded. "The most I can pay is a thousand."

Thank God. He would pay. Hope surged. "Fifteen hundred," she shot back, keeping her face neutral.

"No way." His eyes flared, but only slightly, so she knew he was still in the game. "Twelve hundred. And that's final." His tone and locked jaw confirmed his words. He couldn't pay more.

"Deal," she said. "We'll prorate this month to $600. Pay me on Monday."

"I'll need to shift some funds." He frowned.

"Then make it Wednesday." A concession would make him feel better about the deal. "Thank you. This means a lot to us." She could pay stipends to an assistant and an aide and use the rest for food and supplies.

"You had me over a barrel."

"Only because I was over one myself."

They stared at each other, settling down from the bargaining, weighing the balance between resentment and acceptance and how they would relate to each other from here.

"If you need help clearing the space, Dave Scott can assist you."

"Dave?" He half laughed. "I'll pass. He'll want to give me coaching tips."

"You, too? If he pats me on the shoulder once more and says, 'You're new, you'll learn,' I can't be held responsible for my actions." She was certain Dave had started the rumor that she was going to be fired.

Gabe laughed. "That's where kickboxing is handy. One shot to the family jewels and he'll be at your command."

She burst out laughing, then covered her mouth. "That wasn't very professional. Pretend I didn't laugh."

"Your secret's safe." He smiled and she got that rush of attraction again, saw him reacting to her, too.

"Anyway, Dave speaks well of you. He says you keep his, quote, 'biggest pains-in-the-ass out of my hair,' end quote." Another teacher had praised STRIKE's effect on one of her students. *Plus, the coach is sooo hot,* she'd said. *When he comes into the lounge, I swear I drool on myself.*

"Makes sense he'd like that. The fewer kids he has in detention, the more time he has to plant real-estate signs."

She winced. "I need to talk to him about that. Teachers complain that he disappears from campus to work his side job. Not helpful, especially since I need him on board to fully implement my system."

"Tell him what I tell my boys—work hard or get out."

"I wish it were that simple. I need him on my side. Otherwise, he can foment turmoil and start rumors, make my job much harder. So I have to show him respect while convincing him to do his job. There are nuances."

"Nuances? Jesus. I could never do your job. I wouldn't know a nuance if it kicked me in the crotch."

Her gaze dipped unconsciously to that part of his body, then up to his face. He'd seen what she'd done and heat flashed in his eyes.

She flushed, fighting off her own response.

Gabe cleared his throat. "So...nuances. How you dealt with Alex and the protest had nuance, for sure. It didn't hurt that he's got a crush on you."

"I noticed that."

"Now he wants to know if you need to meet with him again."

"You mean as leader of the rebels?" She smiled. "I could thank him for his cooperation, I guess."

"That'd be good. You can reinforce what it takes to be a leader. The kid's on the razor's edge of trouble. He's got a lot of anger. A friend just jumped into the Double Deuce and he wants Alex to join."

"That's not good."

"Plus, he's been tagging with a crew of toys."

"Toys?"

"Kiddie graf writers. The city's cracking down on graffiti crimes—major fines and jail time. Juvenile hall will wreck him." Gabe's gaze went distant and stormy.

Like with Robert. She was sure that's what he was thinking, with the anniversary of Robert's funeral a day away. Robert and Alex were alike, now that she thought about it—both angry, both artistic, both small. Robert's nickname had been Chapo—*shortie* in Spanish.

Gabe's gaze returned to her. "His mother's useless. His current stepfather beats him. Thanks to STRIKE, he holds his own with his big brother, but now the asshole wants Alex to help him steal cars."

"That's terrible."

"Not unusual around here. So use his crush, throw in some *nuances,* and maybe you can help him stay straight."

"I'll do that." She paused. "You care about him."

"I care about all my guys."

"I get that, Gabe. I do." She caught his gaze and held it. "And I care about my students—not just their test scores."

"Point taken." A connection snapped into place between them—crisp as two pieces of a puzzle. They understood each other better.

"I need to get back to the job. Reheat the gyros in the oven, not the microwave. The pita absorbs more juices that way. Enjoy."

"I will. Thank you. I'm glad we could work this out."

"Me, too," he said. Then he was gone.

She'd gotten what she was after—rent money for her program—even though she had to sacrifice some space. But like every encounter with Gabe, there was more to it than getting the cash. Kicking STRIKE out would have felt wrong. Because of their past? Because his fighters loved STRIKE and he loved them? It didn't matter. Not really. For better or worse, STRIKE was in. She would just have to make the best of it.

CHAPTER FOUR

EARLY THE NEXT EVENING, Gabe parked in the lot behind Giorgio's Grotto for the family dinner before the cemetery visit. He wasn't sure these events were good for his mother. They always made her melancholy. She'd been clean for five years, but Gabe stayed vigilant against a relapse.

Tonight should be more lighthearted, since she and Giorgio were fresh from their honeymoon. Thank God for Giorgio, who'd coaxed her into his life with his good cheer and great food.

Gabe paused to kiss his fingertips, then touched the tattoo of Robert on his arm. "Always in my heart, *hermano,*" he whispered. *"Siempre."*

Inside the restaurant, he breathed in the great smells—garlic, lemon, mint and seasoned lamb. The place won Best Greek Food in every review there was, and it was as homey and welcoming as Giorgio himself. The walls were painted bright blue and sparkling white, the lights glowing golden.

"How is my new stepson?" Giorgio stepped out of the kitchen to give Gabe a hug. The man walked in a bubble of optimism, despite the fact he'd lost his first wife to cancer five years ago. "Myself, I'm a happily married man."

"I'm good. How's Mom?"

"As well as you'd expect today. I respect the sadness

of your family, so no jokes tonight." He made his mouth a straight line.

"Please...we need to laugh tonight most of all."

Giorgio led him toward the private dining room, then put a hand on his arm. "I have to warn you. The girls styled Mary's hair. It's very...modern."

"Okay," he said. When he saw his mother, he was glad he'd gotten a heads-up. Her hair had stripes of purple, orange and black and had been smoothed in waves against her head. "Wow" was all he could manage to say.

"Didn't the girls do...great?" his mother said uncertainly.

"It's...stylish." It looked like a Halloween fright wig. For God's sake, did his sisters have no sense?

"She said we could practice what we needed to practice, okay?" Trina said defensively. "It's temporary color, so pick up your jaw." Trina's hair was in cornrows so tight they had to hurt.

"I didn't say a word."

"But the waves are perfect, right?" Shanna said. "I did those." Her own hair was a cloud of kink reaching to her shoulders. He hoped to hell they were getting good grades. They were certainly *practicing* enough.

"We need to work on you, Gabe," Trina said. "Hardly any guys come into the beauty school for cuts and we need men for our portfolio."

"I'm cool, thank you."

"Come on. One haircut? You've got great thick hair. And so shaggy. You're making me salivate."

"Please, no drool at the table."

"If you get to cut, then I get to color," Shanna said. "You would totally rock blond highlights, Gabe."

"I like my hair like I like my coffee—straight and black."

"You'd look hot."

"I don't need to look hot."

"Yes, you do," Shanna said. "You need to start dating. It's been a year."

"I'm fine." He had dated, though his sisters didn't know. Right after the breakup with Adelia he'd hooked up with women who wanted no more than one-night stands. Before long, the sex had begun to seem pointless. He'd gone without for a while now.

"Wait! That reminds me," Trina said. "Adelia! I saw her at the DMV. She misses you, asked me all about you. She's doing a mural on 20th Street and Indian School. You should stop by and see her."

"I might." Though the breakup had nearly killed him, they were on friendly terms now. He'd thought she was the one, his soul mate. They had the same background, the same world view, wanted the same things in life.

"And she told me that guy was a total mistake."

She'd begun to make a name for herself as a Latina artist and muralist when she cheated on Gabe with a guy who'd bought one of her pieces.

"Could we drop this, please?" Adelia had claimed she'd strayed because Gabe was too closed off to truly *be* hers. Bullshit, he'd thought…at first.

Over time, he'd realized she might have a point. He'd given all he had, but maybe that wasn't enough. Maybe it would never be enough. Maybe he didn't deserve a soul mate. His head hurt thinking about it, so he'd stopped.

"Pretty please," Shanna whined, returning to the subject of his hair.

"Still no." He adored his sisters. He'd taken care of them during the years his mother was out of it. They'd been cooperative and uncomplaining right up until puberty, when they'd been hell on wheels for a while—belligerent, rebellious, secretive.

They'd hated high school, but hung in to graduate. They loved beauty school and wanted to open their own shop one day. He'd love to have enough cash to set them up.

"We'll do any favor you ask," Trina said. "Washing? Ironing?"

"I like to iron." Turning a crumpled wad of fabric into a crisply smooth shirt was stupidly satisfying to him.

"You're so domestic," Shanna said. "You cook, you iron, you keep your house pretty clean. You'll make some girl a great wife."

"Shanna, don't insult your brother," his mother said.

"No worries, Ma. My manhood is secure."

"Ew. Don't talk about your manhood at the dinner table," Trina said.

Meanwhile, Giorgio and a waiter brought out the food: delicate lamb chops—Gabe's favorite—melt-in-your-mouth moussaka, flaky spanikopita and minty dolmas, along with a big Greek salad. Another waiter poured sparkling grape juice for all, since they avoided alcohol around their mother. Giorgio lifted his glass in a toast. "Here's to our beautiful family. Those who are here and those we remember."

They all murmured agreement.

"I miss Robert every day," his mother said softly.

"He used to draw cartoons of us." Trina sighed.

"He was so talented and so smart," his mother said.

"You didn't think so when he got drunk and stole your car," Gabe said to lighten the mood.

"He *borrowed* the car. And that was because of that girl. That Cici."

Gabe groaned inwardly. Cici again.

"She was wild, that one. Always looking for trouble, out all night. Where was her mother? She showed up with the lawyer right quick. Got her daughter off, left Robert to rot behind bars."

Gabe felt a rush of shame. That very afternoon, he'd been casually flirting with Cici, ignoring what she'd done to his family. He looked around the table. What would they say if they knew?

"Tell us about your trip," he said to change the subject. "How was Greece?"

"It was gorgeous, was it not, my love?" Giorgio asked his wife, who blushed. Giorgio and Mary took turns describing their accommodations, the visits to Giorgio's family, the clear blue water of the islands, the boat they'd sailed on, the meals they'd enjoyed.

Gabe let the conversation wash over him, grateful to Giorgio, who was solid, full of love and patient as time. Plus, he was magic with a lamb chop. Gabe ate the last bite, then leaned back in his chair.

Before Giorgio, Gabe would cook supper for his mother and the girls a couple nights a week. He missed that, he realized. His birthday wasn't far away. He always cooked a family meal then. Afterward, he'd start a new tradition, maybe dinner at his house once a month.

After supper, they climbed into Gabe's van to go to the cemetery, each carrying a memento for the grave. The vase Gabe had had engraved rested beside him. They were quiet on the drive. The sky was gold and pink with sunset, but there were dark clouds and the air smelled of ozone. Rain was on the way. Unusual for March.

The cemetery was old and small, tucked into the barrio, colorful with flowers, trinkets and painted saints. There was one other car and a cab parked on the narrow lane, and he spotted a family standing around a grave.

The first few years, Robert's friends came to the cemetery to honor him. At the funeral, Robert's friend Mad Dog, new in the Doble, had muttered about revenge, a piece shoved into his waistband. Gabe had gotten in his face, made him swear not to retaliate. He'd obeyed out of respect for the Ochoa name, but he'd held a stone-cold hatred for Gabe ever since.

Now he ran the Doble.

Gabe put the desert poppies his mother had brought into the stone vase and watered them at a standing faucet. Mary studied the fresh copy of Robert's school photo she'd brought to replace the sun-faded one in the silver frame. "He would be thirty-one. What a fine man he would have been."

"But see what a fine man you still have." Giorgio nodded at Gabe.

"You have always been my rock," she said to Gabe. "If only Robert had had your strength and good sense. You looked out for him."

But not enough. Not nearly enough. He swallowed the lump in his throat and looked out over the grass. The acres of graves always hit him hard. All these people dead and gone. What had their lives meant? What had Robert's meant? His own?

When Gabe gave his boys a place to sleep, a number to call, a loan, a job reference, he hoped he was making up in small ways for failing Robert. Was there more he should do?

Sensing his distress, Trina reached up to run her fingers through his hair. "Look at this mess. Can't you hear your split ends crying? 'Help us. End our suffering.'"

"Cut it out," he said, smiling at her effort to cheer him. His sisters had been his joy during those hard years. They still made him grin.

They started toward the stand of mesquite trees that hid Robert's grave, Gabe leading the way, the marble vase cool and heavy in his hands, followed by the twins. Giorgio held Mary close and they walked more slowly.

Gabe made the turn around the trees, startled to see that a woman knelt at Robert's grave. She'd laid flowers down. They were rust-colored snapdragons—the same flowers Robert used to bring to their mother.

Hearing them approach, the woman turned. It was Cici. He should have recognized the flyaway hair. "What the hell are you doing here?" he said, burning with fury.

"Gabriel!" his mother said from behind him, thinking him rude.

"It's Cici, Mom." He kept his eyes on the interloper.

His mother gasped.

"You need to leave," Gabe said. How dare she invade their private tragedy?

"I came…to…g-give respect," Felicity stuttered.

"Respect?" Gabe's mother said. "You left him to suffer in jail. Where was your respect then?" She advanced toward Cici.

Gabe caught her arm. "Easy, Mom."

"You dare to come here? Boo-hoo-hoo. Poor me. My boyfriend was killed."

"Leave. Now," Gabe said again, but Felicity seemed frozen in place, her face dead-white, her eyes wide and wet.

"When I visited him in jail, he only asked for you," his mother went on. "'Where is she, Mom? Have you seen her, Mom? Has she called?'"

"We…moved… I couldn't… I was… It was…" She was struggling to speak.

"He was just a toy to you. A toy you threw away. He was never the same because of you. Always with gangbangers after that. And mean. Bitter. That was the end of him and you caused it!"

Gabe's mother dropped to her knees in the grass, sobbing. Giorgio kneeled and put his arm across her shoulders.

"Don't cry, Mom," Trina said, crouching down. She clutched a purple teddy bear Robert had won for them at the fair. "Please don't cry."

"I'm so sorry," Felicity said. "I didn't mean to hurt anyone. I just..." She gave him a helpless look. What? She thought he would tell her what to say?

He couldn't bear to see his mother crumpled on the ground, the way she'd been those first few months. Felicity had brought it all back, damn her.

Furious, he scooped up the flowers and thrust them at her. "Just go. You've done enough damage."

"I'm sorry for the pain I caused," she said, a few flowers slipping from her trembling hands. "And I'm sorry for your loss." She gave him a look so anguished he felt an unwelcome stab of regret, then she stumbled across the grass, trailing snapdragons as she went. The waiting cab carried her away.

Gabe dropped beside his mother. "She's gone now."

She lifted her tear-streaked face. "Why did she come here? What is she doing in Phoenix?"

"It's the anniversary, Mom." He wasn't about to mention that she had a job at Discovery, that he was working with her. "But forget about her. We're here to honor Robert."

Giorgio put the vase of flowers on one side of the headstone. "Perfect." he said. "Look, Mary, at how perfect."

"I'll put the picture in." Shanna took Robert's photo from their mother's hands and put it in the frame, while Trina placed the teddy bear.

"Take a look, Mom," Gabe said, but she was too lost in grief to do more than glance at the mementos. Rain flicked Gabe's cheek and the breeze picked up. "The rain's coming. We should go."

"I never wanted to see her again," his mother said.

"You won't have to," Giorgio said, helping her to her feet.

Gabe, on the other hand, would see her the next day. What the hell would he say to her?

GABE FOUND FELICITY'S NOTE when he got to the gym the next afternoon:

> Words cannot express how sorry I am that I upset you and your family. I doubt anything I say will ease your anger toward me, but I hope we can maintain a civil, professional relationship here at school.
> Sincerely,
> Felicity Spencer

He was glad he didn't have to talk to her. He couldn't stop seeing his mother sobbing on her knees, like all those terrible weeks when Gabe had been helpless to soothe her bottomless grief.

It was nine at night now and he was driving cab in the pouring rain. No picnic, considering how Arizona drivers behaved. Used to dry roads and sunny skies, they acted as if the apocalypse was upon them—tailgating, speeding, weaving lanes or testing their brakes with quick slams.

Fridays were usually big cab nights, but not when it rained, so Gabe was about to call it quits when dispatch called in a pickup at IKEA. He was nearby, so he took it, wipers clacking in time to the Latin hip-hop he had on his iPod.

He shared the lease on the late-model Rav4 with his friend Mickey Donaldson, but he was the one who kept it polished, peaceful and sweet-smelling. He liked things squared away.

He liked the rain, too, despite the annoyance, because of how clean and crisp the world looked afterward and how great the desert smelled.

The rain made the blue-and-yellow IKEA colors glow brilliantly against the cloud-darkened sky. He pulled to the curb. The entrance was so crowded with carts and people loading goods into vehicles that he didn't immediately notice the woman who approached his passenger window.

He lowered it and saw Felicity.

"Gabe? Oh." She jerked away, as if the door was electrified. She had several plastic Target sacks in both hands and a loaded IKEA cart behind her. "I had no idea. I'll get another cab."

"Not in this weather, you won't," he said, climbing out. He couldn't leave her stranded. Together they loaded her stuff into the cargo area—boxes of unassembled furniture, bags of pillows and kitchen goods. The Target bags were mostly groceries.

In the cab, Felicity pushed her wet hair from her face. "Thanks. I bought too much to carry home on the bus. I got my security-deposit check from my old apartment, so I went crazy. My place looks too much like a Motel 6 room." She shot him a glance, then stared straight out. "I thought you had a job doing landscaping."

"I do. Whatever puts groceries on the table. No car?"

"Saving up for one."

She was broke? Living in a rinky-dink place? That surprised him, considering how well she dressed. Her family had money.

"So where to?"

She gave him an address not far from the school. After that, a heavy silence descended, broken only by his music and the rhythmic thump of the wipers. Stupid, with such a long drive ahead of them, so he said, "I got your note," in a neutral voice.

She didn't respond. After a few seconds, he glanced at her and was startled to see tears running down her cheeks. He jerked his gaze forward, not wanting to embarrass her.

When she spoke, her voice quavered. "I would never have… If I'd known… I really regret that I—" She stopped and he could tell she didn't want him to know she was crying. She'd hidden her tears the day she'd crashed the car, too.

"Forget it. It's over," he said, wanting to be done with it.

"But your mom… She was so upset."

"She survived." He paused. "Giorgio's good with her."

"Really?" She sounded so relieved he felt a pang of sympathy. She blew out a breath and brushed at her face. "Wow. That rain's really falling." She was pretending it was rain that streaked her cheeks.

"It is." He felt another pinch of emotion.

"I always loved when it rained here," she said softly.

"Me, too."

"Yeah?" She shifted in her seat to look at him.

"Sure. Especially the summer storms."

"Oh, absolutely. It's so magical with the sky brown and yellow and ominous, lightning zipping everywhere, rain in sheets, palm trees rioting and that great wet-desert smell."

"Yeah. All that."

She faced forward again. "It's unusual in March. I'm

glad for the change. March is…hard." He heard her swallow. Did she associate spring with Robert's death the way he did?

He steeled himself against feeling sorry for her. If she'd been so damned devastated, why hadn't she written Robert in juvie? Or given him a number to call? She was just trying to make herself feel better about what she'd done.

"At the funeral, you were so angry at me, I was afraid to go to the graveside," she said quietly. "That's why I went last night. To say goodbye."

Why the hell wouldn't she shut up about this? He remembered her at the funeral—small and pale and scared.

She looked young now, and vulnerable, sitting low in the seat, her wet hair clinging to her face, plastered to her skull. Her candy smell filled his cab as it had her car the day he'd fixed it for her. He remembered how he'd felt that day, that tug inside that told him, *Keep an eye on this one.*

She raised her arm to push away her hair and he saw she had on a candy bracelet. Really? After all these years? That explained the aroma.

He saw they'd reached her building, so he parked, got out and started unloading her stuff, planning to help her carry it up.

She met him at the back of the car, looking troubled. "Do you think it helped your mother to yell at me? Was it cathartic? I know this has been terrible for her. They say it's the worst thing, to lose a child."

"She's okay. Let's get this stuff inside." He lifted out a box that held a flat-packed table.

"What she said about me abandoning Robert…" Her teeth were chattering, but not from the rain, which was warm. "She was right. I did that. I tried to write, but the words were all wrong. I was ashamed and afraid he hated me because I got off. I know I was a coward."

"Just let it go, would you?" He had an armload of stuff now.

But she kept going. "I should have made my mom take me to see him, but she was so furious. We spent all my college money on legal fees. She didn't speak to me for months. I was afraid of her, I guess."

"What floor are you on?" He tried to pass her, but she blocked him. She looked stricken, as if she had no choice but to spill her guts.

"I made Robert take the ride that night to the party. Damien was the only one with a car. Robert said Damien was bad news, but I didn't care. I wanted to get to that stupid party."

"You don't need to tell me this."

"Damien went into the Circle K to buy cigarettes. Robert and I didn't pay attention. We were making out in the backseat. Then all of a sudden, Damien was back, yelling that he'd robbed the store. He drove off like a maniac."

He couldn't stand this, listening to her draw the scene, make him picture it again.

"We tried to get him to pull over and let us out, but he wouldn't. Then that cop, the one who hated Robert, stopped us. And that went all wrong, too."

"For the love of God, stop!" he yelled. "I don't care how it happened. I don't want to think about it. My brother is dead. That's all that matters."

"I'm so sorry," she said, her face crumpling up, crying straight-out now. "I don't expect you to forgive me. You shouldn't. I can't forgive myself."

She stood in the rain, sobbing. It was pitiful.

He couldn't stand to see her suffer. It wouldn't bring

Robert back. "You were fourteen. You were stupid and so was he."

She met his eyes. "No matter what you think, I did love Robert. And I miss him. I still miss him."

"I believe you, okay. It's a long time ago now. Yes, we blamed you, but, hell, you had your own problems, I guess." He thought he just wanted to calm her so they could get the hell out of the downpour, but he realized abruptly he meant it. He didn't hate her anymore. Or blame her.

"I have my own regrets about Robert," he said softly. "They don't bring him back, either."

"Really?" Pinpoints of hope were breaking through the gloom in her eyes.

"Really. Now can we get this stuff inside before the boxes melt to mush?"

"Oh." She jolted, at last aware of where they stood and why. "No, no. I'll carry it all up. You have to get back to work." She fished in her purse, but instead of keys, she held out money. "Thank you so much."

"Save your cash. Buy a car."

"I called a cab. I owe you this."

"Consider it a housewarming gift. Get the door for me." He strode for the entrance with his armload.

She scurried after him. "I don't want to keep you any longer."

"I'm done for tonight."

"Okay, I guess." She unlocked the lobby door. The guy at the night desk nodded at them and they headed to the elevator.

CHAPTER FIVE

GABE SET HIS SECOND LOAD inside the door to Felicity's apartment. She was putting things away in the kitchen. The place was pretty bare. She had rows of books on brick-and-board shelves, a couple pieces of framed art, a laminate laptop desk, a rolling set of plastic drawers, an end table, a standing lamp and a mattress on the floor next to a pile of partly assembled metal pieces.

"That's supposed to be a futon," she said. "I haven't quite figured out the frame. Some bolts seem to be missing. I guess that's why it was on sale."

"That's a drag." Standing with her, alone in the small apartment, he felt the sexual hum start up again, that steady engine idling always when they were together.

Her wet blouse was so translucent he could see where her bra quit and her skin began. She should change into something dry, or at least *thicker.*

He forced his gaze away, noticing her candy bracelet had melted a bit, streaking her arm with color. "Your bracelet's dissolving."

"Oh. Shoot. I forgot I had that on." She licked her wrist, her tongue working against her creamy skin in a way that set off fireworks inside him.

She caught him staring. "You okay?" she asked, mistaking his sexual haze for some kind of distress.

When he could form words, he said, "You used to wear those a lot."

"Yeah. Constantly." She gave a laugh. "I can't believe you remembered."

He shrugged.

"Robert used to keep me supplied. When I saw this one I bought it in his honor." She hesitated. "Does that upset you?"

Only a few hours ago, he would have found it revoltingly phony, but he'd seen true regret and real sorrow in her face when she'd stammered out her story. She'd meant every word. "No. It's fine." Kind of touching.

"They tasted like the best part of childhood to me. When candy was this amazing treat that seemed to last forever and made you so happy." She brought the inside of her wrist to her mouth and bit off a few of the beads.

The sight got him stupidly aroused.

"I know it's ridiculous," she said, "but some of the best things are ridiculous, you know? Halloween parties… roller coasters…bungee jumping…Zumba." She stopped with a short laugh. "I'm babbling. Nervous, I guess."

"No reason to be."

"Want to taste?" She extended her arm.

Oh, yeah. His parts jolted at the prospect. He saw why Robert had fallen for her. She had energy and fire, a sense of mischief and surprise.

He brought her forearm to his mouth and bit off a few pieces, watching her face as he did so. She made a little sound and closed her eyes, slumping a bit, as if she'd gone weak in the knees.

He wanted to pull her into his arms, taste the candy on her lips as well as his own, and that was just for starters.

But he forced himself to release her arm and step back. "So what's Zumba?"

It took her a second to get clear. "Uh…oh…Latin dance aerobics."

"I figured you were a dancer, considering the shape of your muscles."

"You analyzed my muscles?"

"I'm a trainer. It's my job." Damn, he was full of it.

"Your *job?*" She rolled her eyes. "I always wanted to dance. I took ballet when I was little and ballroom dance in college, but I'm too short to ever be serious about it and—" She gave a sheepish smile. "I'm doing it again. Babbling. How about a beer? You're my first guest, after all."

Should he stay? Would they talk? Or do more? He'd made that rule about avoiding meaningless sex, but watching her chest rise and fall with the same urgency he felt, he thought sex had plenty of meaning on its own.

Be sensible. You should go. They had a professional arrangement now and it was tenuous at best. He wasn't sure he'd have six hundred dollars by Wednesday and no way could he give up half the gym.

Then he noticed her bare mattress on the floor surrounded by metal bars and springs. Pitiful. "The least I can do is put your bed together, so, sure, I'll take a beer. Maybe put on some dry clothes." He nodded at her tantalizingly visible chest.

She glanced at herself. "Oh." She blushed. "Be right back." She whisked around a corner and changed into jersey shorts and a tank top.

She fetched two Coronas from the kitchen and held one out to him, her color high, eyes bright, pupils huge and *no bra* under that flimsy top.

Damn. His pulse kicked up, but he fought it down. He tapped his bottle against hers. "To the three most dreaded words in the English language—*some assembly required.*"

She smiled, her small teeth flashing. They looked at

each other, not drinking, just absorbing the energy between them, like the suspended feeling before a rain, when ozone filled the air, thick with expectation. The engine went from idle to rhythmic revs, ready to jet.

"You have the instructions?" he finally said.

"I thought guys didn't read instructions. Isn't that like asking for directions? Just not done." She was joking to cover the fact him staying crossed a line that might not be smart.

"Someone spent hours on it. Worth a skim."

She found the instructions and he read them over, Felicity behind him, looking on, giving off that great candy smell, plus something in her hair that smelled like oranges.

"It's this." She tapped at one picture. "Where the V is, the bolts they gave me are too short."

He looked through the pile of hardware, then noticed brackets with longer screws. "Maybe we could switch these out."

His theory worked and once they reversed the pieces—she'd had them backward—they were in business. Grinning at him from across the mattress, she said, "Let's turn it into a sofa."

But a mattress is so much handier. "Sure."

They lifted from both sides until the latch clicked, locking the mattress into a fold. "Now for the slipcover." She seemed ridiculously excited, tossing him one of the navy-blue pieces and putting the other on herself. When it was finished she dropped onto the couch. "Feels great." She looked up at him. "Come try." She looked so inviting he had to remind himself she meant the futon, not her.

He sat next to her. She was so pretty, with her hair almost silver in the lamplight, her skin pale as moonlight.

It was all he could do not to touch her. Could she possibly feel as good as she looked?

"You'd never know it's a bed, huh?"

Oh, he knew. It was all he could think about.

He pulled his gaze away, then noticed a picture on the wall that seemed familiar. He got up to see. It was one of Robert's wolves in his signature style—sharp angles, bold colors, thick lines.

She joined him. "This was my favorite, so I asked for it."

"I know what you mean." He lifted his shirt to show her the tattoo of one of Robert's wolves he'd had done.

"That's beautiful." She ran her finger over it, making his skin jump.

She shot her gaze to his. Heat flared, but she stepped back. "He was so good, no matter what he tried. Acrylics…watercolor…charcoal…"

"Graffiti." Reminding himself of Robert's flaws staved off the despair he felt thinking about all Robert had lost.

"Yeah. That." She winced. "I went on tagging runs with him. It was so scary, but I wanted Robert to be proud of me."

"Proud of you? For vandalizing buildings?"

"He was my first friend at Central Middle School. I was new in eighth grade, where everybody knew everybody and I was this freakish stranger to pick on."

"Because you were white?"

"No. It was the white girls who shoved me into lockers and trash-talked me. The Latinas and black girls mostly ignored me."

"Different from Scottsdale, huh?"

"We had mean girls. But they were fashion-police mean, not switchblade-in-a-cross-necklace mean."

He laughed. "Good one."

"Robert was kind to me." She shot him a swift smile. "He didn't care that I was white and wore J. Crew. He made his friends accept me. It was such a relief to have people to hang with."

"Yeah. I can see that." He'd never thought through how those days might have been for her. Why would he? Robert had been his only concern.

"I went along with whatever they did—shoplift, ditch, get high, break windows—so Robert wouldn't regret including me. I was kind of a mess. My mom was always out trying to score a rich guy, which disgusted me. When she was home, we fought constantly, so I stayed out when I could."

"You were at the house a lot, I remember."

"Which your mother didn't like. I felt guilty, so whenever Robert brought me snapdragons I made him give half to her."

"So that was your idea? The flowers he gave our mother?"

"Robert knew they were my favorite flowers, so he brought me some every week. He got them from the florist on McDowell."

"Stole them, no doubt."

"I think he coaxed them from the ladies. He could be charming."

"Not that I ever saw. Around me he was pissed off or sullen."

"All fourteen-year-olds are pissed off and sullen. He looked up to you."

"I doubt that. I was always on his case."

She shook her head. "No. He knew what you stood for. He wanted you to be proud of him. He told me so."

Gabe's throat went tight and he couldn't speak.

She held his gaze, her eyes shiny with emotion. "You miss him."

"Yeah." The word felt torn from his throat. "I do."

"Oh, Gabe. I'm so sorry." She lurched forward and hugged him.

He hugged her back, letting the feelings roll through him. Usually, when he thought of Robert, he got mad. Mad at Robert for getting into trouble, mad at the system, at the neighborhood, at the gangs, at himself, at fate.

Felicity had pushed him deeper. Waves of grief and sorrow and loss passed through him, wrenching at first, and raw, then gradually less intense, less painful, until he felt relief, as if he'd let out a breath he'd held too long.

The entire time, they held each other, not moving, just breathing together, hearts beating in time.

When they broke apart, Felicity's face held compassion and sadness. They'd both loved Robert. They both missed him.

He felt disoriented. He'd just been comforted by the girl his family blamed for Robert's slide into gang life, then death. It was a lot to take in. "I should go."

"Sure," she said. "Thanks to you I've got a bed *and* a sofa."

But no table or bar stools. The boxes were stacked by her door. "How about I put together those, while you set up the small stuff?"

"I wouldn't want to keep you."

"I've got nothing else to do." Except sky-high laundry and chits to call in for the rent money she'd extorted from him. Why the hell was he pretending his dearest wish was to assemble her bar stools?

"That would be great."

An hour later, Felicity dropped one final decorative pillow onto the futon. "That's it. Done." She looked around triumphantly.

It did look better. She'd hung more framed posters, added a throw rug, put a sculpture on the cocktail table, along with two white candles she'd lit.

"I like the obelisk," he said.

"You know what an obelisk is?"

"You mean a tall, narrow monument with a pyramid-shaped top built by the ancient Egyptians, but named by a Greek? Name escapes me."

She laughed. "I barely knew what it's called."

"I'm not illiterate, even if I quit college."

"Why did you? Quit, I mean."

"I had to go to work." He wasn't getting into the story of his mother dropping into a pain-med fog and losing her job.

"That's too bad." Felicity assessed him.

Before she could tell him, *It's never too late, there are grants and loans,* he said, "Place looks much better."

She took in the room. "Definitely. Makes me feels less lonely."

"You're lonely?"

"I shouldn't be. I have no time to socialize. I work nonstop and always have. But I had roommates in L.A., so there were people around. I don't know anyone here anymore. I guess I feel a little lost."

"Understandable." He wondered if she had a boyfriend in L.A.

"I'll make friends, I'm sure. Just takes time." But she looked sad. He was a sucker for a brave front, but he'd better get out of here before he did something rash, like offer to rustle up a meal, or, hell, spend the night.

He started for the door.

"Before you go, I want to be sure I can open up the bed on my own. Would you mind?"

He helped her remove the cover, then watched as she bent to pull the bottom and the top together to unhook the catch. It didn't give.

"I think it's stuck," she said.

He leaned past her and lifted hard. The mechanism sprang open unexpectedly and he fell forward, knocking Felicity to the mattress, then landing on top of her.

She laughed, looking at him, her big eyes warm and bright.

He held himself off her chest, but they were inches apart, her breath sweet on his face, her lips just there. He could kiss her almost by accident.

Her gaze settled on his mouth, inviting that very mishap.

They were both breathing hard.

It would be so easy to let it happen, lose himself in her body. All the touches and smells and closeness had worn down his resistance. Plus, he'd lost his resentment of her. She'd been a better person than he'd imagined and she'd cared for Robert.

But staying would be a mistake. The solid part of him knew that. He rolled away and stretched out. "Bed feels comfortable."

"It is." She shifted to her side, smiling, her cheek braced on a palm. He matched her position, so they lay face-to-face like lovers engaged in pillow talk. "Except it occurs to me I could end up folded inside the bed."

"Keep your cell phone with you."

"If I call, you'll come extract me?"

"I keep the Jaws of Life in my trunk, baby." He grinned, picturing it.

"What?"

"I'm just thinking about what the paramedics would say when they broke in and found a talking couch."

She laughed a full-throated laugh. "Help, I've been eaten by my futon." Again he felt the urge to take her mouth, but he resisted. Each time it got harder. So did he.

He scrambled off the bed. "Looks like you're set." She looked so inviting on that big, empty bed. "Maybe put WD-40 on that latch so it'll move easier."

"If I have trouble." She got up and walked him to the door. "You busy this weekend?" She caught herself. "Not for any reason. I'm busy. Working, I mean, just—"

He laughed. "Yeah. Big landscaping job. Driving cab. Couple hours of training tomorrow. We have a meet next Saturday at North Central."

"I see."

"You should stop in at the gym. Work out with us. Get a feel for my program." Maybe she'd drop the idea of him giving up so much space.

"I'm not much for physical conflict."

"Everybody needs to blow off steam."

"I don't need to use my fists to do that."

"You might be surprised how good it feels."

"I don't think so."

"I'm serious. Consider it payment for the free cab ride and furniture assembly."

"Ooh, blackmail again. You're quite the extortionist, Gabe Cassidy."

"I learn from the best."

She smiled. "I'll think about it. Maybe on Monday."

"See you then. Sleep well," he said, an embarrassing amount of warmth in the words. The whole encounter puzzled him. In the parking lot, he looked up toward her apartment window, surprised to see her on her terrace, looking down at him, Juliet to his Romeo.

She gave him the sweetest wave. It hit him hard, like an unexpected kick to the chest, only nicer and more welcome. He felt stupidly sappy and unaccountably cheerful all the way home.

LATE MONDAY AFTERNOON, Felicity pulled on the spandex tank top she ran in, tied the string to her nylon shorts, then checked herself in the mirror of the tiny faculty restroom. Incredible as it seemed, she was about to let Gabe teach her how to kickbox.

She'd practically promised him, right?

Mainly, she was dying to see him again.

The merest thought of that near-kiss sent electricity to her toes—and more relevant spots—all weekend long. The whole evening had felt…big.

She'd never responded to a man so strongly. It kind of scared her. Her professional priorities hadn't allowed time for anything intense.

At least that's how she'd always explained it to herself. For that matter, she had even less time now, with all she had to accomplish.

Still, she'd replayed those moments over and over again. Now the memory was like a friend's hand on her shoulder, a hug to her heart.

Had he felt it, too? Or had she cooked up the power of it out of loneliness and the relief of clearing the air about Robert?

That had been such a good feeling, to hear Gabe say he didn't blame her, that he had his own regrets, that he believed that she'd loved Robert. It was such a miracle. Such a weight had lifted from her she thought she might float away. He forgave her.

You didn't tell him all of it. He'd stopped her, said he'd heard enough. Maybe he was right. At least he no longer hated her.

In fact, he'd nearly kissed her. She had to find out how he felt about that three days later.

She put her fists up like a fighter. The sight made her burst out laughing. Not her at all. Though maybe she would surprise herself as Gabe had said.

She'd entered the gym and barely inhaled her first smell of sweat and detergent when Gabe spotted her.

"You came," he said. "And you look…great." He ran his eyes down her body, making her feel nearly naked.

"Just my running clothes." She glanced around, grateful that the boys were busy training and no one had noticed them. "You look good, too." His white muscle shirt perfectly complemented the brown of his skin. The man was so sexy she could hardly breathe.

"Get a lot done this weekend?" His tone was intimate, telling her she hadn't imagined the closeness she'd felt.

"I did okay." Except when she was fantasizing about him.

"Bed fold out all right?"

"I had to wrestle it a little."

"I wish I'd seen that."

His words burned through her, just as his eyes were doing. "I almost stopped by Saturday morning in case you needed my Jaws of Life."

"I would have liked that." It was as though they'd drawn the closeness of that night around them like a blanket. "I may need that WD-40."

"I might have a can in my office you could borrow."

"That would be great." They were staring at each other, smiling like goofs, saying nothing and everything. "Thanks again. My place feels more like a home now."

She realized that had more to do with Gabe being there with her than throw pillows and obelisks.

"Glad I could help." They stood there, breathing and staring for more long seconds. Through his shirt she could see a word tattooed over his heart. *Terco.* "What's *Terco* mean?"

"Huh?"

She ran her finger over the spot. His muscle shivered under her touch.

"Ah." He took down one side of his muscle shirt to show her the tattoo. His shoulders and chest were gorgeous and the gold cross was pretty in the dip between his pectorals. "It means *stubborn.*"

"Oh, that fits for sure."

"You ought to know." He shrugged his shirt back in place.

"Hey…I prefer *determined.*"

"*Stubborn* not nuanced enough?"

"Gabe?" Neither of them had noticed Conrad standing there. "You gonna spar with these kids or what?"

"Oh. Uh…"

"I can come back another time," she said, embarrassed to be keeping him from his fighters.

"I asked you here. Take over for a bit, Conrad, while I show Ms. Spencer a few basics."

"If you say so." Conrad gave them both a speculative look then walked off.

"Let's get you wrapped up," Gabe said to her.

"Wrapped up?"

"Your fists." Grabbing a roll of red stretch fabric, he led her to a weight bench, which they straddled, facing each other. He took her right hand and began wrapping the stretchy fabric around her wrist, palm, knuckles, then fingers. "I'm using a basic wrap. You'll figure out the style that works best for you as you keep training."

She could hardly think with him so close, gently working over her hand, his fingers graceful and strong. "The reason we wrap is to keep the wrists straight, pad the knuckles and protect the small bones of the hand."

"Sounds hazardous."

"No more than most sports, less than many." He patted her hand. "Make a fist. Be sure it's not too tight."

She did what he said. "Feels okay." Her fist looked dangerous. She realized she could hurt someone with it. It was a daunting thought.

Gabe started on her other hand.

She watched how the tattoo of Robert shivered as Gabe's biceps moved. *Siempre en mi corazón* had been written under it. "'Always in my heart,'" she translated out loud.

Gabe stopped wrapping to look at her. "You speak Spanish?"

"I spent a year *en el barrrrrio,* remember? Come on. Everyone takes Spanish. My accent was better than some of the Chicanos who grew up speaking mostly English."

"Probably better than mine. My mom was bilingual, but she spoke English to piss off my dad."

"Robert said you hated your dad. Is that why you changed your last name?"

"Ochoa was his gang name, so, yeah. I hated what he became for the gang—full of hate, always after revenge, all that macho bullshit. He tried to make it sound honorable, talking about *mi familia, mi gente, mi barrio,* about loyalty and duty, but it's murder and drugs and money."

"Robert admired him."

"No matter what I said, he idolized the guy." He patted her second fist. "Done. Let's go teach you to fight."

"I guess."

"Hey, don't be nervous. I won't hurt you. At least not at first."

She managed a laugh.

He led her to a corner of the gym near a mirror and positioned himself as if to start boxing. "This is fight stance," he said. "Feet shoulder-width apart, one slightly in front, knees bent, on the balls of your feet. This gives you a strong base for balance, but allows plenty of mobility. Try it."

She copied his position.

"Almost." He shifted her shoulders, his hands so warm they made her knees give a little. "Don't bend your knees so much," he said.

"Sorry." She wanted to laugh.

Next he started in on her feet. He knelt and braced her at the hip, while he angled her front foot more, explaining why, though she could hardly follow with his hands all over her.

Finally finished messing with her position, he straightened. "I'm being particular because proper stance is crucial. You don't want to start bad habits you have to unlearn. Get it right and you can cover any move your opponent makes."

He raised his fists and shifted his weight. "Without moving your feet, try to avoid my strikes." He pretended to punch her from different angles. She shifted easily until he surprised her with a left and she leaned too far back.

Before she could fall, Gabe caught her, hand to her back, as if dipping her in a dance, his face inches away. "You've got good reflexes. Great flexibility." She caught a flicker of male awareness. "And amazing BMI."

"BMI?"

"Body Mass Index. Ratio of fat to muscle. I could give you the science, but it's basically the degree of jiggle."

"I jiggle?"

"Only where it counts." He glanced down at her breasts, then cleared his throat and pulled her to her feet. "You've got good muscle definition." He turned her to the mirror and ran his finger along the tops of her arms, standing behind her. "See?"

"Yeah," she said, trying not to tremble. He was all but embracing her, filling her head with his smells—lime, clean sweat and starched cotton. He looked better and sexier to her every minute.

"Let's start with some basic strikes." He demonstrated different punches—jab, cross, uppercut—and had her try them in the mirror, one by one.

"A jab should snap like a snake strike—out and back, fast." He showed her. She tried it. "Better. Keep practicing."

Next he had her move around him while doing strikes, reminding her to keep her fists up, her chin tucked, her elbows in, her feet at the right angle, until she wanted to scream.

"It's a lot right now. When your muscle memory locks on, it'll be automatic. You'll see." He seemed to think she would keep this up.

He watched her every move so closely it was unnerving. "Don't bounce so much—you're wasting energy. Focus your power on the point of the strike. Picture the face you want to smash and aim for it."

She dropped her fists and stared at him. "I don't want to smash a face."

"Come on. Sure you do. Think about Dave Scott."

She smiled. "We had our talk today, he and I."

"Yeah? Show me some combo punches."

She started punching.

"Elbows… What did you tell him?"

She pressed her arms to her sides. "I told him that during school hours his focus had to be on Discovery, not real estate. And if he couldn't be my partner, then we both needed to make other arrangements."

"So, basically, *work hard or get out,* except nuanced."

"Actually, I was pretty blunt. I don't have time to waste." She sensed a clock ticking on Discovery's survival. If she didn't fix things fast, both the school and her career could go down in flames.

"Let me see cross, jab, cross, jab. So did he get the message?"

"I think so," she said, doing the drill, starting to breathe hard. "Because we're a charter school, he knows I can fire him. At the very least he no longer sees me as a naive ball of newbie fluff he can mock salute. God, I hate when he does that."

"You think he'll come through?"

"I hope so. Most of the teachers are on board already."

"Same drill, but quicker this time. How'd you manage that?"

"I made them part of the planning," she said, speeding up her punches. "I carved out time in the school day for the extra work instead of piling it on after school, which also helps."

"Sounds smart. Let's try some kicks." He showed her the snap kick, the side kick and the back kick. Her muscles were aching now, but he kept coaxing more out of her, asking questions that kept her talking and panting between words.

She told him about the extra challenges of an at-risk school—students with a history of failing, parents who were angry or absent, about inspiring the less effective teachers and protecting the brilliant ones from burnout, about how tough it was to make big changes when dealing with the deluge of daily crises, district meetings, memos and reports.

"Sounds like you've got plenty of people whose faces you could punch."

She stopped, midkick. "Never. I won't be like my father." She hadn't meant to blurt that, but she was so physically spent it slipped out.

"Your father hit you?" Gabe went still.

She stopped fighting. "No. He broke furniture and dishes and doors, but he never hit us. Just made us cower before his rage. I was always afraid one day he would snap. It made me feel so helpless."

"When you know how to fight that goes away. You know you can handle whatever comes at you."

"I tried to stay away from him. After the divorce I hardly saw him. Still don't see him much." She bent down, fighting to catch her breath.

"Had enough for today?" he asked.

She nodded.

"How do you feel?"

"Good. Better." She was surprised by how satisfying it had been to kick and hit with all her might. She felt calmer, settled in her skin, aware of her physical strength in a way she didn't get from the gym or jogging. Gabe might have a point about physical confidence.

"You worked hard. You have a lot of drive, lady. A lot of energy." He wanted to kiss her—she could tell. And she wanted him to. Why not finish what they'd started Friday night? They were alone. The kids had all gone.

"We need to go over the tournament schedule, Gabe." Conrad had sneaked up on them again. How did he do that?

"Sure. Be right with you," Gabe said, color darkening his face.

Conrad walked off, shaking his head.

"I'd better go," she said.

"Tomorrow I'll show you some takedowns."

"I'll try to be here."

"It'll be worth it."

"Maybe." She backed toward the door. She was about to ask him to come to her place with the WD-40 when her head hit the door with a thud and the fog cleared.

What was she thinking? She'd be working nonstop to be ready to open the Institute in two days. She had no time for workouts or futons or takedown lessons and she didn't dare forget it.

"Think about it," Gabe called to her.

"I will." All night long, no doubt.

CHAPTER SIX

WEDNESDAY MORNING, the school secretary handed Felicity an envelope that had been stuck through the mail slot. It held a check from Gabe for three hundred dollars with a sticky note: "I'll get you the rest when I can."

On top of that, he'd only cleared out part of the space they'd agreed on, so she had the janitor and Dave take the weight equipment and exercise machines out to the quad and pack up enough mats to make space for the room dividers she was using to mark off the discussion circle, the study area, the computer workstation and a space for workshops or guest speakers.

Not an auspicious start to their deal, she thought with irritation.

As soon as classes ended, Felicity took her place at the door to greet the sixty students who had so far returned After-School Institute permission slips. She had planned six-week sessions of a hundred students at a time for the three hundred pupils at the school. Sixty was a great start.

As the kids trickled in, she motioned them toward the discussion circle, where April Harris was laying out paper and colored pencils for the welcome activity. April had agreed to be her assistant now that Felicity could pay her.

"Are you shittin' me?"

The harsh words made Felicity turn. Alex stood with four STRIKE friends, all dressed to train. When he saw

Felicity, he softened his expression. "Sorry, Ms. Spencer, but our stuff's all missing and shit."

"You'll find most of it on the quad."

"What's it doing there?" Gabe's voice came from behind her.

"We had to clear the rest of the space we agreed on."

He was obviously angry. "Get started on the bags," he said to the boys, who were waiting for him to settle this with Felicity. Reluctantly, they departed.

"Come on, Cici. You saw how we use the gym. That weight equipment needs to be in here."

"We had a deal. Frankly, that broken-down equipment should be hauled away as a hazard."

"That *broken-down equipment* is all we've got, since I'm using my equipment fund to pay your rent."

"What rent? You only paid half of what you owe."

"I need a couple weeks, okay?"

"In a couple weeks, you'll owe me another twelve hundred. Is this how you operate? Ignore the parts of a deal you don't like?"

"I could say the same thing about you. In fact—"

"Do we get to train with STRIKE?" a boy asked, his eyes as big as Christmas morning.

"Yeah, do we?" a girl added. She was a tall Latina with cornrows. Felicity thought she'd seen her with Alex.

"We're in STRIKE now?" another boy echoed. "Damn."

"Really? Wow." Other excited voices chimed in.

"No. Hold on," Felicity said. "The Institute is only sharing space with STRIKE. We're not connected in any way."

"That sucks," the first boy said. Others agreed loudly.

"You'll get plenty of exercise during the recreation period," she said.

More groans and complaints. *STRIKE rocks...recreation is bullshit...boring...dumb...* On and on.

"Can they train with us, Coach?" Alex asked the question standing beside the girl in cornrows, who towered over him.

The crowd of students who'd gathered around stilled to hear the answer.

Felicity jumped into the silence. "That's not possible, Alex. I'm sorry."

"Hold on," Gabe said before the kids could erupt in disappointment again. "How about this? I can do one hour of training for your kids, show them what STRIKE's about. Say, fifteen at a time. One hour per group. Sound good?"

Before she could object, the kids exploded in cheers and whistles.

"Sign up in my office!" Gabe yelled over the noise. He walked away, trailed by two dozen of her students, skipping after him as though he was the Pied Piper of Discovery, enchanting them with boxing gloves instead of a flute.

She could kill the man, which was ironic, since a few days ago she'd wanted to sleep with him.

When it was time to start, she had to blow a whistle to gather the Institute kids from the gym. They slowly took seats in the discussion circle, heads turning to watch the gym action.

Felicity forced a smile, determined to start off on the right foot. "I want to welcome you to Discovery's After-School Institute, where you'll learn, talk, explore and grow. We hope you'll make the most of the two hours you'll be with us each afternoon."

She introduced April and the two aides who would supervise some activities, then explained how they would operate.

It wasn't easy to be heard over the gym noise, and the kids continued to watch the action there. Was Gabe deliberately being loud and interesting?

She introduced the guest speaker, an employment counselor, who would help them prepare summer job applications, then asked them to write down any suggestions for speakers or workshops they'd like to have.

Like a shot, Bethany Milton, the PTO president's daughter, raised her hand. "My mom will teach a craft workshop."

Several kids groaned.

"Shut up," she said, glaring.

"Riley's dad can teach us how to get shit-faced," one boy said.

"Yeah, well, your mom can show us how to work the pole."

Kids all laughed.

"Our first rule is respect," Felicity said, quieting the group. "There will be no insults. No attacks. This is a safe place for all of us." She paused while her words sank in. The kids sobered a little.

"To get started, let's do an activity to get to know each other better. You'll make your personal coat of arms. Who can explain what that is?"

Bethany's hand jerked up. "Like in olden times. Kings had flags and shields with pictures of lions and horses that were their symbols."

"Exactly." She told the students to divide their shield into four parts and create a symbol that represented family background, personality, values and goals, along with a personal motto.

"Damn it, Devin, focus!" Gabe's shout filled the air. The kids laughed.

Felicity shot a quelling look in Gabe's direction.

"Sorry, Ms. Spencer. I'll put a quarter in the swear jar."

Everyone but Felicity seemed to think that was hilarious. Gabe had the nerve to wink at her. *Wink.* It was all fun and games to him.

The students set to work and when most seemed finished, Felicity asked for volunteers to share with everyone. The first hand up was a tall Latino boy's. He told her his name, then started explaining. "My slogan is 'Live by the blade, die by the blade.'" His drawing was in Double Deuce colors and included a nasty-looking knife and a well-rendered automatic weapon. Kids flashed gang signs. One kid yelled, "Doble representin'."

"I should have caught that," April murmured to her.

"It's okay," she said, then turned to the boy. "Gang references aren't allowed in school. You know that, Bernardo."

"You said put what I stand for. That's what I stand for."

"There are no gang affiliations at our school," Felicity said. "Please sit."

He fell back in his chair with a derisive snort and ripped his paper.

"Who else would like to share?"

Kadisha Green, a black eighth-grader who'd been in Felicity's office several times, raised her hand. Kadisha was exactly the kind of student Felicity's system was designed to reach—smart, but bored, at risk of dropping out.

Felicity felt a surge of satisfaction, until she saw Kadisha's poster, which showed a marijuana leaf, a hash pipe, a Rastafarian flag and the motto "Be cool…get baked."

Everyone laughed. Kadisha beamed.

Just great. Felicity should have anticipated this. Middle-school students were more hardcore and more peer-aligned than elementary ones, so of course they'd show off for each other.

"I know you're trying to impress each other with how cool and street you can be," she said, "but in this room we look deeper than that. Underneath the drugs, sex, weapons, gangs and bad attitude, who are you really? Who do you want to be and what do you want out of life? What's really in your heart? That's what we're exploring. If your work gives answers like that, Ms. Harris will put you in small groups to talk about it. If not, start over."

Some of the kids tuned out, she could see. But most were glancing at their friends to see if they would comply. Building trust would take time, she knew. Too bad she didn't have much of it.

When the session ended, she gave the students a snack break, which most of them spent hanging out in the gym.

Again she had to blow her whistle to call them back. Gabe shrugged, as if he couldn't help being so irresistible. Did he think this was a popularity contest and he was getting the most votes?

So infuriating.

The students divided into groups for outdoor recreation, homework help and the job-counselor session. Felicity ached to offer more. She wanted to pay tutors, buy newer computers, bring in mentors, take field trips. That would take time and far more cash than she had, especially at the rate Gabe was paying rent.

They worked through the sessions, contending with the gym noise as best they could. The career counselor gave up halfway through two of her sessions because of the noise and lack of attention.

At 5:30 p.m., when Felicity dismissed the Institute kids, they all raced over to the gym. All over the room, coats of arms and practice job applications littered the floor. Not what she'd planned at all.

There had been flashes of progress—a few new friendships started, a handful of students had drafted résumés or been helped with their homework and the cage-ball game outside had been a hit. But Gabe's gym had wrecked the atmosphere, disrupted the flow, distracted the students from their work and prevented them from taking the Institute seriously.

Discouraged, she sat at a table to read over the kids' workshop suggestions, hoping that would cheer her up. It only made her feel worse. More than half asked for martial arts, kickboxing or Coach Cassidy. She braced her forehead on her palms. What now?

"So that went great, huh?" Gabe straddled a backward-facing chair and dropped stapled pages of signatures in front of her. "Got most of them signed up." He grinned at her.

"Great? Are you kidding me? You created chaos in here."

"Hey. I did you a favor. Once other kids hear about the free lesson, you'll get more signed up for your study hall."

"It's not a study hall," she snapped. "And that was no favor. That was sabotage. Wasn't it enough that you were so loud we couldn't hear ourselves think, that you were a constant distraction? You had to offer to train them, too—take them completely off task?"

His amused expression fled. "Look, it's not my fault the kids were more interested in STRIKE than whatever the hell you were doing. I had to explain to my guys why they lost half their gym. Be glad I didn't tell them about the rent or they'd be pounding the pavement with protest signs right now."

"Is that a threat? More blackmail, Coach? Got *60 Minutes* on the line?"

"It is what it is."

Her throat tightened. "Don't you get it? The Institute is important. It's a way to extend the school day, to get these kids what they need to succeed." She fought to keep her voice level "The kids have to *work.* They have to think, open up, try new things and study *hard.* So you go and offer them playtime."

"My fighters work hard and you know it."

"Not the kind of work I'm talking about. I can't compete with you." Her voice cracked, so she cleared her throat.

He was silent for a moment. "I should have run the free session past you first. They were so into it I got carried away. Would it make you feel better to know my training got shot to hell? My guys were too busy showing off for your students."

She shook her head. "Nope. Doesn't make me feel better."

"How's this? Your beginners will eat up training time when we've got a meet on Saturday."

"You should have thought of that before you blurted your offer."

"Lesson learned." He blew out a breath.

"What now? How do we handle this?"

"Make the best of a bad deal. I'll do what I can about the noise, chase your kids back when they stray, try not to look like we're having too much fun. And you try not to be too boring. Unless you've got a better idea?"

"Not at the moment."

"If my broken-down equipment is going to have to stay outside, then we need tarps to cover it every night."

"I'll get the janitor on that."

He rose from the chair he was straddling. "Now I've got to pick up some fares if I hope to make the rent you expect." He looked as unhappy as she felt.

Their deal had made them both miserable. She felt like a cheerleader waving her pom-poms ragged at a game no one could win.

It's your own damn fault, Gabe told himself, surveying the mess that was his first free lesson for the Discovery kids. Alex was showing off for Carmen, who'd come to the gym dressed like a skank in short shorts and a tiny tank top. She was barefoot. Gabe had made all the girls who'd showed up in sandals or fat wedgies take off their shoes.

Girls changed the whole vibe of the gym. Victor, usually a steady, sensible fighter, was risking torn tendons doing trick moves to impress a girl, and the rest were hyper and loud, fighting wildly, no focus at all.

He looked over to see how Felicity was holding up. The kids were in a circle talking and she wasn't shooting glares at him, so his occasional "Keep the noise down!" must be working.

It was funny, but he was always aware of her. He had this prickle at the back of his neck whenever she was nearby and he kept looking for her in the room. He was worse than his boys.

Training her on Monday had been tough. Putting his hands on her body, adjusting her stance, watching her move… Damn. He'd fought a hard-on the whole time. He hadn't been kidding about her BMI. She was lean and strong and soft in the best places.

He liked her attitude, the way she took his tips to heart, pushed to do better with every punch or kick. The woman had a lot of drive. What she was doing at Discovery sounded impressive, too.

Every time he looked at her, he wanted her more. He kept getting pictures in his head of her naked and him on top of her…or under her.

Not helpful at all.

Especially because she'd done nothing but mess up his life—crowding his fighters, taking over his gym, wasting his time, cramping his style. She even had him babysitting her students.

Shit. Their so-called *deal* got worse every time they talked about it.

Now she was in the middle of the circle, talking, her face animated, her arms moving. Whatever she was saying, the kids were totally into it. Hands shot into the air, eyes stayed with her. This from kids who would rather die than look interested in anything, least of all school.

She lifted her gaze and caught his. For a second, they held on, connected, together, as if they were a team. Which made no sense, except that they both cared about the kids. That was something, he guessed.

"They're ready, Gabe." Conrad had gotten the Institute kids on the mats for Gabe to run some drills with them. They were a motley crew, half boys, half girls, all of them out of shape, most of them overweight. He intended to work them so hard they'd beg to get back to Felicity's program.

He started in fast and fierce, showing them strikes, blocks and kicks in quick order, drilling each move to the point of exhaustion. Right away, they were gasping and groaning, red-faced, sweaty and trembling. Next would come whining and complaining, followed by quitting.

Except it didn't go that way. The kids hung in, giving it their all, despite their lack of fitness, tight clothes or having no coordination whatsoever. His fighters joined in to help without him saying a word and this seemed to spur the new kids on even more.

"Release your *chi,* Sonya," Victor said to a small, heavy girl who was delivering some damn high side kicks. "*Chi* is your energy, your power. Yell out! *Huh! Huh...huh!*" Gabe had to smile at the very advice he'd once given Victor.

"Your punch is good, Sarah," Alex said to a chubby blonde. "Now get on the balls of your feet. Stay loose." She bounced up and down, setting her breasts moving. "Damn, girl. You need an Ace wrap for those things."

The girl stopped, turned bright red and ran for the hall door.

Carmen, standing nearby, slugged Alex. "You asshole."

"What?"

"You made Sarah feel bad about her tits."

"But it's true. She could *bruise* herself."

"Go apologize." She shoved him toward the door.

"Nut up, Kadisha," Digger was saying. He wore mitts and leg guards and Kadisha was doing kick-strike combos.

"I don't have nuts, you douche."

"Whatever you got, use 'em. Hit me harder or go home to your mama."

"Shut up about my mama." Kadisha lowered her head like a bull and began punching right, left, right, left, right, backing Digger to the wall, while kids all around cheered.

Kadisha beamed, her face shiny with sweat.

A while later, he noticed Sarah, the girl with the bobbing breasts, sitting against the wall, head buried in her knees. What now? He walked over to her. "No one sits out in my gym," he said, his hands on his hips.

She didn't respond.

If she were one of his boys, he'd give her hell, but she

was new and he remembered the twins at this age, when they would sob or giggle or explode at the drop of a hat. He crouched down. "What's going on, Sarah?"

No answer.

"Come on. What is it?"

"I jiggle," she said, face still down.

"The more you work out the less you will. Sports bras help. See that girl there." He motioned toward the short powerhouse with the high kicks. Sarah risked a glance. "Only difference between you and her is she's been exercising—turning fat into muscle. You can, too."

She looked at him, wanting to believe, but not ready to.

"I saw your punch. You've got real power."

"That's just because I'm big," she mumbled.

"Who's the expert here? I do not bullshit. Yeah, you've got some pounds keeping you down, but you start hittin' the bag and they'll melt like the ice cream you're gonna stop eating. You feel me?"

"I did like the punching…." She gave a smile as quick as a whisper.

Sensing a presence, he glanced up, knowing it was Felicity before he saw her because of his prickling neck hairs. He focused on Sarah. "Sure you like punching. Girls don't get to use their fists enough, do they, Ms. Spencer?"

"It's entirely possible."

"Look, Sarah. You hit harder and straighter than half the Institute kids already, boys included. Keep at it. Ignore the trash talk. Rock the house."

He held out a hand and helped her to her feet. "Victor!" he called. "Help Sarah here with some kicks." He whispered to her, "Less jiggle with kicks."

She smiled, then headed over to Victor.

"That was good what you said to her," Felicity told him, a thoughtful look on her face. "See that girl at the bag—the black girl with dreads?"

"The one who went after Digger earlier, yeah."

"That's Kadisha Green. She's smart, but always in trouble. She ditches, back-talks, comes to school high. She's close to dropping out."

"Yeah?"

"Look at her go." He watched as she did some rapid kicks, while the girls behind her yelled for their turns at the bag. "She's totally into it."

"Looks that way."

"They all are," she said, looking around the gym.

"I pushed them hard trying to scare them off, too."

"Didn't work."

"Sorry."

She gave him a speculative look. "You were right. We did fill all our slots today. They all want your free class."

"Yeah?"

"So, we need to talk, you and I." She had a gleam in her eye he didn't like. "Can I take you to dinner? When you have a break?"

"I don't know. Talks with you never turn out good for me." On the other hand, maybe over dinner he could get her to reduce his rent. "What the hell? Tonight's a slow night. How about I fix you dinner?"

"Fix me…? You want to cook for me? At your house?" Her eyes were wide with amazement. It made him smile.

"That's the idea, yeah. You okay eating meat?"

"Meat? Sure. I eat any meat. Well, not veal. Or liver. I'm not big on liver." She blushed. "Babbling…sorry."

"Range-fed rib eye sound okay?"

"It sounds great. Spectacular! Who wouldn't like range-fed rib eyes?" He'd really thrown her off. Good.

He'd buy two bottles of whatever wine the wine guy suggested and throw her off more. If he didn't get a rent concession, he could at least score a grace period. "I can pick you up if you'd like."

"No, no. You have to cook. I can take a cab. Unless there's a bus stop?"

"Yeah. Down the block. I'm in from Seventh Ave." He gave her his address. "Come at seven. Be hungry."

He left her looking dazed. He liked that.

CHAPTER SEVEN

IT WAS A SHORT WALK, and the sky glowed gold and pink with sunset when Felicity approached Gabe's house, a pale yellow craftsman bungalow with brick-red trim in a historic neighborhood. Succulent cacti lined the flagstone path—tall euphorbia and puffy aloe, some with bright blooms. The porch held colorful pots of red hibiscus and a swing upholstered in a striped Mexican fabric. Very welcoming. Well tended for a guy's place.

He cooked, too, which had surprised her. Totally not fair to assume all single guys were slobs who survived on pizza. And she prided herself on not prejudging people. Shame on her.

She smoothed the skirt of the red silk dress she wore. It hugged her figure and had a deeply scooped neckline and—

Uh-oh. She'd put on a date dress, not business attire. And she'd worn diamond earrings and the smoky eye makeup and burgundy lip stain that looked good in night-clubs.

Her subconscious hadn't forgotten that her "business meeting" was with a man she'd love to have sex with and had dressed her for that purpose. How embarrassing. At least she'd brought her curriculum materials to show Gabe. Maybe he would overlook her do-me dress.

Mesquite smoke wafted her way from his backyard. Yum. Her mouth began to water and her heart skipped beats along with the Latin hip-hop coming through the screen door.

She was ridiculously nervous.

Before she could ring the bell, a chocolate Lab appeared with a halfhearted woof, wagging its tail too hard to ever be mistaken for a guard dog. Gabe came to the door. "Come in," he said, holding open the screen.

Inside, she set down her messenger bag so she could pet the dog, who looked adoringly up at her.

"Gordo is a sucker for the ladies." Gabe's gaze swept her body in a way that made her feel weak. "I'm with him. Nice dress."

"Thanks. You look good, too." Very sexy in a loose white silk shirt with embroidered panels and crisply pressed jeans. Totally date-worthy, she realized. Maybe his subconscious had been at work, too. To cover her reaction, she held out the wine. "Red's good with beef."

He took the bottle, examined the label, then laughed.

"No good? The guy said it had blackberry notes and—"

"A full-bodied, buttery finish," he said. "I talked to the same guy. Bought two bottles, in fact."

She laughed. "I'm more of a beer person, I guess."

"Me, too. I've got Corona, Guinness and some Tsingtao."

"I've never tried Tsingtao. It's Chinese?"

"Yes. They brew it with rice, so it has a light taste."

"Sounds interesting. I'll have that."

"You bring homework?" He nodded at her messenger bag.

She figured the more he knew about her system, the more likely he'd be to go along with her plan. That said, a man with *stubborn* inked into his skin would not go down easily.

"I brought my materials. Since you showed me yours, I thought I'd show you mine." She put her hand to her mouth. "That sounded bad, didn't it?"

"Not to me," he said, setting off a charge low in her stomach. "Hold that thought. I'll get the beers."

While he was gone, she looked around the room. It was masculine and neat, but lived-in. Books and a stack of newspapers sat on the cocktail table in front of a massive sofa in tan leather on roughly carved wood. A jacket was tossed across a matching chair and there was a pair of work boots near the small fireplace, which was framed in colorful Mexican tiles.

Mexican folk-art accents brightened the space—a tall standing vase, a metal sculpture of a rooster, a colorful throw rug.

The walls held framed black-and-white photos and two large paintings she recognized as Robert's—one of a quetzal bird with an elaborate tail, another of a Mayan warrior standing before a temple.

Gabe returned with two full steins, glowing like wet gold. He passed her one, the handle icy against her overheated skin.

Their gazes met. *"Salud,"* he said, tapping his bottle against hers. *Health.*

"Amor y dinero," she added. *Love and money.*

"Y el tiempo para gozarlos."

"And the time to spend them," she translated.

He nodded and they drank, watching each other over the tops of their mugs. The beer was almost sweet, refreshing and icy.

"Yum," she said, licking the foam from her lip.

He stared for a frozen moment, then said, "You learned booze toasts in Spanish class? That's pretty progressive."

"No. Robert taught me that one."

"When you were fourteen? Great."

"No. It *was* great. Him teaching me that—something from his culture—made me feel special. At that age, every little boyfriend thing was a big deal. I wrote his name in hearts all over my binders."

He held her gaze, clearly thinking about her and Robert back then. This time, the silence was comfortable. Their talk had eased the tension, she was relieved to notice.

"Did you say you bought *two* bottles of wine?" she said. "Were you planning on getting me drunk?"

He grinned sheepishly. "Maybe just…cheerful."

"I'm always cheerful. Now, you, on the other hand, you glower."

"I do?" His eyebrows lifted, amused, his eyes going lighter. "That's a new one. My sisters say I look fierce. And that I need a haircut."

She looked over his deliciously thick, tousled hair. "I don't know. I like it. With your earring, it's kind of pirate-y."

"Is that a good thing?"

"Are you kidding? Check out the covers of historical romances. Lots of swashbuckling going on."

"Swashbuckling? That's what they called it back then?" His voice went low and sexy. A shiver went through her. "You cold?"

"Maybe it's the beer," she said, sipping more of it.

"Maybe," he said, his small smile telling her he knew better. "Think my sisters will buy that I'm going for the pirate look and leave me alone?"

"Why are they so upset about your hair?"

"They're in beauty school and they want to cut my hair for practice. Tonight, as a matter of fact. Thanks to you, I had plans."

"You told them about…me?" The idea startled her.

"I told them I had a school meeting. There's no point getting into the rest." He looked away, uncomfortable.

"That makes sense." She had to admit it also hurt that she was this terrible secret Gabe had to keep from his family.

For good reason, she reminded herself. His family *hated* her. *Blamed* her for Robert's death. She remembered the girls' desperate faces as they tried to calm Mary, who had fallen to the grass at the cemetery, overcome by the sight of Felicity.

She shouldn't let Gabe's forgiveness ease her guilt too much. She'd hurt other people. And there was more he didn't yet know.

"Your home is lovely," she said to change the subject. "Did you decorate it yourself?"

"Guys don't *decorate.* They buy crap."

"Then you bought good crap," she said. Each piece looked lovingly placed and he clearly had an eye for design.

"Thanks. I like it. It's home. Anyway, I thought we'd eat out back, since the weather's so nice." He led her through a French door to a covered patio. There was a punching bag and weight bench in one corner. The other held a grill that was smoking lightly, the source of that mesquite wood smell.

She noticed that the wrought-iron table held a vase bursting with flowers. Burgundy snapdragons. At least two dozen of them.

"How pretty." She turned to him.

"Your favorites, right? I bought enough so you could keep some and take the rest to the cemetery if you want. I'm sorry I threw yours at you."

"Don't apologize." She was so touched. Her nose tingled with emotion.

"You loved him. I know that now."

"I'm glad. It makes me feel better. Thank you." They shared another long, silent moment, wordlessly connecting. This was happening more and more between them.

He looked at her with so much *tenderness,* it made her melt. She'd never felt this way with anyone, friend or lover. Was it the new-job pressure and the old sadness bringing her emotions to the surface? Or was it something about the two of them together?

She didn't know, but it made her uneasy.

She turned to survey the yard. A flagstone path wound through groupings of desert plants, cactus and paloverde trees, with their bright green trunks. A stone fountain graced the center of the small space. There were lights everywhere, so she knew the sight would be magical after dark. In fact, she could see a string of white lights lining the patio roof, too.

"This is really beautiful," she said.

"*Bien firme* for a *vato* from the hood, eh, *ese?*"

"Are you kidding? *Bien firme* for a Scottsdale resort. *Bien firme* means cool, right?"

"You do remember your barrio days, *chulita.*"

"Don't underestimate me, *cabrón.*"

"Hey, I call you cutie and you call me asshole? And I wouldn't dare underestimate you. Learned my lesson the hard way. You've got me paying rent, giving up half my gym and training beginners for free. God knows what you've got up your sleeve now." His tone was very sexual.

But then, everything he said to her lately sounded sexual. She drank the last of her beer, hoping to calm herself down.

"Sit," he said. "I'll get the bread and more beer." He took their empty mugs and brought them back full and foaming, along with a colorful basket of sliced bread.

She took a bite. The bread dissolved on her tongue, leaving an explosion of tastes—tart cheese, sweet basil, tangy green chili. "Wow…this is good."

"Took me a while to work out the recipe."

"You *made* this?"

"The bread machine did most of the work."

"But you made up the recipe. You baked it. Damn."

He chuckled. "Yeah. My sisters say I'd make a great wife."

"Oh, you would. Absolutely."

"Luckily, my masculinity is pretty sturdy."

"Oh, I'm sorry. Did I offend you? Because I didn't mean you were… I mean, you are *very* masculine. Completely, totally virile and all man. God, I sound like I'm in a porn movie."

He laughed. "Relax, Felicity. We're fine." He touched her hand, as if to reassure her. The contact jolted through her, flooding her insides with desire. She wanted to straddle his lap, wrap her arms around him and kiss him until he kissed her back.

Which wouldn't take much, judging by the expression on Gabe's face. He wanted her, too.

But she wasn't here for sex. She was here for work. She retrieved her hand and changed the subject. "So how did you get into martial arts?" she said shakily.

He took a second to shift gears. "That's a long story."

"Tell me," she said, though her body was moaning *do me*.

"It was because of Robert. After he died."

"If you'd rather not talk about it…."

"No. It's okay." He blew out a breath. "I took Robert to a Muay Thai fight for his sixteenth birthday. Turned out he was really into it, so I offered to pay for training if he'd stay clear of his banger friends in the Doble."

"He agreed?"

"Yeah. I found a great coach and Robert loved it. I thought I'd found the way out for him—something he cared about, that he wanted more than gang life." He ran his finger through the condensation on his mug.

"Trouble was he had to cross enemy gang territory to get to the gym. He was on his way to a meet one day when a crew from Fourteenth Ave. called him out. His head got slammed into a fire hydrant. On my way to watch him fight I found him on the sidewalk. He died in my arms. Paramedics said it was a brain bleed." He looked out over his yard.

"I didn't know any of that. The Flagstaff paper just said it was gang related."

"That was true. It was his friend Mad Dog who caused it. He was new in the Doble, trying to make a name, so he'd been challenging the Fourteenth Ave. crew on their borders. Otherwise, they might have let Robert pass. Mad Dog's *jefe* of the Doble now, by the way. A bad kid is now a worse man."

She let the words settle between them before she asked, "So after that you decided to train? For Robert?"

"Yeah. For him. In his place, you know? It helped to have a way to burn off my anger. I competed, won some titles, then earned instructor credentials."

"Did you coach full-time?"

"No. It was a hobby. My job was at the South Mountain Recreation Center. I was running the place before they fired me."

"They *fired* you?"

He smiled crookedly. "They said they had to *let me go.* Supposedly, their policy changed so that center directors needed college degrees."

"Supposedly?"

"A high-end subdivision went up and they needed someone less *street* to draw the yuppies there, instead of to the fancier health clubs."

"You're saying it was racism? Because you could have sued. The city has a minority hiring policy, I'm sure, and the EEOC investigates all claims."

"That stuff is impossible to prove." He shrugged.

"It's a shame, though. I'm sure you were great. It wouldn't be hard to get a recreation degree. There are online classes and night classes for people who work. Maybe a teaching degree. Inner-city schools need strong male role models like you."

"I like my life, Felicity," he said. "I don't owe anybody. I make my own hours. I do what I want. When my coach passed away, he left me his boxing ring and some cash, Charlie gave me the gym space, and I started STRIKE."

"But what happened to you was wrong. You can sue after the fact, you know. You have several years, I think."

"Life's not fair. Why fight it?"

"Because that's how change happens. People stand up for what's right."

"Some people, sure. Not people like me, with my background. No one forgets that Ochoa was my father. I'm as branded as if I had *Doble* tattooed here." He ran his thumb across his forehead.

"But you've got *terco* tattooed here." She smoothed her fingers across his heart. "Don't forget that."

He clasped her hand against his chest so she felt his warmth through his shirt and the hard thud of his heartbeat against the back of her hand. He wanted her. She wanted him. They were alone as darkness settled around them. She started to tremble, all thoughts of fighting city hall gone.

No. Don't do it. She had a mission here. That came

first. With all her might, she brought her mind to heel, her body under control.

Reading her reaction, Gabe released her hand. "Guess I'd better get the steaks."

She might have offended him going on about a lawsuit and college, but she hated seeing someone with so much to offer live such a limited life.

Gabe put the steaks on, then finished the side dishes in the kitchen while Felicity set the table with Mexican folk-art plates, heavy silver filigreed flatware and brightly woven napkins.

Soon they were eating. Gabe had made the preparations seem effortless. The steaks were perfectly cooked, well seasoned and dusky with mesquite smoke. The salad was dressed with a homemade raspberry vinaigrette, decorated with pine nuts and freshly made croutons, while the asparagus had a buttery pecan-and-cheese sauce and the basil-dressed fingerling potatoes practically melted in her mouth. She exclaimed over each dish, asking him how he'd prepared it.

Dessert was farmer's market berries on French vanilla ice cream with hand-whipped almond-flavored cream. She thought she might pass out from pure pleasure.

"That was delicious," she said, pushing her empty dish away. "I don't know why I keep asking for your recipes. It's not like I have time to cook or even want to. Though you make it seem worth the trouble."

"I like cooking for people."

"It shows. Every bite was a gift to my mouth."

"A gift to your mouth?" He shook his head at the hyperbole.

"Over-the-top, huh? I'd never make a food writer." She giggled. "I guess I'm one beer too cheerful."

"Me, too." He grinned and drank the last of his.

"You look so different when you smile. You should do it more."

"I'm with the Russians—all that grinning makes you look like a fool."

"But you're so intimidating, with those brooding eyes of yours."

"Now I brood? I thought I glowered."

"The point is when you smile you seem approachable."

"I get a lot of mileage out of being intimidating."

"Maybe if you'd smiled more you'd still have your recreation job."

"Not that again."

"I'm just saying presentation affects perception and perception controls reactions."

"So I should put on an act, blow smoke, dish bullshit?"

"Put your best foot forward. Focus on the positive. Emphasize strengths over weaknesses. You didn't set out paper plates or plastic forks tonight, did you? Or serve me microwave Hot Pockets."

"I get it. I just don't like it." He leaned forward on both elbows, arms crossed, and looked at her full-on. "I'm so cheerful my smile muscles ache."

"Me, too." And that made it even harder to ignore how much she wanted Gabe. The urge practically throbbed in her veins.

"So what's your story? How'd you end up a principal?"

Relieved he'd changed the subject, she leaned back in her chair. "I took an education class as an elective and the professor was so dynamic I got hooked. His specialty was the behavioral and academic conditions that produce achievement gains in disadvantaged pupils."

"Meaning what makes poor kids get good grades?"

"Exactly. He hired me as an intern. I got a degree in education administration with a focus on curriculum development, then put together a program using what I'd learned. I piloted it at two schools, then opened a consulting business to share it with districts in California."

"Sounds ambitious."

"Sure. I want to make a difference for lots of kids if I can. Then funding tanked and no one was hiring consultants. So I had to close up shop."

"Couldn't your folks have covered you for a while?"

"My stepdad offered, but I pay my own way."

"Sure." But doubt flickered in his eyes.

"I mean that. I had scholarships and worked to get my teaching degree and took out a loan for graduate school. Not a dime from my parents."

"Hey, if you've got money, spend it. I would if I had it, believe me."

"Money messed up my family," she said. "When my dad went broke, my mom basically abandoned him. I mean, he was an angry, gloomy man, but he loved my mother. It turned out the only reason she'd stayed with him was his wealth. After that, she hunted down a rich guy—my stepdad. He's nice and all, but I *won't* spend his money. Not with my mother's attitude. I make my own way, like I said."

Gabe didn't speak, but she could guess his response: *Easy to say you don't care about money when you have plenty of it—or at least access to it.*

She didn't want to argue about it, so she kept talking. "After that I applied for jobs in California and Arizona, hoping to strengthen my reputation so I can open up my business again, when money in California frees up."

"And Jefferson district offered you the job at Discovery," he said.

"Yes. Because of my program, *not* my uncle. I made

sure he had no involvement with hiring before I accepted the job."

"I believe you," he said.

"You didn't before."

"Sorry. I was pissed about Charlie."

"You'll see why they hired me when I show you my system." Here was the chance to get to her purpose for coming. She started to rise, but he gripped her arm, his hand warm and sure, making everything inside her go still.

"No need. I get that you're good. Just tell me what you want. I might be cheerful enough to take it." He gave a resigned smile and released her arm. "Give it to me straight. No nuances."

"Okay, here goes. I want to make STRIKE part of the After-School Institute."

"You what?"

"My students could choose STRIKE as their recreation component. You'd teach them one hour a day."

"Are you crazy? You hate fighting."

"I still do. But you might have a point about motivation. You reached Kadisha when I couldn't. Or at least not yet. And these kids don't have time to waste. We have lots of kids like Kadisha at Discovery."

"But what about their studies, all the work you say they should do?"

"That's the genius part. They'll have to *earn* STRIKE sessions. By doing well in school and participating fully in the Institute. STRIKE will be a privilege."

He stared at her. "So I would have the mess I've got now every damn day? No way. I've sacrificed too much training time already."

"One hour a day. That's all. And if your boys help

coach my kids—didn't you say the master learns from the pupil?—they would still be training."

"Now you're using my words against me."

"Whatever it takes. If the lost time's a big deal, you could keep STRIKE open an hour later."

"My guys have places to be. And I have other jobs. Now that I owe rent, I can't afford to lose any income, remember?"

Time for her ace in the hole. "What if you didn't owe rent?"

"What?" He leaned in, very interested now.

"I'd charge my students five dollars a week for your class. If enough students enrolled, I could replace your rent money, no problem."

"No rent, huh?" He eyed her. "What's the catch?"

"No catch."

"You've got time to cook one up." He assessed her. "I'll have to think about it."

"I know it will work, Gabe. It'll be great. You can talk to the kids about staying out of gangs, too."

"I train fighters. I don't give speeches."

"So you mention it here and there. Also, I was thinking about those techniques you had Alex work on with Devin. Ways to deal with bullies. You called it hop-something."

"Hapkido. It's a defensive martial art. Mostly blocks and escapes. It's used in self-defense training for women."

"Perfect. You can teach the kids that. Is it difficult?"

"No." He studied her. "I can show you a few moves if you want."

"Really?" There was a gleam in his eye she wasn't entirely comfortable with. "But I'm in a dress..."

"I noticed," he said, low and sexy. "Don't worry. I won't tear it."

"Okay, I guess."

He stood and reached for her hand. "Come inside. I'll find something soft to throw you onto."

"You're going to…throw me?"

She was just cheerful enough to let him.

Inside, Felicity dug her bare toes into the wool of the sheepskin Gabe had dragged from his hearth to the middle of the room, concluding it was thick and soft enough to cushion her fall. Standing in her bare feet, she was vividly aware of how much taller and broader Gabe was than she, and it made her breathless.

"Hapkido is based on simple mechanical physics," he said, all serious. "We use pressure, joints, levers and momentum to defeat an attacker."

"Physics. Got it," she said, though she was too caught up in his closeness to listen very well.

"Grab my forearm like you want to drag me somewhere," he said.

Like to bed maybe? She'd barely taken hold of him when he twisted his wrist, grabbed his hand and yanked it down, as though it was the handle on a slot machine. Her grip broke instantly.

"You're stronger than I am," she said. "Of course you can get away."

"That's not it. I used my arm as a lever." He gripped her forearm. "You try it now."

She turned her wrist and yanked down on her hand. His grip broke. "Wow. It works."

"It's the laws of force and motion. Combine that with strategic strikes with the body's hardest parts—crown of the head, heel of the hand, elbow, knee and heel—to its most vulnerable spots like the nose, eyes, groin and instep and you can escape any hold and disable your attacker."

"You're going to use your hardest parts on my most vulnerable places?" she said, feeling nervous.

A slow grin spread on his face and she realized what she'd said. "You make that sound like a bad thing."

She flushed. "I didn't mean…"

"I know what you meant," he said. "I won't hurt you."

"Then I'm in your hands."

"Yeah?" The flare of heat in his eyes told her he was fighting sexual urges, too. "Let's stick with physics…for now."

He demonstrated a few moves, positioning her gently, stopping each blow before he made contact. Seeing his reined-in power and pinpoint control made her dizzy with desire.

"Let's try an easy throw," he said. "Pretend to come at me with a knife."

When she did, he grabbed her attacking hand, turned her and tripped her, catching her before she hit the sheepskin. Her neckline gaped and she knew he'd seen her bra. She'd worn the sexy one, thanks to her busy subconscious.

He yanked her up fast, as if to end the temptation. "Did you get that?"

"Not quite. Do it again…slowly." She knew she was playing with fire, but she was dying to see what might happen.

"You sure about that?" he breathed, catching her meaning.

She nodded, her heart pounding in her ears.

He did it again, but this time he lowered her to the rug, going down on one knee, his body over hers.

She was so aware of him—his muscles, his brown skin, the lime of his cologne, the mesquite smoke in his hair, his intense eyes. He was all man and he had her in his power. He could crush her if he wanted to, break her in two, but he never would. He would protect her, keep her safe always. Her primal self liked that.

Her dress had slid off one shoulder and ridden high on her thigh, but she had no urge to cover herself. She wanted him to see her…to not be able to stop himself from stripping her. She wanted him to take her, vanquish her, subdue her… Oh, her subconscious was having a field day.

He lowered his face. He was going to kiss her. Was he going to fulfill her fantasy? She held her breath, her heart skipping beats.

But he went for her neck and *sniffed.*

What the…?

"I gotta ask. Why do you always smell like candy?"

"It's my chemistry," she said. "Every perfume goes sweet on me."

"Hmm. So does it make you taste sweet, too?" He leaned closer. "Gotta find out, I guess." He kissed her.

Thank *God.*

A charge shot through her, electrifying every nerve ending. He took her head in his hands and let his tongue graze hers, the contact so thrilling she made a needy sound that should have embarrassed her, but didn't.

He broke off the kiss, assessing her reaction.

"Well?" she asked shakily.

"Sweet as hell," he murmured, then dived in again before she'd even caught her breath. Again she was deluged by sensations—the way he tasted, how his lips moved on hers, the smell of him, the sounds he made against her mouth. Flames licked her insides, hotter every second until she feared she'd burn right up. How did people survive this kind of onslaught?

Kissing her the entire time, Gabe shifted her on top of him, lowered her zipper and unclasped her bra as smoothly as a hapkido move. She'd barely registered that her breasts were free before his palms covered them.

Surge after surge of new desire poured through her and she rocked her hips against him, feeling his hardness, knowing he wanted her.

This was like a sex dream come to life, only more vivid and so *real.* Oh, what were they doing? It was crazy, but she didn't want to stop. *Ever.*

A ringing sound distracted her. Had all this fire actually set off an alarm? Gabe ignored the sound, but Gordo began to whine.

The ring sounded again. The doorbell. Someone wanted in. Gordo whined louder. The caller began pounding on the door. "Gabe, come on," a female voice yelled. "We know you're back. Your van's in the carport."

"Damn." Gabe sat up. "It's my sisters."

"They're here…*now?*" She was so shocked she simply sat there.

Gabe hooked her bra for her and zipped up her dress. "I'll try to get rid of them, but for now why don't you wait in the guest room? First door on the right."

"Oh, okay, sure."

He thrust her messenger bag at her. "I'm sorry."

"No, it's good. I get it." She stumbled out of the room and down the hall, feeling like a sitcom cliché. Except there was nothing funny about this situation.

She felt humiliated—sent to hide in the closet because she would horrify his sisters. Then she felt ashamed that she'd behaved as if all had been forgiven and they were merely two people who wanted to sleep together.

How could she forget who they were and what she'd done? Or the cemetery, the way Mary had yelled at her and sobbed at the sight of her. The twins' stricken faces as they tried to soothe their mother.

Gabe had told her not to blame herself, but he didn't know everything she'd done.

She'd put him in a terrible position now, having to chase his sisters away. She hadn't given it a second thought. *You are a selfish jerk, Felicity.*

You are a complete CABRÓN, Gabe told himself, watching Felicity stumble from the room, her face wearing the same dazed anguish as when he'd chased her out of the cemetery. He felt sick.

His sisters' arrival was a bucket of ice tossed over his head, waking him up instantly. He'd been about to have sex with the woman who had destroyed his brother and torn his family apart. And he'd exposed Felicity to possible humiliation at the hands of his outspoken sisters, now pounding down his door, made her cower in the guest room praying she wouldn't be found out.

He and Felicity had eased some of the guilt they both felt, but that didn't make things right. There were others whose feelings had to be considered.

"Let us in!" Trina shouted.

For a flash he resented that. He'd spent his whole life taking care of his sisters and his mother. Robert, too. Pushing down his own grief, desires and dreams to take care of them, make sure they were okay.

Screw self-pity. Family meant everything to him. Family came first.

"I'm coming," he called, shaking his head clear. He went to the door and pulled it open a few inches. The girls both had their little hair tool boxes with them. They wanted to give him that damned haircut.

Gordo whined wildly, since he adored the twins. But then they hadn't threatened to cut *his* hair.

"What took you so long?" Trina said.

"I'm busy, okay. And I don't need a haircut."

"It won't take long, we promise," Trina said. "Just a cut. No color."

"Another time," he said.

"We've got a portfolio check tomorrow. And we're here now."

Gordo shoved the door open to get at the girls, who pushed right on in, petting the dog.

"What's your problem?" Trina demanded. Then she looked him over. "Wait a sec. That's your date shirt. You said you had a meeting. Was it a *date?*"

Shanna sniffed. "And I smell a really sweet perfume. Is she still here?"

"If she's not, Gabe's got something to tell us." Trina picked up one of Felicity's heels from the floor. He'd forgotten he'd had her take off her shoes. He had to cop to having a woman in his house. Maybe he could keep her identity a secret.

"You got me. Someone's here. And we'd like some privacy."

"Later. Bring her out so we can meet her," Trina said. "Maybe she needs a haircut. Does she have fine hair? We need texture work."

"It's okay. You can come out!" Shanna said, starting for the hallway.

Gabe grabbed her arm. "Don't. Stay here."

"God, what's with you?" Shanna shook her arm loose, looking at him as though he'd lost his mind. He felt as if he nearly had.

"What's the big secret?" Trina asked, then lowered her voice. "Is she, like, too young? Or old? That waitress at Giorgio's? She's got a major thing for you. Wait, is it Adelia? You don't have to hide Adelia. We love her, don't we, Shanna?"

"Except for the cheating part," Shanna muttered.

His sisters were relentless. Damn. He would have to tell them and hope to hell they wouldn't attack Felicity. "Sit down so I can talk to you."

"Why? Is it serious? Are you engaged? Is she pregnant?"

"Would you calm down and listen to me," he yelled.

"*You* calm down," Trina said. "We just want to give you a *haircut* and you're getting all fierce and yanking our arms and all."

"I'm sorry. I need to explain what's going on. Hear me out, please."

FROM THE GUEST-ROOM doorway, Felicity heard the dread in Gabe's voice when he asked his sisters to hear him out.

She was the one who needed to explain, to apologize, let them yell at her if they needed to. It wouldn't be easy or pleasant, but it was the right thing to do. So she would do it.

She threw back her shoulders, opened the door and headed out to face the girls.

"It's me who needs to explain, not Gabe," she said, forcing her wooden legs to take her to where the girls sat—one on the love seat, the other at the opposite end of the couch from Gabe. Feeling light-headed, she gripped the mantelpiece for balance.

"Cici? Again!" The girl on the couch pushed into the back of it. Her hair was darker with bleached ends. Trina, Felicity thought.

"You're dating *her?*" the other girl said. Her hair was a rainbow Afro. Had to be Shanna, who'd had natural curls as a child. "What the hell, Gabe?"

"You don't have to do this," he said, standing to go to her, probably to hustle her out the door.

"Yes, I do." Felicity waved him back to the sofa. "I

know this is a shock, girls. Gabe and I *were* having a school meeting. I'm the new principal at Discovery and we had to work out the details about STRIKE. Your brother was kind enough to ask me over for dinner." Her mouth was so dry her lips stuck together.

"You *cooked* for her?" Shanna demanded, turning on Gabe.

"You dress like *that* for a *meeting?*" Trina motioned at Felicity's dress.

"Don't be rude," Gabe snapped. "Have some respect."

"Why should we? What respect do you have? For Mom? For Robert? For us?"

"That's enough," Gabe said. "I won't allow you to—"

"I'm very sorry, girls." To Felicity, this wasn't about respect owed to her. It was about saying her piece and sincerely expressing her sorrow. "I'm sorry about what happened and—"

"You're *sorry?*" Trina snapped. "After what you did to Robert, to our mother, you think *sorry* cuts it?"

"No, I don't. But it's all I can think to say." She swallowed, trying to get the words out, feeling numb and sluggish. Maybe what she'd written in the note. "I know I hurt your family and I doubt anything I say will make up for that, but—"

"You're right," Shanna said. "Nothing you say fixes what you did. You put Robert in jail and then you broke his heart. When he came out he was not the same. He was mean all the time. Because of *you.* What you did."

"That's not the whole story," Gabe said. "They were both young. Fourteen. They were stupid. They made mistakes."

"Do you believe he's saying that?" Trina asked Shanna.

"You just walked away," Shanna said to Felicity, leaning in, hatred in her eyes. "How could you do that? He was in jail. You were free. You couldn't be bothered to visit him, to write, to take his calls."

"It was terrible, I know." What would make this right? Her mind buzzed with white noise. Hearing their words brought it all back. "I was a coward. I was ashamed." She swallowed. "I was afraid Robert hated me."

"You were afraid. You were ashamed," Trina mimicked Felicity. "Wah, wah, wah. Robert was in jail—ugly, stinking jail, all alone and so small. Crying himself to sleep on a cement ledge with a blanket thin as a tissue, terrified someone would beat him up. And he begged our mother to call you, find you, get you to talk to him."

Anguish poured through Felicity and she blinked back the water in her eyes. She deserved this. This and more. "You're right. If I could do anything to fix this—"

"Bring back our brother. Give him the life you stole from him. Can you do that?" Shanna said.

"That's enough, girls," Gabe said. "Cici apologized. It's been seventeen years, fifteen since Robert died. It's time we let it go."

"Is that all it takes, Gabe?" Trina said. "She says she's sorry, all is forgiven, so you can jump her bones?"

"That's enough," Gabe snapped. "You need to leave."

"She's the one who should leave," Shanna said. "You're choosing her over your family?"

"She's right. I need to go," Felicity said, her voice choked. "They have every right to hate me and no reason to forgive me."

"You're wrong. Trina, sit. Felicity, too. No one's leaving."

Trina huffed a breath and sat with folded arms.

Felicity sat on the edge of a painted hardback chair beside the fireplace, wanting only to leave before she broke down completely.

"Felicity knows she hurt us. She's not making excuses. She admitted she was wrong. She stood here and let you beat up on her. Enough is enough. What more can she do?"

The girls glowered, arms folded. They looked a lot like Gabe at the moment. She remembered Mary at the cemetery. Her hair had been strangely waved with odd colors. The girls must have practiced on her. The way this little family clung to each other made her ache inside.

"Since when have you two been so holy?" Gabe continued. "Did you forget the Shakira concert? You were fourteen, if I recall. Mom said no because it was a school night. Also, you were going with older boys she didn't know. All the way to Peoria."

"Yeah. So?" Trina squirmed in her seat.

"And what did you do? Stole her keys, sneaked out and let a high-school guy drive Mom's car to the stadium."

"We had tickets, okay?" Shanna muttered. "We saved up babysitting money."

"As if that wasn't bad enough, you stayed after for a party, got drunk, ran out of gas and tried to come in at five in the morning."

"We didn't want to wake Mom up."

"But she was already up, wasn't she? In total panic. She called the police. She called me. She was hysterical."

The girls were quiet, glancing at each other.

"Did you give one thought to how scared she would be? Or what that might do to her sobriety? How hard she fought for that? After losing Robert, where her mind would be going?"

They didn't answer.

"Of course you didn't. You were fourteen. Fourteen-year-olds do stupid, selfish, thoughtless things. Cici was fourteen. So was Robert. They did stupid, selfish, thoughtless things. The only difference was you two didn't get arrested."

"But we didn't—"

"Break the law? How about underage drinking? Your boyfriend was driving drunk. Did he even have a license?"

The girls dropped their heads.

"Don't forget that Robert was in trouble before he met Cici. She didn't make him screw up."

"I can't believe you're saying this to us," Trina said, but it was obvious Gabe's words had an impact on her.

"Lots of kids got out of juvie and straightened out."

"Now you're dissing Robert?" Shanna said.

"No. I loved Robert, but he was no angel. Cici didn't cause his death. Neither did juvenile hall. A lot of things got him there, most of all the choices he made. It's easier to blame someone, but it's not right. And it doesn't help." He stopped, as if overcome by emotion. "It just doesn't. And I'm done with it."

The girls seemed stricken by how upset he'd gotten. They looked at him, then each other.

Felicity sat very still, her muscles tight, brain on hold, waiting to see how the girls would respond.

"That was bad what we did to Mom," Shanna said softly. "What were we thinking?"

Trina shrugged. "It was mostly Ramon and Dario, remember? We had crushes, but they just wanted the car. The jerks ditched us at the gate."

"Yeah. That was bad."

The girls seemed calm—their fury gone as quickly as it had flared.

"You see my point?" Gabe said.

"You don't need to rub it in," Trina said.

Shanna looked at Felicity. "You used to give us candy necklaces all the time, I remember."

She nodded.

"And you made Robert quit hogging the Nintendo," Trina added. "He was always doing that. *One more life... Let me beat this level... Please, please.*"

"He adored you girls," she said. "He always talked about how smart you were, how funny and how sweet."

"We weren't that sweet," Trina said. "Once we got mad and took all his controllers to school. The teacher confiscated them. He was *so* mad."

"Didn't matter to him," Felicity said.

"Yeah, he spoiled you like the rest of us," Gabe said.

"Shut up, Gabe," Trina said. "We're getting compliments here."

The girls were quiet then, thinking it all through. Felicity's breath rasped in her ears as she waited for them to vocalize whatever they had left to say to her.

Gabe caught her gaze, steady and calm, sending her support.

"Fourteen is a messed-up age for sure," Trina said finally.

"Yeah," Shanna said. "Totally messed up. Dario was a skeev."

"I guess if Gabe is okay with you, we are, too." Trina spoke slowly.

"I'm sorry I caused your family so much pain." Felicity's voice caught.

"We get it," the girls said in unison, then grinned at each other. "Jinx, you owe me a Coke," they shouted together, punching each other in the arm, while they counted to six, then gave up.

Felicity smiled. Gabe rolled his eyes.

The girls looked at her seriously. "We're cool with this. Kind of. But you better not tell Mom," Trina said to Gabe.

"The cemetery thing was messed up," Shanna added. "Let her settle down from that."

"Probably wise," Gabe said.

One day, Felicity wanted to make things right with Mary, too. But one step at a time.

They all blew out deep breaths.

"So, that's settled." Gabe slapped his legs then stood. "If you girls wouldn't mind, we'd like to finish our meeting."

"*Meeting?* Oh, please," Trina said.

Meanwhile, Shanna was staring intently at Felicity. What now?

"Check it out, Treen," she said, coming over to Felicity's chair.

Trina followed her. They fingered Felicity's hair, then looked at each other. "Perfect," they said at once.

"Oh, no, you don't," Gabe said. "You're not cutting her hair."

"We *have* to," Trina said. "She has fine hair. You're cool with it, right?" she asked Felicity, her expression eager.

"I could use a trim, I guess," she said hesitantly. A bad cut made her look like a featherless baby bird. But if a haircut cemented the girls' goodwill toward her, she would happily risk a bald spot or two.

"Damn it, Cici. You've unleashed the hounds." But he was smiling and that was enough for her.

CHAPTER EIGHT

GABE SAT ON A KITCHEN STOOL across from Felicity with a striped bath towel around his neck. She wore a matching one. Damn. How did he get here? The events of the past hour had his head feeling like a piñata a couple swings into the party—shook up, dizzy and dented.

The confrontation with the girls had been intense. Felicity had been brave to come out and take their abuse. He'd gotten through to them, thank God, and they'd made peace with her.

It was funny, but as he'd given them the lecture, he'd felt it sink into him, too, registering even more than that talk in the rain, peeling away another layer of pain over his brother's death.

And now here they were, letting the twins experiment on their hair. He could tell Felicity was nervous, but she'd put on a brave front. That made him smile. He liked her more and more.

Wanted her more and more, too.

Take that incident on the sheepskin. Not smart. Not with all that was going on between them at the school. Her offer of no rent in exchange for training her kids was tempting, but he didn't want to lose more time with his fighters. He was already worried that his neglect would hurt their chances at the Saturday meet.

Besides, Felicity had a nasty habit of changing the rules midgame, and he'd had enough of that.

"What do you think, Shanna?" Trina said, picking up a strand of Gabe's hair. "The scythe or the shredder?"

"The what?" Gabe said, ready to bolt.

"Relax." She slapped his shoulder. "Those are nicknames."

"Scythe first, then the shredder for a thinning taper."

"Just nothing...extreme," Gabe said faintly. A thick wad of hair dropped in front of his face. He gulped.

"Hair grows back," Felicity said cheerfully, but she didn't look as sure as she sounded. She kept grabbing her shortened locks. The girls had been talking her ears off about beauty school. She'd fit right in with them, which might not be a good thing.

"So how's Gabe as a big brother?" Felicity asked, winking at him.

"Gawd! He's terrible!" Trina said. "*Sooo* overprotective. Makes us show our pepper spray before we go out. Wants to know who's driving and if they drink. We're twenty years old."

"Like Adelia said, we can't learn to fly if we don't spread our wings," Shanna added.

"Adelia's Gabe's ex-girlfriend," Trina explained to Felicity.

Great.

"Ex because she cheated on him," Shanna added. Shanna was a broken record on that subject.

"She does murals," Trina said. "You know the one at Buen Vecino? She did that. She's a really good artist. And a great person."

"Except for the—"

"We got it, Shan," Trina said. "Anyway, it's been a year and still Gabe just sits around the house baking bread and *ironing,* if you can believe that. He gets all hot about creases in his jeans. He's so homeboy Mexican that way."

"I'm sitting right here, girls."

They both shrugged, as if that didn't matter.

"Forgive my sisters. They never met a secret they could keep."

"Secrets suck," Trina said.

"Are you about done here?" He reached up to feel what was left of his hair, praying he didn't look like a dog with mange.

"Let me style it already."

"Guys don't get styled."

"The hot ones do." She squirted some goo into her hands, then applied it through his hair, rubbing strands together as if she was trying to start a fire.

"How bad is it?" he asked Felicity.

"It looks good."

"You mean gay? Not that there's anything wrong with that. I'm just…not."

"I'd say more metrosexual." Felicity grinned.

"You mean *pretending* to be gay."

"Oh, stop." Trina slapped him on the head with her comb. "Why do you pay our fees if you think we're that bad? Here. See for yourself." She gave him a hand mirror.

Damn. His hair stuck up in messy spikes like some idiot news anchor. "Coaches don't wear mousse," he said, handing her back the mirror.

"It makes you look friendlier. Don't you think he looks too fierce, Cici?"

"He can be intimidating," Felicity said.

"With that square jaw and dark eyebrows and black, black eyes, always scowling?"

"He does tend to glower." She was almost laughing. "And brood."

"See, Gabe? Even Cici thinks you're too scary. We should thin your eyebrows."

"Forget it. I already look like one of those tools on *The Jersey Shore*."

"You watch that?" Felicity asked.

"Saw a commercial," he mumbled. He'd watched a couple episodes since the boys talked about it so much. He was sounding gayer by the minute.

"Done," Shanna declared, handing Felicity the mirror.

"I like it," she said, sounding relieved it wasn't terrible. "What do you think?" she asked Gabe.

"It's good." It looked sophisticated—shorter, closer to her skull, though he kind of missed the feather float.

Then Trina got her camera for the portfolio photos. She took a few individual shots from all sides, then wanted some of them together.

"Put your arm around her," Trina instructed him.

He did. She seemed so small beneath his arm, her skin warm and soft as butter, it was all he could do not to crush her into an embrace. The woman set him off like crazy.

He'd been hot for Adelia, but not like this, not craving her, following her around the room with his eyes all the time, picturing her naked, dying to explore every inch of her candy-sweet body.

Maybe the intensity with Felicity was tied up with their history, with that old, old attraction, or because of what they'd shared about Robert, this new ease he'd begun to feel. Whatever it was, it *bothered* him. He felt out of control and he did not like it.

He was actually glad his sisters had busted in on them with scythes and shredders. He intended to keep them around until Felicity left—insurance against his weakening will.

"God, Gabe, you're all tense," Trina said. "Look at her and smile, would you? Act like you *like* her."

He turned to Felicity, so pretty, with pink in her

cheeks, a soft smile and her big blue eyes lit with pleasure. He liked her all right. He liked her too damn much. After the camera flashed, he blurted, "You two do the dishes, while I walk Cici out. To pay me for this." He tugged at his sticky hair.

They groaned, but headed for the kitchen.

He walked Felicity to the door. "Whoops. I forgot the flowers," she said.

"I'll slip out back and bring them around to the porch. Otherwise we'll get the whole this-is-a-date bit."

He went to the backyard then returned and handed her the vase.

"These are so beautiful. Thank you again." She held his gaze. "Want to walk me to the bus stop?"

"I forgot you don't have a car. I'll drive you home. It's late."

"The bus is fine, Gabe. Really."

"Not tonight, it's not," he said. "Come on." He led her to his van. Maybe she'd invite him up to her place. Maybe he would go.

Maybe he should bring the twins along.

"That was a complicated night," Felicity said, holding the flowers on her lap. They practically filled her side of the van.

"It would make a decent three-act play. Dinner…huge fight…then haircuts…with an epilogue of sneaking out with flowers."

"Don't forget the hapkido lesson," she added softly.

"Never could." He remembered her breasts in his hands, her gasps of pleasure, the way she'd pushed against him, showing the same urgency he felt. He felt the heat rise between them again, the engine revving louder than ever, barely held back.

"Me, either. It makes me dizzy thinking about it."

There was a long silence and he could hear them both breathing. He could almost hear their hearts pounding. Maybe the bus would have been better. Or maybe they should just finish what they'd started.

"I'm sorry my sisters gave you hell," he said. "Blunt runs in the family."

"They were honest. It was right. A good reminder that being sorry doesn't erase the terrible thing I did."

"I meant what I said. It's time to let it go."

"Thank you for defending me. That meant a lot." She swallowed, clearly fighting emotion.

"Thanks for letting the girls cut your hair." He pulled up at a light.

"It looks okay, doesn't it?" She turned to him, tugging at a strand.

"It looks great." She was so pretty to him.

"Yours is good, too."

"If I wash this gunk out will it lay flat?" He fingered the sticky strands.

"If you use your natural part, yeah." She ran a fingernail down his scalp, then flicked his hair this way and that. As she moved, her breasts shivered before him. He itched to pull her close, taste her mouth again.

Someone honked. The light was green.

He accelerated with a sigh.

"It was nice to see you with your sisters. You seem really close."

"We are. I took care of them when Mom was in bad shape."

"What happened?"

"After Robert died, she got hooked on pain meds. That's why I left school. She couldn't cope. She lost her job and couldn't handle the girls at all."

"I had no idea. I'm so sorry."

"She struggled off and on, but she's been straight for five years now."

"That's good." But he could tell she was upset.

"That wasn't your fault. Lots of people grieve without dropping into addiction. We dealt with it. And Giorgio makes her happy, so that's good."

"I'm glad." But she seemed too quiet.

"I shouldn't have told you that."

"I'm glad you did. I need to hear the truth."

"I'd have thought the twins gave you enough of that. Telling you how I overprotect them and about my cheating girlfriend." He shook his head.

"That must have been hard."

"Because she cheated? Yeah, but it sucks to get your heart broken no matter how it happens."

"I wouldn't know. I've never experienced that."

"Yeah?" He glanced at her.

"I've been lucky, I guess. We either drifted apart or broke it off by mutual consent."

She'd never been in love. That seemed sad to him. For all the pain with Adelia he wasn't sorry he'd loved her. Maybe he didn't have what it took to sustain a relationship, but he knew what it was to love someone.

He pulled up to Felicity's apartment building and stopped the van. He got out to open her door, but she beat him to it and met him on the sidewalk.

"Thanks for the dinner, Gabe. It was incredible."

"Glad you liked it."

She leaned in to kiss him goodbye, staying long enough to send the blood rushing below his belt and stop all hope of a clear thought.

"So what do you think about making STRIKE part of the Institute?" she asked him when she broke away.

"What do I think…?" He was thinking about getting

her naked, but she looked at him with so much damn *hope* brimming in her eyes.

What was the point of fighting it? She was as relentless as his sisters, he already knew, so she'd never let this rest. "We can try it, I guess."

"Really? Oh, that's great. I can't wait! You'll see. I know you will." She hugged him. He hugged her back. Almost immediately it went sexual and he felt a shiver pass through her. Why resist it? They should go upstairs and let nature take its course.

She broke away. "I don't think we should do this, Gabe."

"Do what?" *Have mind-blowing sex? Why the hell not?*

"Get physically involved. It would distract us from what's important—our work with the students—tie up too much energy."

"So sex is too much trouble? Jesus. I must be losing my touch." He'd managed a joke, but he felt as if he'd gunned the engine and she'd jerked the hand brake on him and now he smelled smoke.

"No, your touch is…amazing." She shivered, nearly closing her eyes remembering it. "That's the problem. It's too amazing and I'm afraid it would be all-consuming. And that's not… I mean, I've never been…um, in that situation." She stopped, flustered by her admission.

Damn. Who were these lukewarm losers she'd been sleeping with?

"Anyway, I can't risk it. There's too much at stake." But her eyes were full of longing and she was breathing funny. He knew if he pulled her close and kissed her, she'd drop her defenses as if he'd paid her to throw the fight. As much as he was tempted, he couldn't do that.

"I get it," he said. "You're right."

She blew out a shaky breath. "I'm glad you agree."

She backed away reluctantly, giving him a little wave. "Good night." She went inside, leaving him feeling even more like that birthday piñata than ever, this time with a couple of limbs dangling. He'd not only let her get her hooks into STRIKE, he'd let her convince him that sex was a *time-suck*. Damn. He *was* losing his touch.

THE NEXT AFTERNOON, after the Institute was over, Felicity sat at her desk staring at one of the haircut photos Trina had emailed—the one where she and Gabe were smiling at each other. They looked so good, so into each other—like two people falling in love—that Felicity's heart turned over in her chest.

It was just a picture, not reality, she knew. But saying goodbye to him last night had felt like saying goodbye to love. Which was dumb.

She'd been a little scared by how intense her feelings for Gabe seemed to be. What if it was a snarled-up reaction to the past? What if she was reliving her first love, turning Gabe into Robert in her head? That was too weird.

And, anyway, as she'd told Gabe, this was no time to get emotionally overwrought. That was definitely true.

She hovered over Delete on the email, then chose Close. She could be tricky that way.

The roller coaster of a night had stayed in her head. The sexual part, of course, but also the meal he'd prepared for her, getting to know him better and, after that terrible confrontation, spending time with his sisters, seeing how they teased each other, feeling the love they shared.

As an only child with difficult parents, Felicity had never experienced that kind of affection, and it had felt good to be part of the warmth and fun.

Best of all, Gabe had agreed to include STRIKE in the

Institute. She had announced it first thing that morning and by 10:30 a.m., kids had filled the roster for the next Institute session. Today, the Institute kids had worked their butts off, clearly wanting to qualify for STRIKE, which would begin on Monday.

It was Friday, the end of her second week as principal, and she felt as though she'd turned an important corner.

Then Beatrice Milton, the president of the PTO, marched into Felicity's office, looking grim. She held the STRIKE flyer in one hand. Felicity could tell from the handwriting on it that her daughter had filled it out.

"When Bethany brought this to me I thought it was an April Fools' joke two weeks early." She flung the paper on Felicity's desk. "You are forcibly exposing our children to this street-fighting gangbanger? Why weren't parents consulted about this?"

Damn. She should have met with the PTO. Normally, she would have, but she'd been so desperate, so anxious, she'd forgotten the basics of organizational change—involve all stakeholders, especially active parents.

"I'm sorry this has upset you. Please…have a seat."

Beatrice sat, her back stiff, face stern, arms folded, eyeing the items on Felicity's desk with suspicion.

"Feel free to use the toys. People find them soothing."

"I'm not interested in being soothed," Beatrice snapped. "Not when this school is falling apart. I enrolled my daughter here because of the focus on academics and the personal attention of a small school."

In fact, she'd enrolled Bethany after the girl was expelled from her regular school over a Facebook bullying incident, but Felicity knew better than to correct her.

"And you were right to do so. I should have met with the PTO. Especially because of the negative misconceptions some people have about STRIKE. Let me explain more about it."

"I know all I need to know."

"First, the STRIKE class is voluntary for students whose parents want it. No one is being forced. We see this as a way to motivate the students to work hard in school and the After-School Institute, since they have to earn the STRIKE sessions by doing well in both."

Beatrice seemed unmoved.

"I've already heard from teachers that students are buckling down so they can participate."

"I fail to see how a gangster teaching fistfighting helps with grades."

"Coach Cassidy is not a gangster. He's strongly anti-gang, as a matter of fact. He gives students the skills and confidence to resist fights."

Beatrice rolled her eyes.

"I had my doubts, too," Felicity said with a smile. "Then I saw for myself the difference he can make. I think you'll see that, too. Can I take you to the gym to watch STRIKE in action?"

"Are you telling me you intend to go forward with this?"

"We've had tremendous interest. I think if you give us time, you'll see what I mean."

"Our kids don't have time. Neither does Discovery, from what I hear. My husband serves on the mayor's civic-improvement council with Leonard Lancaster, your landlord, and he says the neighborhood is falling apart."

Felicity stiffened at her words.

Beatrice looked smug. "He's spent thousands replacing windows and cleaning off graffiti. Meanwhile, there are gangs selling drugs on every corner."

"One window was broken and only the plywood was

tagged. The school is safe. You're here often, so you know he's exaggerating." Or out-and-out lying. The man was playing poor-me about minimum maintenance costs.

"Well, we won't stand for this." She got to her feet. "And by *we,* I mean the parents of your top students, the only hope that Discovery's test scores won't stay in the basement. If you insist on this fight club, we'll be forced to take our children elsewhere."

"I hope you won't act in haste," Felicity said levelly. "Give the program a chance."

"I'll do what's best for my child. We all will. You'll hear more about this, I promise you." Beatrice stalked out, leaving Felicity in despair. Beatrice could bad-mouth Discovery enough to lose students, which would be a PR disaster, not to mention a funding loss. If only Felicity had laid the proper groundwork with the PTO.

She felt sick to her stomach.

Then it got worse. Tom Brown called her at home that night, not even bothering to apologize for the late call. "I just got off the phone with the school-board president. He told me a crazy story about you starting a fight club. With a gangster? Tell me that's not true."

Her face went hot and her heart raced. Beatrice had tattled to the president of the school board. She explained the whole story to Tom, admitting her oversight with the parents, promising to settle the situation as soon as possible.

"It's too late for that, I'm afraid," he said. "With the board up in arms, you'll have to close that gym. Get it off campus altogether."

"I can't do that, Tom. For one thing, I promised the coach he could stay. For another, the kids and their parents are ecstatic about STRIKE, which will be a crucial achievement motivator. And lastly, the program pays for itself. You took away my budget, remember?"

"I'm sorry, but that's the way it has to be."

"One ill-informed parent complains and you fold?"

"When that parent's husband plays golf with the school-board president, yes. I despise the politics involved, but I can't ignore them. Tell your people the district shut you down. It's the truth."

"I don't believe this." How could she comply? She'd be letting down the kids, the parents and her teachers, breaking her deal with Gabe and, with no rent money, losing the After-School Institute, too.

"I can't do it, Tom," she said. "It means too much to everyone." There was a long silence, during which Felicity felt her heart pounding in her ears. She had some autonomy, but she was basically defying her boss.

"I appreciate your disappointment, Felicity, and I admire your persistence, but I have to insist. Our alternative schools are already under the gun. If you don't shut it down, I'll be forced to ask for your resignation."

"You would fire me?" Her entire body tensed.

"Don't let it come to that. I know we robbed you. I regret that a lot. Drop this now and I'll push hard for next year's budget."

"This year is what counts." Discovery might not exist next year.

"Think it over this weekend. Let me know your decision on Monday."

She hung up, totally devastated. If she wanted to keep her job, she had to cut STRIKE from the Institute and kick Gabe out.

No. She wouldn't take back the eight weeks she'd given him. She'd stand firm on that, tell Tom that Gabe was looking for a new location until the promised time ran out.

STRIKE would have to be cut from the Institute. Without rent from Gabe—and she could hardly ask for it now—she'd have to close the Institute. She would have the rest of her system, at least, which should have a significant impact on achievement. If progress was decent, Discovery might hang on another year, when Tom would come through with the funds to fully implement it.

That didn't make her feel better. It felt like surrender. Charlie Hopkins had stood up to the district and gotten fired for it. Should she follow his lead? Stand by her program and lose her job? Or stay to fight another day?

She wished she had someone to talk to about this. Her friends in L.A. were too far away, her teachers too close to the situation. And she hadn't had time to connect with any other principals on a personal level.

There was one person who came to mind. *Gabe.*

He would help her sort out the pros and cons—probably as devil's advocate. She knew where to find him tomorrow—North Central High for the Muay Thai tournament his fighters had been training for. She would watch the matches, hang out, wait for a time they could talk. Hard as the conversation would be, she knew it would help her decide what to do.

CHAPTER NINE

THE NORTH CENTRAL GYM was brightly lit and echoing with noise when Felicity walked in Saturday morning, foggy from lack of sleep and heavy with dread.

The space had several marked-off fighting areas with brightly colored mats. Parents and kids sat in clumps in the bleachers, near tables with club banners draped in front. Teams of fighters wore T-shirts and shorts in all colors of the rainbow.

She picked out Gabe immediately—partly because he stood out from the crowd, being tall, well built and strikingly good-looking, but also because she had a kind of radar for him. Whenever they were in the same place, she felt this tickle of excitement, a vibration just under the skin.

When he saw her approach, he grinned and his face lit up. "You came."

"Thought I'd see what this was all about," she said, trying to sound as though she had nothing on her mind. She looked at the bleachers. "You've got a lot of fans."

"Today, yeah. Mostly Discovery kids who signed up for the STRIKE class and their parents checking us out. It's nice."

Her stomach twisted. "Not many of your fighters' parents come?"

"My guys are used to that. The rewards come from fighting a good fight."

Victor came up to Gabe, looking worried. "The guy I'm fighting took first place last time."

"So what? He didn't fight you, did he?"

"He's got techniques I never saw before."

"And you've got dead-solid timing. You can nail him."

Victor nodded soberly.

"Fight your fight, not his." He squeezed Victor's shoulder once before the boy walked to the fight area.

"Will he win?" she asked Gabe.

"If he keeps his confidence up. Not easy for him. His parents have told him his whole life he's a loser. The kid does algebra in his head, but thinks he's stupid."

"That's awful."

"STRIKE's helped him some. He's learning to judge his performance objectively—in the ring and also in class. He tested into advanced math so that's good." He read her face. "You okay?"

"I didn't sleep well, I guess."

"Futon acting up?" he asked, smiling.

She smiled back. "I've got a lot on my mind." Before she could say more, a buzzer sounded, signaling Victor's match was about to begin. The three rounds went by so fast, she could hardly follow. In the end, Victor won. The STRIKE kids and audience went wild.

Victor glowed, shoulders back, grinning with pride. Felicity wanted to hug him. He walked straight to Gabe, who slapped his shoulder in congratulations, then said, "What'd you learn?"

Victor seemed ready for the question. "Keep my focus. Don't be intimidated. Fight my fight. I watched my timing."

"You beat him to every strike that third round."

"I did. Yeah."

"What you just said, lock it in here—" He jabbed Victor's temple. "And here." He poked his chest. "Use it every time."

For every bout, Gabe gave the boys last-minute tips and afterward asked about the lessons, win or lose. In between, he told her about them—their families, their challenges, their fighting strengths and issues.

"I don't see Devin," she said.

"His mother thinks the meets are too stressful. I'm working on him to stand up to her. He backed off a bully the other day—stared the kid down. He was about to burst with pride."

"That sounds wonderful." If it weren't for Beatrice Milton's narrow mind—and Felicity's oversight—STRIKE could help so many kids like Devin.

Felicity introduced herself to the Discovery parents in the bleachers and spoke to the kids she recognized. They were all excited about STRIKE, which made her heart even heavier. Sarah was there. Kadisha had brought a posse. Carmen was hovering around Alex.

"Excuse me, Ms. Spencer?" A tall Latina touched her arm. "I'm Carmen's mother. Delores."

"Pleased to meet you."

"I want to thank you for what you're doing. Carmen is so excited about being trained for STRIKE."

"I'm glad to hear that," she said faintly.

"The coach is a great guy, from what I hear. Carmen says he's taken Alex Gomez in when there was trouble at home."

"They seem to be close."

"Yeah. I hear he does a lot for the kids. Takes them to the doctor's for physicals, talks to their teachers, finagles food stamps when there are snags. I guess he knows some of the caseworkers and cops."

They both looked over at him, where he was crouched

giving advice to a fighter, looking so handsome Felicity's heart melted.

"Easy on the eyes, too," Dolores said. "You know if he's single?"

"I believe so," Felicity managed to say, feeling a stab of jealousy. Totally ridiculous, but her attraction glowed as steady as a pilot light, not even close to going out.

"He's one of the good ones. He drives an older lady from my church to the market every week, no charge. Goes into neighborhoods where lots of cabs won't."

As the hours passed, she saw more of what Delores was talking about. Gabe promised one boy ear drops because his mom wouldn't take him to the clinic, told another he'd call a store owner about a summer job and warned a third that if he didn't raise his math grade, he'd be out of STRIKE.

Throughout the day, Felicity's eyes would meet Gabe's and for those seconds the gym, the noise, the people faded and it was only the two of them, connected the way they had been from the beginning.

The STRIKE fighters seemed to be doing well until Alex lost his bout. He lost his temper and yelled at the ref. Whistles blew and Gabe marched Alex out of the gym, then returned a few minutes later, walking with him to the judging table, where Alex apologized.

Afterward, Felicity heard Gabe talk with him. "What's the lesson?"

"Control my temper or it controls me," Alex muttered. "But that ref hates us. He calls us down all the time. He thinks we're thugs."

"So what? You fight every asshole who judges you by where you come from, you'll spend your life behind bars or six feet under."

There were no breaks where she could talk to Gabe, so

she invited herself to the pizza parlor where they went to celebrate their three first-place, three second-place and four third-place wins—an impressive showing for a small club—hoping to get him alone somehow. And, hell, for the fun of it.

Gabe looked pleased but puzzled by her interest. At the restaurant, Gabe said, "Pony up. Let's see what we can buy." The boys emptied their pockets, tossing crumpled ones and coins into a pile Gabe counted.

It broke her heart. They'd worked so hard and now they had to scrape up dimes to have anything to eat?

No way. "Discovery is hosting the party," she announced. "Pizza and drinks…and tokens for the arcade."

The kids looked at her in amazement.

She turned over a flyer on the table to use the back and set down a pen. "List your orders. Whatever you want." Then she gave Victor three twenties. "Divide up the tokens."

The kids wrote down what they wanted and she took it to the counter.

"This is coming out of your pocket, isn't it?" Gabe said, clearly not pleased or the least bit grateful.

"The kids deserve it." Scanning the menu board, she figured a rough total. Ouch. She'd eat ramen noodles for a while. So what? Totally worth it.

"They have to learn to spend what they have and no more. Charity doesn't help them."

"I'm treating them for pizza, not buying their souls. They shouldn't have to spend every cent to have that."

"They need limits. The shortcuts are too tempting—selling drugs, stealing or conning rich white ladies into paying their way."

"Nobody conned me. I offered. And I'm not rich."

"Come on. You know your family would cover you in

a heartbeat if you got into trouble. These kids don't have a safety net." There was superiority in his tone, as if he dismissed her, thought her a fool.

She stared at him, angry now. "This isn't about what's good or bad for the boys, is it? This is about me. You think I'm a spoiled Scottsdale brat slumming in the barrio."

"Privilege is the water you swim in. It's not like that for these kids."

"That is so unfair. You don't think I know what it's like to be—"

"Ms. Spencer?" Victor held out the bills she'd given him. "We're teaming up on *Ultimate Fighter.* We can go forever. Buy some churros maybe? For dessert?"

"You got it," she said. When he left, she turned to Gabe. "See? They could have pocketed that cash. You don't give them enough credit. It's pretty hypocritical of you to go on about how the boys have to tough it out, no breaks, no favors. They do have a safety net. You. You give them money, take them to the doctor, let them stay at your place, talk to their teachers, whatever they need."

"That's just good sense. If they're sick or hungry or afraid to go home, they can't focus on fighting."

"Oh, please."

The cashier yelled their number so they headed to the counter. She paid the hefty bill, while Gabe glowered in the background. He carried the tray of soda pitchers and she grabbed the pizza boxes, carrying them to the picnic table where the boys had gathered.

The argument had hurt her feelings. Gabe clearly didn't get her at all. He was the last person she should confide her dilemma in. Seeing the boys happy with their food, she decided to scoot out the door and grab a bus home.

"You're leaving, Ms. Spencer?" Alex said. "You didn't eat any pizza. We've got space. Move down." He shoved the kid next to him, then scooted, making room on the end for her.

"That's okay. Ms. Spencer and I will sit over there," Gabe said, nodding at a small round table. "Have a seat. I'll bring pizza," he said to her.

She went and sat, not happy about being trapped with him, but what else could she do?

Gabe brought paper plates with slices and two drinks and sat across from her, their knees meeting beneath the small table. "Okay," he said with a sigh. "You're right. They did deserve this. Thank you."

"You're welcome," she said, her hurt fading a little.

"It means a lot, you coming. To the boys." He paused. "And to me."

Her heart jumped. "It meant a lot to me, too."

"I'd like to help pay for it." He pulled out his wallet.

"I said it was my treat," she said firmly, then softened. "Let the privileged white lady do her act of charity."

He gave a sheepish smile. "Got it."

They ate in silence for a while, listening to the boys tease and insult each other, talk about the meet and how they'd performed, what they would do next time.

As she listened, glancing now and then at Gabe, Felicity thought about the lessons the boys learned from Gabe, how they analyzed each fight, how he'd helped Victor see he was good at math, how Alex had apologized for his outburst. She thought about the parents who'd been there, how their kids were dying to start STRIKE.

By the time she'd finished her second slice of pepperoni, she realized she didn't need to weigh pros and cons or have Gabe be devil's advocate. The day's events had made her decision for her.

She would not give up STRIKE or her job. Not without a fight. Like Gabe's team, she had strengths to tap—her people skills, her flexibility, her creativity, her determination. And she had Gabe.

"Looks like you're thinking pretty hard over there," Gabe said.

"I am. And we need to talk."

"Again?" He groaned. "Damn."

"Can you give me an hour sometime this weekend?"

"Depends on what you're wearing."

She felt the charge all the way to her toes. "What did you have in mind?"

"Anything like that red silk number would do fine. How about drinks at Buen Vecino, Sunday at six?"

"Perfect. I'll wear something you'll like."

GABE PARKED AND HEADED TOWARD Buen Vecino to meet Felicity. He was sunburned and muscle-sore from spending the day planting olive trees on the grounds of a new hotel, but he looked forward to seeing her, even if she had some cockeyed idea to torture him with.

The popular restaurant was no-reservations, so diners waiting for tables spilled outside the door. He picked Felicity out right away. She was elegant and sexy in tight black pants and a silky black top. Very money. He liked it just fine.

He'd been out of line to hassle her about the pizzas yesterday, but at a gut level it had hit him as an insult: *Let's give these needy barrio kids a thrill—buy 'em a slice and a Coke.* Deep down, he probably resented the advantages she took for granted, especially when there was so much he wanted to do for his boys—and his sisters—that he could never afford.

He walked closer. She was studying Adelia's mural—

tropical flowers surrounding a crowd of black, brown and white faces—a decent accent for a restaurant whose name meant *good neighbor.*

Gold hoop earrings added to the sleek look of Felicity's shorter hair. He did miss her flying feathers, which had made her seem sweet and young, but she looked amazing.

She spun to face him, though he hadn't called her name, smiling so big she seemed to glow. Or maybe it was just how he'd started seeing her. He'd been moved by her appearance at the meet, the way she'd watched and listened so closely to him and his boys.

"Hey, there," he said.

"Hey, yourself."

They smiled at each other for a moment, happy to be together. Then he took her arm and led her into the restaurant. They slid onto bar stools at the small, brightly tiled bar.

Santiago, the bartender, greeted him and Gabe ordered Coronas in bottles. Once they arrived, he tapped his against hers, looking into the vivid blue of her starlit eyes. He could get lost in their depths, find himself saying yes when he should mean no. Make that *hell no.*

They each took a drink, then set their bottles down. Felicity licked her lips, which made his mind blank and his blood go south, so he didn't quite catch her first words. "Say that again."

"I said I know you hate small talk, so I'll cut to the chase. Tom Brown told me I have to evict you or lose my job. Beatrice Milton complained to the school board president about STRIKE being part of the Institute and that was that."

"Damn." He'd been sucker punched. He motioned to Santiago. "Tequila shot with lime and salt. Felicity?"

"Sounds right to me."

"Dos. Pronto."

When the drinks came, he handed her a lime wedge and shook salt for her. She licked it, tossed back the shot, then bit the lime. Slamming down the glass she gasped for air. "Whew. Wow. That's strong."

"That's the idea." He went through the same ritual, welcoming the warm rush in his blood. "So, I figure you've got a plan. Spill."

She angled her knees toward him. "I won't give up STRIKE. It means too much to my kids."

"They'll fire you."

"Not if I can change Beatrice's mind."

"Sounds risky."

"It is. But I believe in this. If I get fired, I want it to be for something that counts." She looked determined and scared at the same time. He had the urge to kiss her.

She shifted on her stool, bumping his leg. "Sorry."

"I'm not." He held her leg in place, then moved closer, intertwining their thighs.

She sucked in a sharp breath. "You're making it hard to think."

"Maybe that's better. Maybe we've done too much thinking already."

"Another round?" Santiago asked.

"Please," Felicity said.

Gabe grinned. "You sure? Tequila sneaks up on you."

"Good. We're celebrating and I'm terrified."

Santiago brought two more beers and filled their shot glasses.

Felicity did the shot, then frowned. "I hardly felt that."

"Trust me, you will. Maybe wait on the beer."

She nodded. "So all I've got to do is make Beatrice happy. She'll call off the school board and Tom won't have to fire me."

"And how will you do that?"

"By using hapkido."

"You're going to stomp her instep and run?"

"I'm going to use her power against her. She loves to be in charge—she runs the PTO. Half of her anger is because she didn't know about STRIKE in advance. That was my mistake. So I'm going to rectify that."

"How?"

"By holding parent and family workshops and asking her to be in charge—put out the flyers, make the calls, generate support."

"What kind of workshops?"

"Things she'll like—self-defense for women and dealing with bullies."

"And when you say *we,* you mean *me?*"

"Mostly. I'll share research, too. But she needs to see you in action, realize what a good guy you are. It doesn't hurt that you're really hot."

"Pretty tricky, Cici."

"Human behavior has rules just like mechanical physics, I guess."

"You're good."

She was. She had him agreeing to give the workshops and to speak at a PTO meeting about gangs if it came to that. Worse, she made it sound fun.

He noticed the bar was jammed with people. "We should free up these stools," he said.

"Sure." She hopped to the floor. "Wow…I'm kind of wobbly."

He caught her arm. "We should get some food into you."

"I've got it! Come home with me and I'll make you supper. It's my turn!"

At least that way he'd be sure she got home safely. And

he would be okay driving her the short distance to her place. He was a big guy and he hadn't touched the second beer.

Outside, she stopped at the mural. "Your ex-girlfriend is *soooo* talented. I'd *looove* her to do a mural at Discovery. How much does she charge?"

"These days, plenty. When she did this, she traded it for meals and beers. The owner was sick of all the tags on his building and she convinced him taggers would leave the mural alone out of respect. She was right."

"That is very cool. Would she talk to our kids? About real art as opposed to tagging? Would you ask her?"

"I'll try. But she's pretty busy."

"You know she'll say yes to you." She stood on tiptoe, leaning against him. "You're irresistible."

"And you're drunk." He half laughed.

"Just *very* cheerful. But I've been so scared and now I've jus' decided to go for it and it *feelssogood.* Plus, I like you…." She sighed with so much longing, he felt it down deep.

"Yeah?" He felt the same about her, more now that the tequila had burned down some of his defenses. He ran his hands down her upper arms. Tiny bumps rose. "You cold?" Her nipples had tightened beneath the thin fabric that covered them.

"No. I'm hotter than hot." She gave him a look she meant to be sultry, but looked goofy instead.

"Let's go soak up some of that alcohol."

If he were smart, he'd walk her to her apartment and leave, but he had the feeling that there was enough tequila and testosterone running through him to make him really, really stupid.

When he turned onto Central Avenue, a group of lowriders cruised by, hopping their struts, chrome bumpers reflecting light like a laser show. Gabe signaled approval with a nod. These guys loved their rides. He'd hung with a lowrider club for a bit. Just beers, gears and good times. No hate, no guns, no drugs.

At her apartment, Gabe guided Felicity by the elbow into the lobby.

"Hi, Abel!" she called to the guy at the desk.

"Everything okay, Ms. Spencer?"

"Everything's great! This is Gabe. My friend."

Abel eyed Gabe like he'd roofied Felicity and intended to have his way with her upstairs. He tracked them all the way to the elevator, looking concerned.

"Why was he staring at us like that?" she asked.

Gabe almost laughed. "Let's just say I don't look like your type."

"But I don't have a type," she said. "I like who I like. And I like *you.*" She stuck a finger in his chest. "It's probably that he's never seen me drunk before."

"Maybe." Could she be that naive?

"He's a champion bass fisherman. Can you believe they actually have competitions in fishing?"

"I take it you're making friends now?"

"I am. There's a girl named Candee who runs early like I do. We talk. She's a bank teller. She's on a celery diet, if you can believe that. Where's the protein, I ask her? Protein is vital. Vi-*tal.*"

On her floor, Felicity fished out her key, opened the door and waved him inside. "Check it out. I did a little more decorating."

"I can see that." There was more art, another lamp and an entertainment center, empty except for a few books.

"That's for when I can afford a TV. Abel put it together."

"Abel, huh? I thought *I* was your some-assembly-required guy."

She laughed. "You're funny when you're...*cheerful.*"

"You're pretty cheerful yourself, *chica.*"

"I know. Anyway, when you helped me set all this up... you made me feel like I could live here...and be okay, you know?" She gave him a tentative smile. "And at your house the other night. That dinner...your sisters. I felt like I fit in...kind of."

"That's good."

"I'm babbling from the tequila, but it's true. So I'd better see what I've got that's edible." He followed her to the kitchen.

She ducked her head into the fridge. "Not much... sorry. Takeout leftovers. But there should be some..." She opened the freezer. "Yep, triple-chocolate chunk. Calcium and protein." She turned to him, holding the carton, but he was staring at the vase of snapdragons on her table.

"They look nice."

"They're beautiful. I need to take some to Robert's grave." She frowned, studying the blooms. She shot her gaze to him. "What you said to me? About Robert? And with the girls? About letting it go? It made some of the bad past fade. I actually like spring again."

"Me, too." He realized it was true. The fresh smells and new life didn't sink his mood anymore.

"That's good, isn't it?" She didn't look convinced. "I hope so." She turned away to get spoons from a drawer, then dropped into a chair and plopped the carton on the table.

He sat with her. She tore off the lid and clicked her soup spoon against his. "To the ice-cream hangover cure!"

They dug in.

"Mmm, this tastes good." She closed her eyes with

pleasure, her pink tongue working over the spoon in a way that ought to be illegal.

She caught him staring at her mouth. "What? Do I have ice cream…?"

"No. It's just how you're…enjoying it." He cleared his throat.

"It's hitting the spot. I was getting a little woozy there."

"I could see that."

"I like that you watch out for me. Maybe that's lame, but it makes me feel good. Safe, you know?"

"I do." He did feel a strong urge to take care of her.

"I felt that way back then. Like that time you fixed my mom's car without me saying a word."

"I remember."

"My mom screamed over every dime I cost her, so you saved me. I never forgot that."

"Neither did I."

"And always after that, whenever I saw you…"

"Yeah. Always after that…" It was there, the attraction, the connection.

"And now?"

"And now…we have to remember what's important. So I should go."

He didn't know where he got the willpower, but he put down his spoon, got to his feet ready to do the right thing.

GABE WAS LEAVING. Very smart, since, though the ice cream was helping, she was still feeling boozy enough to risk a triple-chocolate-chunk kiss or two.

Her eyes landed on the flowers and she got that jolt of guilt. She hadn't been to the grave yet because she would remember everything, the blame she carried that Gabe didn't know about.

"If you'd like, I can drive you to the cemetery. Save you cab fare," Gabe said so innocently.

"I couldn't ask you to do that."

"I chased you away before. The least I could do is to drive you back, now that we're square."

"But we're not," she said softly. "We're not square." The truth burned through her, tightening her insides, making her eyes sting. They'd had this lovely time, put their heads together to save her job and STRIKE, but she couldn't pretend things were square.

"What do you mean? We talked it out. We let it go."

"Not all of it. You don't know all that happened."

He sat. "What is it?"

She looked into his face. He deserved to know. He could judge her as she should be judged. "That night we got arrested…"

"Yeah?" He stilled, tense, braced for her story.

She closed her eyes, seeing it all again.

Damien roared out of the parking lot, then tore around the corner, too fast, wheels screeching, car tilting. Horns honked. Then another corner and another, the car skittering to the side. Sirens sounded. Felicity, terrified, crashed into the door handle, then the back of the front seat, her body liquid with fear, braced to hit another car, to die, to get shot. It was so strange. Some of it happened lightning quick. The rest was slow as running in the quicksand of a nightmare.

Someone kept screaming, "Stop the car! Stop the car!" After a while, she realized it was her.

"Shut up, bitch! Shut up!" Damien screamed back.

Police lights behind them, in front of them. A police SUV blocked the road and Damien swerved up the curb onto the sidewalk and slammed on the brakes, banging Felicity's head against the seat. "Don't say a word," he yelled at them over the seat. "There's no proof. They don't know what happened. We stick together. We get out of it together. Shut the hell up."

"We didn't do anything," she yelled. "You robbed the store, not us."

"Shut up, bitch, or you're dead." Pure hatred twisted his features.

"Don't talk to her like that," Robert said, lunging at him to hit him.

Through the back window, she saw cops approaching. "One of them's Diaz," she said in despair. He was hateful to all the Chicano kids, but especially Robert, constantly searching him, shoving him around, insulting him.

She felt as if she would throw up.

The car was harshly lit from the cop car's spotlight. Then the cops started shouting, "Driver, remove the keys from the ignition with your left hand. Put your right hand on your head. Passengers, open your doors. Right, then left." It went on: do this, do that, step here, kneel, hands here, hands there.

She was so confused, scared any minute the cops would lose patience with their sluggish actions and shoot them dead. She could hardly breathe and her thoughts raced and stalled and stuttered.

"When the cops stopped us, Damien wanted us to keep still, not talk, stick together," she said to Gabe, her mouth so dry, her lips stuck to each other between words. She rubbed sweaty palms on her pants. "The cops were yelling at us, making us kneel, pushing us around, and I saw Officer Diaz going after Robert."

"Diaz was always on his case," Gabe said grimly.

"I saw Robert's face. I could see he would argue, make it worse. Which would be horrible. We hadn't done anything except get trapped in Damien's car. I couldn't stand it, so I yelled, 'Damien Hidalgo robbed the store. He kidnapped us. It's all him, not us. We're innocent.'"

She glanced at Gabe. There was distance in his gaze and she knew hearing the story was not easy for him.

"Then Damien lunged at me, knocked me down. He wanted to shut me up. He put his arm against my throat." She remembered the grit of the sidewalk scraping her arms, fighting for air, the cop lights flaring all around her while her vision began to fade.

"Robert went for Damien. Diaz threw Robert down and tried to cuff him, but Robert went nuts, punching and kicking like an insane person. He hit Diaz in the face, kicked him."

"Fractured an eye socket, broke two ribs," Gabe said. "Assaulting a police officer meant mandatory time in juvenile hall."

She nodded. "And it was because of me," she said roughly, her throat tight. "He was defending *me*." A sob tore from her throat, almost an animal cry. She felt as if her insides were tearing.

She saw it again.

The flashing lights like an evil carnival, the squirming bodies, the fists, kicks, contorted faces, the dark cop uniforms, light flashing off metal, the gleam of a nightstick, everything out of control, as if the world was tumbling to its destruction.

"It was my fault. All of it. My fault we were in Damien's car. My fault Robert hit the cop and got juvenile hall. Then I abandoned him. You forgave me, but you didn't know all that I did."

Gabe's eyes were full of turmoil as he struggled with this new information. He swallowed hard. "It could have been adult prison. For the attempted robbery. Damien confessed or it would have been."

"My attorney put the deal together. That was one good thing."

He looked at her, took a slow breath, clearly trying to calm down.

"I'm sorry. I know I can't fix it. I should have told you before, but I was so relieved that you forgave me, I pushed it back, tried to forget."

He didn't speak.

"You don't have to say anything." Her voice was shaking. She felt dizzy from holding her breath. "I wouldn't blame you if you never spoke to me again."

"No," he said, then had to clear his throat. He shook his head. "That doesn't change anything. You were scared that night. You were trying to help Robert."

She shook her head. "And I wanted to save myself. I was stupid. From the beginning I was stupid. I went along with everything, all the bad stuff. I could have fixed it. If I'd said, let's be good, go to school, stay straight, Robert might have listened. But I didn't even try. I wanted him to love me."

Gabe was silent for a long time.

"Now you know the kind of person I am." She felt sick. "Being sorry doesn't fix it."

Gabe shook his head slowly. "You don't think I play what-if? If I hadn't ridden Robert so hard when he got released, he might not have avoided me until he was too deep in gang stuff to get out. If only I'd left class earlier that day, or got Mom to take him to the gym, or loaned him my car…" He looked so lost and full of pain.

"Yeah, you were stupid," he said. "So was I. So was Robert. But enough. Guilt is acid in the gut. Robert had choices. He made bad ones. Ultimately, that's why he's gone. Maybe we let him down, you and I, but that can't be helped. Our job is to do better from here."

"Do you really believe that?" Felicity said.

"I'm trying to." He ran his thumbs across each of her cheeks. Until they came away wet, she hadn't known she was crying.

CHAPTER TEN

FELICITY'S FACE broke his heart. Her cheeks were wet, her blue eyes cloudy, her lips trembling. He'd hated being yanked to that terrible turning point in his brother's life, but hearing her agonize over every word and deed, all he wanted was to take away her pain.

He really had forgiven her. He was ready to let go.

He stood, helped her to her feet and pulled her into his arms, holding her and letting her hold him. It was as if a storm had been raging and the wind suddenly died, leaving a calm silence.

He felt Felicity's heart beat against his chest, her ribs swell and subside. He felt her gradually relax, soften against him, steady within herself.

She pulled back to look at him, her eyes asking the question.

"Yeah. It's okay. Forgive yourself. And I'll do the same."

"You are a good man." She pressed her face against his chest and held him tight. As the seconds ticked away, the feeling between them shifted. Peace and comfort fled, replaced by heat and desire. He wanted this woman. He wanted her more than anything he'd wanted in a long time.

He was aware of her candy scent, the curve of her hips under his hands, the sharp intake of her breath as she noticed the change, too. Her fingers dug into his back, as if to keep him close, and she pressed her hips against his.

They looked at each other. The wonder and want he was feeling shone back at him from her eyes.

"Please," she whispered.

"Yeah," he said. It seemed inevitable, as right as absolving each other of guilt over Robert, and he took her face in both hands and kissed her.

She began to shake, but held on tight, as if she feared he might pull away. Not going to happen.

They kissed for a long time, tongues sliding and tasting, pushing and coaxing. She felt like heaven. Tasted like it, too.

She urged him backward, into her front room. *The bed.* They needed the bed. Except when his legs hit the frame, he remembered it was a couch he'd have to flip open.

He broke off to do that.

"Don't stop." She grabbed his neck to pull him back.

"Making...the...bed," he managed to say.

"Right. Yeah."

They both threw off the slipcover, clicked the catch and fell together onto the sheets. He lay over her and kissed her again. She lifted her hips against him, grabbing his backside with her fingers.

He should say something, make sure she wanted this, that he wasn't pushing her, but all he managed was, "Protection?" He had no condoms on him.

It took her a second to catch on. "I'm on the Pill. Are you...?"

"Healthy? Yeah."

"Me, too."

That meant they didn't need to stop. They looked at each other for a moment, letting what they were about to do settle in. He started to reach under her shirt, but she stopped his hand and pulled off her top and bra.

He took in the sight of her naked to the waist, her skin golden in the lamplight, then put his hands on her breasts. They were firm, the skin soft as butter. Her nipples tightened against his palms as she made a sound and pushed into his hands. "Damn, you're beautiful," he breathed.

"Take off your shirt," she said, tugging at it.

He obliged her, removing it.

"You're beautiful, too. Also strong—" she ran her fingers over his biceps "—and sentimental." She brushed the tattoo of Robert. "Stubborn—" she traced *terco* with a nail, making him shudder "—and fierce." She slid her palm to his belly where Robert's wolf drawing had been tattooed. "And I want you so bad."

A current poured through him, completely unstoppable. He wanted her, too. And he intended to have her.

"Show me the rest of you," he said.

FELICITY GOT OFF THE BED to take off her clothes for Gabe, her heart beating so hard she feared she'd break a rib. Gabe stared at her. He was so beautiful, so exotic, so different from her—big where she was small, brown where she was pale. She could hardly believe this was happening.

She kicked off her shoes, undid her zipper and shook her pants to the floor. She trembled in her second-best pair of bikini-cut panties.

"Mmm, I was right," he murmured. "Sensible, but sexy."

"You guessed about my panties?"

"Trust me, every man who looks at you does. After that, he's figuring how fast he can get you out of them. It's how we're wired. What can I say?"

She flushed, unsettled about random men lusting after her, but loving the thought that Gabe had.

Gabe moved to the edge of the bed and took her by the hips, his hands big and strong and warm. He pulled her close and kissed her stomach, his mouth firm, his breath hot. She shuddered. Then he traced her navel with his tongue, sending erotic charges along her nerves, making her throb and ache.

Slowly, he pulled off her panties. He kissed her stomach, then moved down, slow and sure.

He was going to kiss her *there.* "Oh…" she breathed, not sure she was ready for that intimate act. When his tongue found her with one sweet stroke, her knees gave out.

"I've got you," he murmured, making his hands a chair for her. He nuzzled her between her folds, teased her clit, tugging it, rolling it with his tongue, sending pulse after pulse along her overloaded circuits.

She couldn't feel her legs anymore, only what his tongue was doing. Her hips rocked into his rhythmic strokes. All she could do was surrender, trusting him to hold her, to pleasure her.

She wove her fingers into his hair, holding his head, making needy, breathy sounds, not caring about anything except what this man was doing to her body.

Oh, this was what the fuss was about. This was passion—hot and hungry and not to be denied.

And then she was coming. She gave a sharp cry as she exploded, rocking hard against his mouth, flying free, full of joy, shaking and shaking with the waves of it. When she stopped, Gabe lowered her to the bed.

"That was amazing," she said, looking at him, fighting for breath. "It was so… I can't…talk."

"Then don't. It's time to *do.*" He took off his pants

and underwear. His cock rose, golden in the lamplight, and she took his shaft in her hand, sliding her fist up and down its length.

"Nice hands," Gabe said, watching her work, shuddering a little as she quickened the pace. "Mmm. I want inside you." He separated her thighs with his knees. She positioned him with her hand and he eased inside her. His eyes flared. "I've wanted this for a long time."

"Me, too," she said, surprised that she was already aroused again. She ran her hands down his arms, the muscles tight, the skin smooth, the dark ink of the tattoos looking dangerous. She felt the bulges and shifts of his back muscles, then slid her hands to his butt as he withdrew, then thrust deeper inside her.

"That feels so good," she said.

"Yeah," he said, beginning a slow rhythm of thrusts. She could tell he was holding back, being careful not to hurt her.

He lowered his mouth to kiss her, pressed fingers into her back, lifting her against him, so she felt all of her body against all of his, all the while continuing to thrust, each movement delicious, exquisite, building the pressure, the urge, the tension.

"You're getting there," Gabe said softly. "I can see it in your face, feel it in your body, how you're breathing."

"I am. Oh, I am. What about you?" Her muscles tightened, prepared for the waves to come.

"Oh, I'm there. Don't worry about me." He stopped moving for a moment, as if waiting for her to reach the top, then he thrust hard, pressing his hips at the perfect angle to take her over the edge. She shattered again, stronger than before. He cried out, too, and his body shook as he pulsed inside her.

She floated for many seconds, light and happy and content. Life was good. She was where she belonged, with this man holding her, cherishing her, needing her.

Gradually, she settled down, became aware of the mattress beneath her, of Gabe's breaths alternating with her own. When he reached past her to pull up the sheet, she noticed a tattoo in the middle of his back and stopped him to study it.

It was a red rose in full bloom, velvety and vivid, on a thorny stem outlined by the words, *De la espina crece la flor.* "What does *espina* mean?"

"Thorn."

"'From the thorn grows the flower.' Meaning beauty comes from struggle."

"My grandmother used to say that."

"And you believe it."

"It's what I hope. That tough times make us stronger. Otherwise, suffering is pointless."

He pulled her onto his chest, covered her with the sheet, then began to stroke her hair, as if to soothe her, to comfort her.

They lay in an easy silence, but questions rose in her head: *What does this mean? What do we do now? Is this all or have we only just started?*

No. She closed her eyes. She would not drive herself—or him—crazy with questions. This felt good. That should be enough.

But it was such a surprise. They made an unlikely pair. Gabe was cynical where she was hopeful, stalled while she kept striving, quiet while she was bubbly. Was that the attraction? The friction? The opposition?

Stop analyzing. Enjoy the moment.

"Sleepy?" Gabe asked drowsily.

"Soon," she said, so wound up she doubted she'd drift off at all.

Did he feel the way she did, that something big had happened between them?

When they were making love, he'd looked at her so intently, so deeply—as if they were meant for each other—that she believed he did.

They would talk in the morning. She couldn't wait.

THE ONLY PROOF GABE had been in her bed was a brief note scribbled on a napkin and left on the table by the door—a last-minute thought when he was sneaking away:

Got an early job. See you this afternoon. We'll work out the details. G

The message was clear: *Don't call me and I sure as hell won't call you. See you at work, business as usual. This never happened.*

She sat at her kitchen table, blinking against the sunlight pouring through the window, making her hangover worse. Or maybe that was the effect of the note.

He hadn't felt anything close to what she had. She balled up the note and tossed it at the trash can, missing, and it lay there like an accusation: *You fool.*

What did she expect? Breakfast in bed? A note signed *mi vida, mi alma, mi amor,* like some character in a *telenovela?*

She wasn't going to sit there and mope. She jumped up, grabbed the balled-up note and slammed it into the garbage. *Done and done.* Better to know now than later, after she'd gotten her hopes up, started to make plans.

She'd never felt this way about a man. That was true. But then, she'd never been with anyone like Gabe before. He was intense, passionate, serious about everything he did. Sex, too, evidently.

They'd had a one-night stand, sparked by the tequila and fueled by the talk about Robert. Gabe had forgiven her—again—and for all of it this time. Of course she would feel emotional and read too much into what had happened.

She knew zero about love. Her parents had been no example, and she'd certainly never fallen in love with the guys she'd dated. The last boy she'd loved had been Robert—and that had been when she was all of fourteen.

She would heed Gabe's note. At school, she would be cool and casual and professional—ball up her hurt like his note and toss it out for good.

"YOU HUNGOVER?" Carl asked Gabe on Monday, handing him a rake for the pile of palm fronds they were loading into the truck.

"Nah." Trimming palm trees was hot and dizzying, but that wasn't what had Gabe dazed. It was Felicity. He could not get her out of his mind. He kept hearing her cries, feeling her quiver when he'd had his mouth on her and seeing the pure joy on her face when she climaxed.

The woman had rocked him to his bones.

He'd awakened at four, too flipped out to sleep longer, so he'd left. It took ten minutes to decide what to write on the note. He'd gone for neutral and friendly, so she wouldn't feel awkward when she saw him again.

He didn't know what to do about what had happened. It felt as though the sex had slipped into something big and deep. He'd gotten that slammed-bolt, locked-in-for-good sensation.

Had he gone so old-school he'd turned great sex into a lifelong match, like wolves mating for life?

With Felicity? Unlikely. The only history they shared was a painful one. They had little in common except their jobs, and that was by accident. He didn't get her at all and he knew he puzzled her.

That emotional talk about Robert had started the connection. They'd held on to each other too long, maybe due to the tequila. Add to it the fact that he hadn't had sex in a while and Felicity was lonely in a new city.

There was the undercurrent of his growing respect for her—she was risking her job over STRIKE—but that wasn't enough to turn his life upside down. Or hers.

What did *she* think? She'd been quiet afterward—no questions, no *what does this mean, when will I see you again?* Maybe he'd been her walk on the wild side and now her curiosity had been satisfied, so she'd want to forget about it.

He tried to lose himself in physical labor; he couldn't stand not knowing what she thought, so he left the landscaping job at 1:00 p.m. to meet with her about the new STRIKE setup and the PTO-lady plot. On the way, he talked to Adelia, so he had that to tell Felicity, too.

He swung home, showered, then drove to the school. In the hallway to Felicity's office, he found himself sweating as if he'd been rolling sod all day. What the hell was he so nervous for? His heart banged his ribs and adrenaline spiked his bloodstream. *Get hold of yourself, homes.*

At her office door, he looked in at her. Damn, he was glad to see her. *A sight for sore eyes.* Wasn't that the saying? He tapped at the door.

She looked up. "Oh, hi!" She half stood, then sat, her breasts bouncing.

"Is this a bad time?"

"No. Come in." She sounded nervous.

He sat across from her. "You okay?" Her cheeks were splashed with color.

"Why wouldn't I be okay?" she snapped. "What about you? Are *you* okay?"

Damn. She was *pissed.* About the night or the note? He took a guess. "My note upset you?"

The color on her cheeks deepened. "Why would it? It had the pertinent data. You had a job. We'd talk this afternoon. It's this afternoon, so let's talk." Anger sizzled beneath every word.

"Look, if I said the wrong thing or—"

"The plan with Beatrice seems to be working. She's putting together a flyer about the workshops. We need to choose the nights. Thursdays are slow cab nights, right? Seven to nine?"

"That'll work," he said.

"Good. I'm thinking that our approach should be..." She rattled on about the workshops, turning a Tinkertoy dowel end to end, faster and faster.

"Felicity," he said, catching her hands, "I'm sorry I upset you. You were great. I just...didn't know—"

"I'm *fine,*" she said firmly. She tugged her hands away, interlacing her fingers on the desk, squeezing so tightly her knuckles went white.

"You seem freaked."

Her shoulders sagged a little, admitting the truth. "I'm a little embarrassed. I mean I was *sooo* drunk. That tequila sneaked up on me, all right." She gave a fake laugh. "I hope I didn't say anything stupid." Her gaze was bouncing around like a pinball, landing everywhere but his face.

"You were perfect, Felicity. Amazing."

She met his gaze. "Oh." She flashed him a smile of pleased relief, then blew out a breath. "So no harm done. We can move on."

"Right." He felt punched. To hide that, he picked up

that stupid magic wand and tilted it so the glitter slid like slow, pink sand. He would never kiss her again or hear her sighs or feel the fingers she'd clutched together so tightly digging into his back.

"So we're clear?" she demanded.

"We are. Clear." Their gazes locked. He wanted to lunge across the desk and kiss her right out of that designer suit and whatever panties she had on today.

"That's that, then." Did she look sad? He wasn't sure.

He remembered his news. "I called Adelia. She's willing to speak to your students, but she wants to meet first. I'll set that up if you'd like."

"Really? That's great." She gave a genuine smile for the first time since he'd walked in. Progress. They were back in business again.

Next they talked about the STRIKE session. She had figured out how to group the kids to train every other day, with Friday as a bonus for the top students. She'd decided to combine her computer lab with the study area to give him more room.

"My guys won't be happy about losing the first hour to your kids."

"I hope you can present that in a positive way."

"You mean, we do this or we're evicted?" He smiled wryly.

"More like this is a chance to share the STRIKE philosophy with more students and an opportunity to hone your coaching skills."

"You do know how to shovel the shit, don't you, Cici?"

"Go with your strengths," she said. "Like you tell your guys." She was joking again, a good sign. "Beatrice will be observing later in the week. Please charm her."

"I'll do my best. No glowering or brooding." Felicity

had put her job on the line to save his program. He would do whatever she asked.

"So, good. We're squared away."

"We are." Except for the fact he wanted her more than ever. She'd said no and all he could think about was yes, yes, *yes.*

GABE LOOKED AT FELICITY through the passenger window as if he thought she was crazy. "You called a cab? Your apartment's down the block."

"I know. I can explain." Felicity climbed in, hoping Gabe wouldn't object to her idea.

"Okay. Go," he said exasperatedly, but he was fighting a grin. He seemed happy to see her, at least. She'd hated the distance that had come between them since the night they'd slept together.

"Put the meter on and start driving first," she said, setting the grocery sack at her feet. She'd had him pick her up from the store.

"Where to?"

"Papago Park. The Buttes. It's pretty up there. That should give us enough time."

"Time for what?"

"For our meeting. It's been two days and we need to debrief, see what adjustments we need to make in the program."

"You want me to drive you around so we can talk? That's crazy. I can spare a few minutes."

"No, you can't. You've sacrificed too much work time already. Plus, I brought sandwiches from the deli counter. For your supper break. If I'd had time, I'd have gone to Giorgio's."

"I don't know...." He shook his head, but he started driving.

Silence settled around them, as they adjusted to each other.

I miss you. That's what she wanted to say, but she knew better. If only she were cool enough to just sleep with him, be content with that. She'd almost suggested it in her office on Monday. She'd been close to climbing across her desk and attacking the man. But he'd sat there calmly tipping the magic wand up and down, totally relaxed, completely cool about being *clear* and *done.*

It had kind of hurt, she had to admit. Proof she'd been smart to back off.

"This cab looks like you," she said.

"I look like a cab?"

"You know what I mean. It's clean, polished, feels peaceful. Smells good." Like starched cotton and lime. She loved that smell. Latin hip-hop played from the stereo.

"I like things squared away."

He'd hung miniature boxing gloves from his mirror and clipped a photo of his mother and the twins to his visor.

"You do," she said. He had the two of them all squared away, too.

"Alex didn't show up at STRIKE today," Gabe said. "Victor told me you suspended him from school. Is that right?"

"He threw a chair at his art teacher, Mr. Salazar."

"He loves art. Why would he do that?"

"The teacher objected to a mural he drew. It was an update of a Diego Rivera piece about the Mexican revolution. He included AK-47s."

"Alex went nuts over that?"

"He says he only shoved the chair near Mr. Salazar,

not at him. It was something about his art being his soul, his people."

"Which is ironic, since Alex isn't even Chicano. *Gomez* was his last stepdad. The guy respected him, taught him about Latin pride. He left to do construction in Vegas when Alex's mother divorced him."

"He seemed really angry at me, too."

"That's about the gym. My guys are pissed about the changes. They blame Alex, saying he's a shitty leader, that he let you walk over him."

"Should I talk to them?"

"Leave it alone. They'll adjust. But the last thing Alex needs is more hours on the streets."

"Mr. Salazar wanted him expelled, so a three-day suspension was the best I could do. I can't show leniency, since I'm new and the teachers want me to be strict. Alex will want back into STRIKE, so he'll behave, don't you think?"

"I hope so."

She blew out a breath, as worried as Gabe seemed to be. "Anyway, we should debrief."

"I don't know. I'm more of a boxers guy."

"I remember." She pushed away the mental picture of him with no shirt on, watching her undress.... "So how did the last two days go?"

"We were crowded, even with the extra space. Kids had to wait their turn, which led to goofing off."

"What would help?"

"More equipment. Another coach. But that costs."

"Maybe a sporting-goods store would give us a discount. I'll make some calls."

"Conrad's going to set up circuit training for tomorrow. That will handle a bunch of kids at once."

They talked through more details and had just finished

planning for Beatrice Milton's visit the next day when they reached Papago Park and pulled in. Gabe reached for the meter.

"Don't turn it off. We're still working."

"I'm not charging you for this, Felicity."

"You have to," she said. "I mean it."

"Now who's stubborn?" He shook his head, but he left the meter running.

CHAPTER ELEVEN

GABE TOOK FELICITY'S GROCERY sack and they started up the path to the distinctive formation of windblown caves in red volcanic rock. It made him think of Mars. The air was cool and there was a pleasant breeze.

Felicity pointed at the moon. It was full and glowed so brightly it looked fake. "Gorgeous, huh?"

"Uh-huh." But he was looking at her, remembering her body lit by the moon through her thin curtains, smooth as marble, until he touched her and found her warm and soft and giving.

He wanted her again right now, the desire stronger than ever. He *yearned* for her, like some brooding hero, bemoaning an unrequited love on some windy cliff above a pitiless sea. Damn, he was losing it for sure, writing bad fiction in his tortured mind.

The trail narrowed and he let her go in front, leaving him the sight of her backside, looking so good it was all he could do not to grab it and take a bite.

She glanced at him. "You're staring at my butt, aren't you?"

"Because you're waving it in my face."

"They're black silk with red piping, FYI."

She meant her underwear. "Ouch," he said, feeling actual pain.

"Not sensible at all. So there." She started walking

again. He caught up with her and noticed her breath quickened.

"Sensible can be sexy." She'd be sexy in a trash bag with leg holes.

"Yeah? Well…" She opened her mouth, closed it again and walked on, clearly flustered. He liked that.

They stopped at the first cave and sat on its lip, legs dangling toward the gentle slope below. Their thighs touched and he held his there. The city lights were a twinkling blanket of colored jewels rolling out to the horizon.

She blew out a breath. "This is nice. I get so caught up in work I never relax."

"You do seem pretty wound up."

She jerked her head to him.

"Not an insult. That's how you get so much done. All that energy."

"Exactly." She reached into the sack and brought out the food—ham sandwiches, chips and soda. "Supper."

"Always prepared. That's another thing."

"Isn't this better than wolfing it down in your car?"

"As long as the meter's running, sure." But there was no way she was paying him for this trip.

They ate, looking out at the scene, glancing at each other every few seconds, smiling like idiots.

"How did you know that Adelia was the one?" she asked, catching him as he was about to take a bite. "That you were in love?"

He put down the sandwich. "You're asking about my feelings? Shit, Cici. I might cook and iron, but I'm still a guy. We don't do feelings."

"I really want to know."

"Okay." He looked up at the huge moon. "We understood each other, sometimes without words. We had a lot in common—same background."

"Because you're both Chicano?"

"Partly. I'm only half, remember? Ethnic stuff is important. My dad was a Chicano gangbanger from the barrio and my mom was a white hippie rebelling from her middle-class parents. Talk about nothing in common."

"But my parents came from the same background and they were a disaster. Did your parents love each other?"

"I guess. But so what? All they did was fight. She hated that the gang was *familia* to him, that she wasn't first in his heart. Plus, she resented his machismo. He kept secrets supposedly to *protect* her—also very Latin. Once she had kids she wanted a settled life, regular hours, dinner on the table. She started hating the late parties, my dad's crew, all the drugs and guns around. She got jumpy about police raids."

"But your father was a criminal. People from different backgrounds can be good together—if they're open-minded and willing to compromise."

"It's the day-to-day differences that mess you up. How you handle money, where you live, who's in charge, how you raise your kids, your church. That's what eats away at what made you want to be together."

He tossed a small stone down the hill. It clicked quietly against a few rocks, then went silent.

"I don't know why I'm arguing about it. What do I know?"

"You've really never been in love?"

"Not since Robert, but I guess that was puppy love. I never clicked with anyone that strongly." She sounded so sad.

"You haven't met the right guy."

She kept staring straight out. "That's what I told myself, or that the time wasn't right. But I don't think love works that way." She turned to him, her eyes big in the moonlight. "Busy people fall in love. They go for it, no matter how bad the timing is. Maybe I'm just not equipped, you know?"

"I doubt that. You've got a big heart."

"If she hadn't cheated on you, would you have married Adelia?"

He gave a short laugh. "I used to think that, but probably not. She said I was too closed off, too wrapped up in my head to really be with her, and that was why she strayed."

"Do you believe that?"

"She had a point." He threw another stone, then smiled at her. "We're a pair, you and I. You've never been in love and I couldn't stay there."

"Yeah. We are."

He noticed crumbs near her mouth and brushed them off, letting his hand linger on her impossibly soft skin. The night breeze lifted her hair, bringing spring smells that no longer saddened him. Now they made him think of Cici and how much pleasure he got holding her…kissing her….

She leaned into his palm, cupped it with her own and closed her eyes.

"Cici…" he whispered and went after her sweet mouth, so giving and soft against his own. With a little moan of relief, she turned and pressed herself against him. He slid his hands down her back, going after those panties she'd mentioned. He was about to strip down and use his clothes as a blanket over the packed earth, when a boxing bell went off in his pocket.

Felicity jerked away with a gasp. "What is that?"

"My ringtone," he said ruefully. "End of round one. Stay right here." He put his arm around her, pulled her close and flipped open the phone.

FELICITY LIKED GABE holding her close while he took his call. It felt right. So had his kiss. So had kissing him back. What about her decision to not do this? They'd been *clear.* But when they kissed, *clear* got all muddy in her mind.

They were a pair, like he'd said, both uncertain about love. Maybe together they could figure it out.

Maybe they shouldn't give up yet… Maybe—

Gabe stiffened, dropped his arm and leaned into the call. "When?…Yeah…Damn it. I'll be right there. Thanks for the heads-up, Coop."

He clicked the phone shut. "That was Coop Carter, a detective on the gang squad. They picked up Alex tagging the school."

"You're kidding. Why would he do that?"

"God only knows." He got up, held out a hand for her. "I've got to get him, try to keep them from filing charges. I'll drop you off on the way."

"Take me with you. I'm the principal of the school he vandalized."

He looked at her.

"Better me than Leonard Lancaster. Maybe I can help. I could arrange for him to paint out the tags, maybe do community service. Would they allow that?"

"Worth a try," he said.

At the station, Gabe introduced her to Detective Carter, who was clearly a friend of his. "Handy you were giving the principal a ride when I called," the officer said, giving Gabe a speculative look.

"What's the story, Coop?" Gabe asked.

"A crew of tykes sprayed the length of the building. He was with them. Sent them off and took the hit himself."

"If he gets charged, it'll be Adobe Mountain for sure. His mother's useless and broke. If he goes behind bars, you'll just get another Duecer, Coop. You want that?"

"You can't adopt these kids. We talked about this."

"I have an idea, Detective," Felicity said. "What if the school has Alex clean up the graffiti, then do some community-service hours in the neighborhood? I'll supervise him, track his hours. However many you think appropriate."

The detective studied her, arms folded.

"He's got a lot of potential," she added. "We don't want to lose him."

"This bleeding-heart deal contagious?" he said to Gabe. He turned to her. "I'll talk to the prosecutor, but no promises."

He led them to the small interview room where Alex sat, his head on the table. The room reeked of alcohol. When they entered, he sat up, terrified, then he saw Gabe and turned his head to hide his tears.

"You are one lucky *vato,* Gomez," Detective Carter said to him. "These two are willing to take responsibility for your sorry ass. My opinion? Your folks should pay for the buff-out and you should spend thirty days at Adobe Mountain scrubbing toilets with a toothbrush."

"My mom can't pay," he said, slumping in his seat.

"Should have thought of that before your little homies did a grand's worth of damage. Sit the hell up and show some respect to these people vouching for you."

Alex lifted his shoulders, but he couldn't meet their gazes.

"It's up to the prosecutor to charge you, but your principal's got your punishment figured out. Thank her for it."

"Thanks," he said faintly.

"Goddamn it, say it like you mean it. Use her name and look her in the eye."

"Thank you, Ms. Spencer," he mumbled, glancing at her.

"Any of your shit-bird tykes get caught tagging, the deal's off," Carter said. "Now get out of here before I change my mind."

"Yes, sir." Alex jumped to his feet, his chair scraping the floor, his expression clearly showing how ashamed he was.

They got into the cab, Alex in the back. Gabe turned to glare at him. "You reek like the john in a dive bar. What the hell is wrong with you? You trash the school and drag shorties into it?"

"They'd tagged it up by the time I got there."

"Yeah, right. Blame it on them. And you throw a chair at your teacher?"

"I didn't throw it. I shoved it. He's a race hater. I have free speech. I'm an American citizen. My art is my story!"

"Not in school, you don't have free speech. Ms. Spencer could have expelled you, but she didn't. And how do you thank her? You pollute her school."

"They weren't my tags."

"They were your crew. You control them. You represent STRIKE. You scarred our rep. I should kick you out for good."

He looked up. "I'm sorry, okay?" he said, near tears. "My brother stole my cash. I can't make up the tests I miss while I'm suspended. I'm gonna fail two classes. I got mad so I got high and drank some shots."

"Bullshit excuses. Be a man. We cut you slack and you throw it in our faces like it's nothing." Gabe was raging now. It was too much. If he kept yelling, piling on all Alex's screwups, the kid would shut down.

"I know how it feels to tag," she said, making both of

them stare. "I did it when I was your age with my boyfriend." She glanced at Gabe, but he shook his head. *Don't mention Robert.*

"You did?" Alex's eyes went wide. "Damn," he said, as if in respect.

"Don't be impressed. We were vandals. My boyfriend got caught and ended up in juvenile hall. It wrecked him for good." That wasn't exactly how it went, but she had to make the point. Then she had a thought. "You know who Adelia Flor is?"

"She did the Buen Vecino mural. Yeah."

"I've asked her to talk to Discovery kids about her art."

He seemed interested, at least.

"Tell him his punishment," Gabe said.

She explained about painting over the tags, doing community hours, and added that he would help Mr. Salazar over his lunch break.

"Be at school at seven to help the janitor pick up the paint," Gabe said. "The school's broke, so you're kicking in some cash."

"What about STRIKE?" he asked quietly.

Gabe was silent for a long moment. Felicity squeezed his thigh, trying to tell him to have mercy. He frowned. "If I get a good report from Ms. Spencer when the week is out, I'll think about letting you back."

Alex nodded, clearly relieved.

In a few moments, they pulled up to his house. Cars were parked all over the place, including the dirt front yard. Hip-hop blasted from behind the screen door, hanging from one hinge on the sagging porch.

Alex got out of the car.

"You going to be okay in there?" Gabe asked.

"They're partying. I can sneak in without my stepdad seeing me."

"The STRIKE fighters respect you. Don't let them down. Or yourself."

He turned and headed up the walk.

"Tagging is so stupid," she said to Gabe. "It's like dogs pissing in corners."

"When you feel invisible and powerless, it's a way to strike back, to say, 'I own this street. See me. This is mine.'"

"Will his stepfather hit him?"

"Nothing we can do about that now. You have to disengage, Felicity."

"Like Coop tells you?"

He gave her a sad smile. "Look, an art talk and some cleanup will not solve Alex's problems. You need to prepare yourself for it to turn out bad."

She didn't have the energy to argue, especially as they drove through Alex's neighborhood. It was full of neglected houses, bars on every window. Groups of men drinking from beer bottles or pints of liquor stared at them malevolently from porches, wielding their music loud enough to be a weapon.

She heard a helicopter circling overhead, spotlight burning down at the street. This would be a hard place to grow up. That's why school was so important. It was a safe haven, a way out—the only way out.

She thought about saying that to Gabe, but he looked too upset.

As they drove away, though, they both seemed to relax, managing some casual conversation. When they reached her apartment, she saw that the meter showed zero. "I hope you wrote down what I owe you." She reached into her wallet.

"I won't take your money, Felicity."

"We made a deal. This was a meeting and I—"

Gabe stopped her with a kiss, hot and strong, making

her forget everything else. "I'll figure out a way you can pay me back. Sleep well."

He drove off, leaving her weak in the knees, lips still tingling. She watched until his taillights blinked out on the horizon.

You haven't met the right guy, he'd said. What if she had, but it turned out all wrong, anyway?

"THE CONTENT CLINICS are fizzling, at least in the English department," April said the next afternoon. She'd followed Felicity to her office after the Institute ended. "The kids who need the clinics can barely read. My teachers teach literature, not phonics."

"I understand. Dave tells me the math teachers are struggling, too. Two of them are science teachers, without much math background." To cover the curriculum, a third of her teachers were teaching subjects they weren't experts in. At least Dave had been doing better at his job, though he seemed to delight in giving her bad news about her program.

"I have no funds to hire remedial teachers, so we'll have to do the best we can. I've requested in-service training from the district and I'll hold a troubleshooting meeting with department chairs to see how we can spread our skills more effectively."

"That should help some," April said. "People are getting discouraged."

"I know. And I'm sorry." She was discouraged, too. The built-in problems of a last-chance school had become roadblocks to the success of her system—unmotivated students with few basic skills, teachers tackling subjects out of their area, lack of learning materials.

"Anyway, Beatrice Milton seemed pleased with her visit," April said to cheer them both up.

"Gabe charmed her socks off."

"I think she was impressed when he got on Bethany for using a disrespectful tone with her."

One mark on the win side at least—Beatrice's big smile when she left the Institute. So Felicity wouldn't lose her job over STRIKE. Now, if she could overcome the obstacles keeping her system from working. Without positive results soon, her teachers would lose faith.

"What you did about the graffiti was great," April said. "Seeing Alex Gomez out there painting when they got to school made the teachers feel better about the mess."

"I'm glad to hear that." Alex had arrived on time with three crumpled twenties to help pay for the paint. "Speaking of that, I need to let him go for the day." Felicity stood. "I appreciate you hanging in with me on the Institute, April. It's a lot of responsibility for not much pay."

"I can see the impact, so it's worth it to me. Kadisha Green turned in all her back homework today and the girl can *write.*"

"That's good. We've hit some bumps, but we'll keep going." Though at times it felt as though they were driving on the rims of four flats.

After April left, Felicity headed out to release Alex, passing through the gym—empty, since the boys were working on the outdoor equipment with the coaches. Gabe had told her Coop said Alex would not be prosecuted for the graffiti, though any further screwups would mean serious trouble.

As she neared the door to the street, she saw through the window that teens had gathered around Alex, yelling and gesturing. They wore the big white T-shirts, baggy shorts and brown-and-green do-rags of the Double Deuce. Felicity's blood ran cold.

She rushed out the door. "What's going on here?" she said, using her most authoritative voice.

"Nothin'," Alex said, looking scared. "We're just talking."

The gangbangers glared at her. The tallest kid, the one in Alex's face, had snake-hard eyes and there was a bulge under his shirt—a gun, no doubt. He gave her a nasty up-and-down, clearly trying to intimidate her.

A car angled into the street was blasting rap, the driver watching out the window with a grin.

"Just go, Ms. S," Alex added.

"Ooh, *Ms. S. Just go,*" the lead boy mocked.

The others hissed profanities about her and Alex. One of them called the leader Chuco.

"You better come, homes," another boy said. "Mad Dog ain't chill wid you, you don't show."

"It's his funeral, Li'l B," Chuco said. "Let him burn."

"Bring in the paint gear, Alex," she said loudly. "You're finished for today."

"Mind your *damn* business, *puta,*" Chuco said, strutting up to her, inches from her face, shifting side to side, eyes hateful, mouth tight. He smelled of sweat, pot and too much cologne.

"This *is* my business," she said, her heart pounding wildly. "I'm the principal and you're threatening one of my students."

The guys standing around began to laugh and jeer.

"We *threatenin'* you, pussy?" Chuco asked, still staring at Felicity.

"Nah, Chuco. It's cool." Alex's eyes begged her to leave.

"It's not cool with me. Coach Cassidy expects you inside." If they knew Gabe was near, they might back off. She would not show weakness.

"You're buffin' out righteous tags, A," Li'l B said. "That's for shit." He kicked over a paint can, sending a river of yellow paint down the sidewalk.

The door opened and she turned to see Gabe standing there. Thank God. "Think you all better back off," he said, low and serious.

Chuco took a step back, clearly intimidated, but trying to act cool. "Jus' gettin' your boy here. He owes us time."

Gabe looked at Alex, reading him. Then he said, "Handle your business. Be back in an hour for that job, Alex."

"I'll be there," Alex said, sounding relieved. Chuco walked backward, eyes on Gabe, hatred in his stare, all the way to the car, where Alex and the others had gone.

After they drove off, Gabe stalked to the high-pressure hose to start washing the paint from the sidewalk.

"Why did you let him go with them? The *business* they're up to is criminal and you know it."

"I gave him an out that doesn't cut off his damn balls," he said through gritted teeth. "He'll take it or he won't."

"This is no time to disengage, Gabe."

He turned on her, his eyes flashing fire. "You have no idea what you just did, do you? You don't draw down on bangers on their turf. You disrespect them, and they hit back ten times harder."

"I won't be intimidated on school grounds."

"Intimidated? You could have been killed. You looking to be a martyr? Joan of Arc of the barrio?"

"Gangsters are bullies. It's a head game. You said so yourself."

He laughed harshly. "They're bullies with nine-millimeters. You think you're in some Lifetime special—crusading principal turns gang-infested shit hole into college-prep academy? Forget it. You put Alex in a world of hurt with those thugs. Now they think he's weak, hiding behind your skirts."

"At least I tried to protect him."

He glared at her, breathing hard, opened his mouth, closed it, then shook his head. "I'm not doing this with you." He grabbed the sprayer and a couple of buckets and stomped inside.

He was so arrogant, so disapproving, she was breathless with outrage. Who the hell did he think he was?

THE MINUTE THE DOOR SHUT behind him, Gabe regretted yelling at her. But damn it, there were rules. And limits to what anyone could do. Alex had to want to stay legit. He had to be determined. He had to be strong. You could drive yourself crazy trying to run interference.

He turned back to go apologize and saw the door was jiggling. He pulled it open and found her bent over, trying to haul in some paint trays and buckets.

"Give me that," he said, bending down to take a bucket.

"Forget it." She elbowed him out of the way. "Let the clueless idiot finish the job." Her face was red, her eyes crackling with fire, the silver stars glittering like the diamond stud in his ear.

"You look like you want to knock me flat." He almost smiled.

"Yeah, I do."

"Then come on. I've got spare shorts and a T-shirt. Let's see what you got."

Her gaze flew to the ring, then back at him. "All right. Let's go." She jutted her jaw.

He turned away to hide his grin. He liked how fierce she got. He'd sent Conrad and the boys home, so they had the gym to themselves, at least.

She changed her clothes and did a decent hand wrap.

Even cinched up, the shorts hung past her knees, but he'd found an extra-small STRIKE T-shirt that fit great. Real great. He handed her a helmet, then adjusted the clasps under her chin, breathing in how she smelled, noticing the way her eyes crackled like a bonfire. She'd kept her mad on, he was glad to see.

"Where's your helmet?" she demanded. "You don't think I can land a punch?"

"I'll take my chances."

"Suit yourself." She threw a jab he barely had time to block.

"Not bad. Better tuck your chin. You tend to stick it out, being *terco* like you are."

She made a derisive sound, but she tucked her chin all the same. Angry as she was, she wanted to fight as well as possible.

"Okay. Give me what you've got, *chica.*"

She exploded at him with jabs and crosses and elbow strikes in combinations they hadn't even practiced. She meant business. "You had no right to talk to me like that," she spat.

"Try some kick combos—high, then low, so my defenses lag."

She nodded, starting in. "I know there's danger, but I know what I'm doing." *Wham, wham, wham.* High, low, high, as he'd instructed. "You have no respect for me, always pulling the street card."

Jab, elbow strike, snap kick, cross, jab, jab, jab. Emotion took over, messing with her aim.

"Keep your focus. You're getting sloppy. Sure, I respect you. But if I see you in danger, I'm gonna intervene."

"Yours isn't the only way, you know." She swung wild, he dodged and she started to fall sideways.

He caught her before she hit the mat and pulled her to her feet. "The truth is I saw those bangers circling you like jackals and it was all I could do not to tear them limb from limb."

She stared at him, her face red, sweat pouring down, breathing hard, taking in the fact that he'd wanted to protect her. He saw it register, saw her soften, moved by his gesture. For a second, she wore the look she'd had as a kid when he got her bumper fixed for her.

"You've got to toughen up if you're going to survive this place," he said.

"I am tough. Don't you see? You have to be tough to have hope."

Her words hit like a punch.

She pulled off her helmet and dropped it to the mat. "My job is hard, Gabe. Really hard. I feel like I'm climbing a mountain in flip-flops. My teachers doubt me. I doubt myself." Her voice cracked.

"I don't doubt you," he said. "Not for one minute. You can turn this school around if anyone can. Charlie was a good guy, but he didn't have your fire or your savvy or your drive."

"You really believe that?" Her eyes were so big, so earnest, so anxious.

"Completely."

"Your faith means a lot to me."

"*You* mean a lot to me," he said, his heart doing a belly flop in his chest.

Her eyes got shiny, her smile shaky.

He found himself going for it, saying what was in his heart and head. "I can't stop thinking about you. I smell you, taste you, hear your voice constantly."

"Me, too. Oh, I feel the same way. I have these dreams..."

That was all he had to hear. He pulled her into his arms and kissed her. She was warm and damp and tasted of salt and candy and he never wanted to let her go.

They kissed for a long time, only stopping when Felicity lost her balance, and then he helped her to the mat in the center of the ring, laws of physics being what they were. Horizontal was the position they needed most.

"What do we do now?" She was breathing hard.

They could stop. Let this be it. That would be the smart thing to do. "Your place is closer," he said. "Let's go."

CHAPTER TWELVE

Felicity clung to Gabe for the ride to her apartment, not speaking, just dying to *get there.* Her heart raced, her blood pounded and her parts ached as though they might break if he didn't touch them soon.

It had taken forever for her to get dressed, even longer to drive to her apartment. Then they had to greet Abel politely and fight not to grope each other for the seven-floor elevator ride with a woman and her shih tzu.

Finally, *finally* they were at her door. Once inside, Gabe shoved her against the closed door, kissing her hard, his hands all over her. He wanted her as much as she wanted him. He wasn't backing off or acting cool and controlled. It was such a relief to share this, to feel the same.

She'd left her bed unmade, thank God, so it only took seconds to get out of their clothes and be naked together on the rumpled sheets, skin to skin, kissing, legs entwined, staring into each other's eyes as if that was all they ever wanted to see.

"Are you sure?" Gabe asked her, his lips hovering above hers. He was breathing hard and she could feel his heart pounding against hers.

"Very sure," she said, grabbing his backside as she lifted her hips, inviting him where he belonged—inside, where she was warm and wet and dying to feel him move.

He entered her slowly, watching her face, reading her

response, his pupils wide and black with arousal. “Damn, you feel good.”

“Oh, you, too. Very good,” she said, lifting her hips to meet his thrust. Each tiny movement reverberated inside her.

“I want to go slow,” he said, but his face showed strain.

“Don’t you dare.” She dug her heels into his backside, urging him deeper.

He thrust into her, pulled out and thrust in again, making her gasp and shudder as he moved, speeding up. They held each other as the tension built, moving in a sweet rhythm, climbing to the edge, then flying over, both of them crying out.

This felt good and right. This felt like home.

Gabe rolled to the side, pulling her onto his chest. “Cici,” he breathed.

“I can’t believe we just did that.”

“Me, either.” He looked at his watch.

“Do you need to get going? To work?”

“Damn, girl. You think I’m going to have sex and run?”

“I didn’t think you were going to have sex and leave me a lame note, either.”

She felt him cringe. “I didn’t know what to say. You knocked me flat. You did it again. And I’m guessing you’ll do it next time, too.”

“Next time?” She pushed up on an elbow.

He turned on his side, facing her. “What do you think about giving this a try?”

“Depends on what *this* is.”

“Good question. I like being with you.” He ran his hand along her hip, then traced a nipple, making her shiver. “I feel good when I’m with you.”

“I feel the same.”

"This will be a time-suck, you know," he teased.

"Okay, so I didn't know what I was talking about. I still don't. I just…don't want to stop yet." It was a concern, though, with all she had to do. What if she let her work lag, sacrificed it to this intensity?

"You have doubts," he said, reading her. "So we'll see how it goes. Be together when it feels right. Call it off if it interferes too much."

"That could work," she said, though it sounded far more calm and rational than she'd felt twenty minutes ago. Post-climax, she could be sensible. Back then, she was ready to push the lady and her dog out of the elevator and go at it on the floor.

Gabe groaned. "I do need to get to my cab pretty soon."

"Sure. But there is something I want to run past you."

"Damn. I should have run when I had the chance."

"So, this afternoon," she said, ignoring his joke to get to the important part, "I went to some businesses to see about cleanup for Alex's community-service time and I was surprised at how leery they were of our kids. They think they're all gangbangers. The guy who owns the dry cleaner's thought we were a juvenile correctional facility."

"People make assumptions."

"Like Beatrice and STRIKE, exactly. So I had this idea for an event that would let the community get to know Discovery and give our students a chance to strut their stuff—build pride, you know?"

"Yeah?"

"We'd call it Discover Discovery Day and it would be a festival and carnival, with rides and food and games, student displays, STRIKE demonstrations, music, whatever we wanted. What do you think?"

WHAT DID HE THINK? He had no idea. All the while Felicity talked, Gabe kept getting lost in her face, the blue of her eyes, the way her lips moved around her words. Her hands danced and her hair floated over her ears. He wanted to make love to her again before he went to work, kiss that mouth that was going a mile a minute….

"So…will you do it?"

"Will I what?" He'd zoned for a bit.

"Be my codirector? It would be great PR for STRIKE.

"We'll get tons of publicity. I'll invite city leaders, district officials, social-service agencies. You'd only have to do what you could fit in. If the teachers like the idea, they'll handle most of the logistics."

"I don't know…"

"Come on. We'll make money—maybe even enough to buy you some equipment or pay an assistant coach."

"I'll do what I can, but I can't promise much."

"Great. Terrific." She kissed him, long and slow, making him forget the cab, his mortgage payment, his next meal. "I need you to set up that meeting with Adelia. I have an idea for the festival that I hope she'll be interested in."

A few minutes later, he was headed to the cab garage, his head in a total fog. He'd been run through a candy-scented wringer, agreeing to weeks of hassles, but he didn't seem to mind.

They'd figured out a way to be together. It was more than just sex, but less than lifelong love, of course. Something in between that would last…awhile? He could deal with that. Sounded as if she could, too. And it had worked out way better than a note scribbled on a napkin.

EVEN BEFORE GABE CALLED her name, Felicity knew the woman who had entered Buen Vecino was Adelia Flor.

She was gorgeous, with almond-shaped eyes, full lips, skin the same mocha as Gabe's and thick black hair halfway down her back. She carried herself with the aura of a celebrity.

Gabe waved her over to where they'd been waiting for an hour. Adelia was "squeezing them in" between a newspaper interviews and a photo shoot related to her newly finished mural.

Adelia wrapped her arms around Gabe's neck and kissed him on the mouth. A surge of unreasonable jealousy made Felicity avert her gaze.

Gabe broke off the kiss, flushed, then turned to Felicity. "Adelia, I want you to meet Felicity Spencer, the principal at Discovery."

He'd introduced her as the *principal.* Reasonable, she supposed. She'd hardly earned girlfriend status in three days, but it hurt that he hadn't acknowledged that they were at least friends.

"Encantada." Adelia held out a hand to shake. *Enchanted.*

"I so love your work," Felicity said. "It's amazing, so moving, so vibrant…" Now she sounded like a fan girl.

"Thank you," Adelia said in the impersonal tone stars used to keep groupies at bay. A hand on his shoulder, she leaned against Gabe. "So how are you, *vato?* What's with the uptown hair?" She played with a few strands.

"The twins were practicing haircuts."

"They should keep practicing."

"You're telling me."

The two of them looked beautiful together, and their connection was obvious, though Gabe kept glancing at Felicity, as if to include her in the cozy chat. "Let's get you a drink." He motioned for the bartender. "The usual?" he asked Adelia.

"*¿Como no?*" she said. *Why not?*

"For the lady, a mojito, double rum, extra lime. Thanks, Santiago."

Gabe remembered Adelia's drink. Felicity felt stupidly left out.

"Sounds like you're busy these days," Gabe said.

"I am." Adelia assumed a less flirtatious tone. "The big news is we're setting up a gallery and studio in an old warehouse downtown. It'll be a co-op for Latino artists. You'll come to our opening, right?"

"Send me a notice."

"I'll call. Maybe we can have dinner first."

"I'm glad things are going well for you," he said, ignoring the dinner invitation, probably because Felicity was standing there.

The drink arrived and Adelia took a sip. "Mmm. *Perfecto.* Try it." She held it out, but he shook his head. "Too girlie for G?"

Adelia got to call him G. Felicity felt another jealous pang.

"Felicity, tell Adelia about your idea," Gabe said, clearing his throat.

"Happy to. Gabe told me that the mural you did here stopped gang taggers from vandalizing the wall. We'd like to do the same at Discovery, except with student art. We plan to unveil the murals at a festival in a month. I hope to have lots of media there." She figured that would appeal to Adelia.

"Sounds smart." She sipped more of her drink. "Mmm. Seriously, you're missing out, Gabe." She waved it under his nose. He shook his head.

Felicity continued. "So, I'm hoping you'd be willing to advise the students when it's time to paint the murals. Give them your perspective."

"I thought I was going to speak to an art class. I've got the gallery show coming up and a new mural project in Chandler."

"We'd value whatever time you could spare," Felicity said.

"One of my kids has been tagging, Adelia," Gabe said. "He admires you as an artist, so you could have an influence on him. And the other kids. You could really help us out here."

"Us? You're involved in this, Gabe?"

"I'm doing some stuff, yeah. I'm kind of the codirector."

"Interesting." She studied him, then turned to Felicity. "If you kicked Gabe out of his rut, you're doing something right." She took a card from her purse and handed it to Felicity. "Call me next week. I'll see what I can do."

"Thank you so much."

"I try to give back." She downed the rest of her drink. "Gotta go prance around for the cameras. Want to come along?" she asked Gabe.

"Thanks, but I have to drop Felicity home on my way to my cab."

"Oh." Adelia shot her gaze to Felicity, assessing her as a rival now. "Rain check, then," she said to Gabe. She leaned in for a goodbye kiss. "I was an idiot," she said softly, her fingers lingering on his cheek.

With a final look at Gabe, she swept off, trailing men's gazes all the way out the door, including Gabe's. Did he still love her?

He turned to Felicity. "So, she said yes. That's good, huh?"

"She's beautiful." She paused. "She wants you back." She'd tried to sound light, but it came out sharp.

"Grass is always greener." He shrugged.

"You seem to still have feelings for her." Now she'd really overstepped, but she couldn't seem to stop herself. "You looked good together, comfortable."

"What, are you jealous?" His eyes twinkled and he was grinning.

"Making an observation," she said. "You share so much—culture, attitudes, worldview. If she's your soul mate, maybe you should try again, be more open this time."

"Cici..." Gabe said. "There's nothing left between us. What's this about?"

"I don't know. I just...felt like a third wheel. It was dumb." With a jolt, she realized what it really was. She was falling in love with him.

She wanted more—a relationship, something serious. Which made no sense, when all they had in common was a crazy attraction, their work at Discovery and their shared sorrow over Robert.

They'd agreed to sleep together until it stopped feeling right.

Like now? If she was getting jealous over old girlfriends, making more of this than was possible, maybe it *wasn't* right anymore.

"You're the only woman I want," he said, pulling her closer. "I'd like to show you how much right now," he murmured in her ear. "I'll start my shift late. Who needs money when I can get naked with you?" His eyes lit with desire, sparking a response she was not capable of resisting. And maybe that was the problem.

TWO WEEKS LATER in a downtown parking garage, Felicity patted the lapel of the blazer she'd helped Gabe buy, along with the oxford shirt, rep tie and dark pants. "You do clean up nice."

"I can't believe you talked me into this monkey suit so I can kiss up to a bunch of politicians and blowhards."

"This is important to both of us." They were headed to a hotel conference room for a meeting hosted by United Giving. It was a mixer for schools applying to the charity's Adopt-a-School grant program.

Tom Brown had urged her to apply for the grant after she'd told him about the festival. The application was rigorous, the competition stiff, but United Giving favored alternative schools and new ideas, so Discovery had a chance. Winning meant thousands of dollars and corporate support. Winning would guarantee Discovery would stay open and her career would soar.

"You sure you want to set me loose in there?" Gabe said. "Tatted-up *cholo* with a fight club and a glower?"

"Show them your bighearted, gentle side."

"You mean act fake."

"Emphasize your strengths."

"No paper plates for company. I get it, but that doesn't mean I'm good at it." He stretched his neck in the collar. "I can't breathe. Wait. Should I lose the earring?"

"No. It makes you look sexy."

"I don't think sexy's what we're going for."

"Depends on how many women are on the committee."

"You are shameless, aren't you?"

"For my school, you bet."

They left the garage and headed for the hotel. It was late afternoon and the sun was warm. "Remember to use anecdotes," she coached. "They love stories they can put in their fundraising brochures. Like Alex, for example. The way he went from tagging the school to coordinating the mural contest."

"You have to twist Salazar's arm on that?"

"Pretty much. But Alex is doing a good job, especially

because Adelia's been around a lot. I think he's shifted his crush to her. She's been at school every day, practically. She got other artists involved and they're donating all the paint, which is saving me a lot of cash."

"That's great. People are into this whole festival thing."

"I know. I've got all the teacher volunteers I need already. I asked Beatrice to coordinate the booths and offered her one for her crafts."

"Smart move. And, I forgot to tell you, I got Los Tres Luchadores to perform for free."

She smiled. "I don't know who that is."

"Are you kidding me? The Three Wrestlers do retro rock and some hipped-up ranchero stuff. They perform in Mexican wrestler costumes. Very popular. You'll see."

"Thanks for all you've done." Gabe had gotten a guy he knew to donate some carnival rides and he'd rounded up raffle prizes, including offering a hundred dollars in cab rides himself.

"I said I'd do what I could."

"You did a lot. More than I asked. I wish I'd done as well. Sorry about the boxing gloves." She'd been excited to get a sporting-goods store to donate two dozen pairs of gloves, but they'd arrived that morning and turned out to be pink with breast-cancer slogans.

"Eh. I told the kids pink's just a color. It's the fist inside that matters."

She smiled. "Look who has a way with words now."

They stopped at the intersection to wait for the walk signal.

"I'm learning from the best." He pulled her into his arms for a kiss, and they crossed the street arm in arm.

They'd been together almost every night—not easy with how busy they both were, but they'd managed it. Busy people made room for passion in their lives. And for love? That was getting ahead of herself. That wasn't part of the deal. At least so far. And she wasn't about to be the one who brought it up first. She was too unsure of herself in this area.

They found the conference room and stood in the doorway. The noise was deafening. The place was packed with United Giving decision makers and Discovery's competitors.

"Not sure I'm ready for this," Gabe said.

"Sure you are. It's like boxing. Fight your fight, not his. Keep your hands up, stay on the balls of your feet, watch your stance and your timing."

"I don't know how I feel about you feeding me my own advice."

"The master learns from the pupil."

He laughed. "You are too much, you know that?"

She'd had a great idea for Gabe, though it was too soon to mention it. If Discovery got this grant, she would hire him to run the After-School Institute. He'd get to work with kids full-time. It would almost be as good as the rec job he'd lost. She couldn't wait to see his face when she told him.

GABE WAS AMAZED BY HOW WELL Felicity worked the crowd, easily talking about her program, bringing him into each conversation in a way that let him shine, then gracefully escaping to join the next group.

They met judges, city-council members, CEOs, business people and school officials from all over the Valley. He noticed that while other principals whined about budget cuts, Felicity focused on what she'd accomplished. Each small audience melted in her hands. It didn't hurt that she was gorgeous and men helplessly flocked around her.

He was proud of himself, too. They'd been at it an hour and he'd managed not to step on his dick. When she left for the ladies' room she told him to keep at it. He strode across the room, looking for an entry point somewhere, planning to use Felicity's tips.

When he heard someone say "Discovery," he headed over, thinking that was his cue. Except he saw that the group included Leonard Lancaster, Felicity's landlord, a sleaze he couldn't stomach.

"So you rent space to the school?" A woman with a notepad asked Lancaster. Had to be a reporter.

"I do. I consider it a civic duty, though it's not easy, with gangs taking over the school as they have, spray-painting death threats on the walls."

"Really?" The reporter scribbled. "Death threats?"

He couldn't let that stand. "That's not true," Gabe said, keeping his voice level. The group turned to him. "There are no gangs at Discovery. There was a minor tagging incident that's been painted over. As you know, Mr. Lancaster, thanks to the new principal, the students will be painting murals to beautify your property at no cost to you."

Lancaster turned red.

"And you are...?" The reporter leaned toward him. Her name tag said she was with the daily paper. *Balls of your feet, watch your timing.*

"Gabriel Cassidy. I coach martial arts as part of the principal's after-school program, which is really motivating the students to do better in school." That was a Felicity line if he'd ever heard one.

Lancaster cleared his throat. "Fresh paint and good thoughts are no match for the forces at play. With your background, Mr. Ochoa, I'm sure you know this."

"It's Cassidy," he corrected, wanting to throttle the man for trying to bring up his father.

"Your background?" the reporter asked Gabe.

"I grew up near the school. And we can beat those so-called forces. All it takes is cash and the belief that brown and black kids deserve safe neighborhoods and good schools as much as white ones."

"Are you saying city leaders are racist?"

"I'm saying that what money gets spent is to get someone elected or ease a few consciences."

Lancaster rolled his eyes.

"Take renting a worthless property to a school to get the tax write-off and the publicity," Gabe continued, "then failing to fix the AC while blaming *forces at play.* I'd say the forces at play are greed and neglect."

The reporter was fighting a grin, her eyes glittering over this argument. "What about that, Mr. Lancaster? Is there any truth to what he's saying?"

Lancaster's face was nearly purple now.

"As a business owner, Mr. Lancaster has to deal with economic pressures we know nothing about," Felicity said from behind Gabe. "I'm Felicity Spencer, the principal at Discovery. Mr. Cassidy feels pretty passionate about our cause." She smiled, asking the group to forgive his outburst.

"Once a fighter, always a fighter," Gabe said, trying to help her out and step away from his dick.

"Like the rest of us, he's frustrated by all the need he sees, which is why United Giving, by filling in the gaps, is so important to the city."

Everyone relaxed. Felicity had snapped the tension like a dry twig.

While Felicity fielded questions, Gabe checked out the name tags. There was a city councilman, a staffer from the mayor's office and two people from United Giving. He'd picked the wrong group to get blunt with.

When they'd walked away, Felicity grabbed his arm. "How the hell did that happen?"

"Lancaster was trashing Discovery. I had to step in."

"You can't beat people up over failure. It makes them feel helpless and they shut down. You have to tell them what works, what makes things better, give them hope."

"You should have left me tied up in the yard, snapping at intruders."

"No." She sighed. "You needed to be here. I think we mitigated the damage. Let's hope the reporter was appeased."

"Are we about done here?" He was worn-out by it all.

Felicity looked around the room. "I think we've talked to everyone I wanted to. I got email addresses, so I can invite them all to the festival."

"You never miss a trick, do you?"

"I can't afford to."

They were close to the elevators, about to escape, when Felicity froze. "Oh, God. That's my uncle."

"The superintendent?"

"Let's go." She started to pull him away.

"Why? Say hello."

"Too awkward. He doesn't even know what I look like." Before she could turn away, the man called her name, smiling.

"Hello," she said, turning bright pink.

"Good to see you." The guy had that empty, glad-handing expression politicians wore when they pressed the flesh. "I understand you're stirring things up out there. Hope it works out for you," he said, moving on to shake the next person's hand practically before he finished his line.

Inside the elevator, Felicity turned to Gabe, looking totally freaked out. "What did that mean, *hope it works out for you?* Am I in trouble?"

"He was making small talk. He's a politician."

"Tom must have told him about me. God, did he hear about the protest the district people thought was a riot? Is that what he meant about me stirring things up?" She sounded so frantic, so insecure, not like herself at all.

"Come on. You're doing a good job. Who cares what he thinks?"

"I have to. He's the head of a major school district. Superintendents talk. They have conferences. If I want to start consulting again, I need positive word of mouth. I can't be seen as a troublemaker."

Gabe was startled by Felicity's reaction. She sounded as if she was clawing her way up some bullshit success ladder. That wasn't the Felicity he'd grown to respect. That Felicity knew that what mattered was her work for the kids and the school. She didn't cower in front of some clueless official.

He didn't like this Felicity much. He thought she was better than that. Counted on her to be.

He tried to settle himself. So what if she was ambitious? It wasn't as if they were making a life together. Why did it matter so damn much to him?

CHAPTER THIRTEEN

GABE WAS TOO QUIET as they drove away from the United Giving meeting. He looked upset and kept shifting in his seat.

"Don't worry about the reporter," she said. "I think I softened your quotes enough."

"Softened them?" His gaze shot to hers. "I told the plain truth. And don't give me that crap about not serving paper plates for company."

She stared at him. "Why are you angry? You know why we went there."

"To fluff up your résumé, right? Give you bragging rights? 'I fixed this miserable school. Hire me to fix yours'?"

She felt slapped. "Of course I want to do well for my career, but that's not the reason. You know that."

He looked straight ahead, a muscle ticking in his jaw.

"You think I'm a fake? Like the politicians you despise?"

"I don't know, Felicity, with you *softening* my quotes and *mitigating the damage* and twisting words to suit the purpose of the moment. You remind me of Leonard Lancaster, who's trying to sound like a beleaguered civic crusader instead of the sleazeball slumlord he is."

"You're comparing me to *Leonard Lancaster?*"

Gabe blew out a breath and shook his head. "You're not that bad."

"Not...that...bad?" That worsened the horror she felt.

"I didn't like you getting so insecure over what some big shot thought about you. It was like his opinion mattered more than what you'd actually done. You're better than that."

She opened her mouth to argue, but his phone sounded its boxing-bell ringtone. He stopped at the light and answered it.

She was glad for the reprieve. Her cheeks stung from his accusations. Comparing her to Leonard had been ugly and totally unfair. But the rest of his words echoed in her head. Was he right? Had she folded in the face of her uncle's negative opinion?

It *did* matter. He *could* affect her career. But even if he thought she was a rabble-rouser, would she change anything she'd done?

Of course not. What she *did* mattered more than what people *thought* she'd done, even people who held her career in their hands.

Okay, so she'd let her values slip for a moment. Gabe had called her on it. Harshly, for sure, but she'd needed the reminder.

He finished his call as the light changed. He accelerated across the intersection. "Trina's got some papers I need to sign at Giorgio's. Mind if I run in on the way?"

"Not at all."

They drove in silence for a few blocks, while she gathered herself to admit she was wrong. It wasn't easy. Finally, she said, "No matter what Phil Evers thinks, I'm proud of what I've done."

Gabe gave a short nod. "I shouldn't have said what I said in front of that reporter. Even if Lancaster is a phony asshole—and he is—I shouldn't have been so blunt."

"Blunt can be good. It depends."

"It's all timing, right?" He gave a quick smile.

"And rhythm and stance."

He laughed. "You're good. Really good." He squeezed her thigh in a way that was friendly and possessive. She liked it a lot.

"I think we just had our first fight," she said.

"We do all right?"

"I think so." She felt pretty good about it, actually. When you cared about someone, you wanted them to be the best they could be. And if you trusted the person, you took heed, tried to improve.

He turned in at the restaurant and parked near the door. "Come in. We can grab dinner while we're here."

When the hostess saw Gabe, she grinned. "Go on back. They're in the private room."

"Should I wait out here?" Felicity asked.

"Nah. Come say hi to the girls. We've got a cover story. I'm in a suit, so we're obviously together for business, not pleasure."

He hadn't told the twins they were dating, which stabbed her with disappointment. But why would he? They weren't serious. Why invite all the questions and comments the girls would offer? They were relentless, for sure.

That reminded her about Gabe's mother. They'd agreed not to tell her that Gabe was working with Felicity, for fear it would traumatize her again.

Traumatize her. Send her into sobs of anger and grief. That gave Felicity fresh chills.

She and Gabe were having a secret affair, a short-term fling that would burn itself out before anybody important had to be told. That was clearly what Gabe thought. But it hurt. It made her feel unimportant, dismissed, the way she'd felt with Adelia. Again, she wondered if she was in over her head.

At the end of the hall, Gabe opened the door to the dining room.

"Surprise!" The room was full of smiling people. Overhead, a banner that said Happy Birthday had been hung with clumps of helium balloons.

Felicity's blood turned to ice. This was Gabe's surprise party.

"Happy birthday!" Shanna and Trina yelled. Then they saw Felicity. "Oh! Wow! Cici!" They looked horrified—just as they had at the cemetery—and rushed to their mother's side.

"You!" Mary said, totally shocked. "You!" she repeated.

"I'm s-sorry," Felicity said. She'd crashed another family event. She spun around and left the room.

Gabe followed and took her arm "Wait." He looked as shocked as she felt.

"I'll call a cab," she said. "Go back to your party."

"I want you to stay."

"Are you kidding? It's your birthday party. I didn't know—"

"Neither did I. My birthday's next week. They wanted to surprise me, I guess. Look, get a beer at the bar. I'll talk to her and come get you."

"And tell her what? That I'm the principal where you work? You sure can't tell her we're dating. Your sisters don't even know. And your mother hates me. She has every right to. So leave it alone. This is a mistake. *We* are a mistake. I can't handle this. I don't want to be a secret. I don't want to be ashamed."

"Let me straighten this out. Stay here."

"You can't, Gabe. It can't *be* straightened out. It's gone

too far for me. I'm in love with you, okay? As stupid as that is. I know that wasn't our deal, but it happened."

Gabe stared at her, stunned, his jaw hanging.

"Say something," she said.

"Uh...don't leave. Get a beer. Give me a few minutes." He turned to go down the hall as if in a trance.

She'd definitely blown it. And every word she'd said had been correct. She had to get away from the humiliation. She turned and ran, brushing past the hostess and out the door. Up the block was a bus stop with people waiting. It would be faster than calling a cab, so she jogged there and dropped onto the bench, fighting the urge to burst into tears.

She felt sick. She'd had no choice but to tell him. She couldn't be casual anymore. He might as well know now. Her heart hurt like crazy, but she'd done the right thing. Gabe knew it, too. It was clear in how stunned he'd looked, how caught off guard he'd been.

Ten minutes later, as she stood to climb onto the bus, she heard her name shouted from a distance. She looked over and saw Gabe running up the sidewalk. "Don't do it! Don't go!" he yelled.

Her heart in her throat, she ran to meet him halfway.

CHAPTER FOURTEEN

"I ALMOST MISSED YOU," he said, winded from running. "When I came back and saw you'd gone, I was… I felt…" He swallowed hard. "Ah, hell. Screw the deal. We need a new one."

"We do?" she asked, hope surging in her chest.

"Stupid as it is, I love you, too."

"Really?" Her heart sang. *She wasn't alone.* She wasn't alone. Gabe loved her, too. Thank God.

Gabe pulled her into his arms and kissed her hard, holding her so tightly it was as if he couldn't get close enough. She melted against him, holding on, too, with all her might.

When they'd had enough for a public sidewalk, Gabe broke off the kiss and leaned back to look at her. "Come to the party. I want my friends and family to meet the woman I love."

"Wait… You told your family? Your mother?"

"I told her about working together…and the girls chimed in about that night. Mom's pretty shaken up. I told her that we'd talked, I told her some of your side of the story. Trina and Shanna threw in about the Shakira concert and how rotten fourteen-year-olds are. Giorgio reminded her about forgiveness and fresh starts. And I told her what a good person you are…and that we were dating."

"You did? You told her that?"

"God help me, I did. So come with me."

"How did she take it?"

"Not well. I get some of my stubborn from her, too."

"Maybe we should wait. Do it another time, when it's less public."

"It's already started. Let's get through the worst."

"If you're sure."

"I'm sure."

At the party, Gabe walked Felicity straight to his mother and her husband. He introduced Felicity to Giorgio, whom she recognized from the cemetery. He smiled kindly. Mary's stare froze her in place.

Okay, here goes. Here was her chance to apologize. "I'm very sorry that I hurt your family," she said, her heart racing. "I regret it with all my heart. And I know this must be a shock—seeing me with your son."

"A shock? It's a waking nightmare."

"Mary," Giorgio said in a warning voice.

She waved him down. "I know. Forgive and forget. But that's you, Giorgio, not me. You don't know."

"I don't expect you to forgive me," Felicity said, braced for more accusations. "What I did was unforgivable. I was selfish. I hurt Robert and—"

"You don't need to go through this again, Felicity," Gabe said firmly. "We all made mistakes—including Robert."

"You can decide it's over, but that doesn't make it over," his mother snapped at him. "Robert was my son. I lost him for no good reason. I won't forget that, no matter how many years go by."

"I'm not asking you to forget Robert," Gabe said. "I'm asking you to give Felicity a chance, see her as an adult, not a messed-up fourteen-year-old."

"Fourteen-year-olds are idiots," Trina threw in. She'd joined them. "Remember, Mom?"

Mary sighed. "Quit ganging up on me. This is a lot to take in. You keep this terrible secret from me for weeks and now you want me to be happy for you? I can't do that. I don't work that way."

"We don't expect that," Gabe said. "Just give us a chance."

"I know how hard this is," Felicity said.

"Do you?" Mary's gaze flew to Felicity's. "I don't think you do. You took one of my boys from me and now you've got hold of the only one I have left." Tears rose in her eyes. "I swear to God if you hurt him…" Her eyes dug in, as intense as Gabe's, though pale blue where his were brown.

"Mom, stop," Gabe said gently. "Nobody wants to hurt anybody." He gave her a hug. After a few seconds, she patted his back and they separated.

"I don't want to ruin your party," his mother said to him. Then she leveled her gaze at Felicity. "Time will tell about you. That's all I can say."

"That's all I can ask," Felicity said.

There was a flicker of hesitation in Mary's face, as if she saw for the first time there was more to Felicity than she'd once believed.

"So, good. That's settled. Now let's eat," Giorgio said, hugging his wife against him. She gave him a small smile. Felicity could see what Gabe meant about Giorgio being good for her.

Gabe led Felicity away, his arm around her. "You did great," he whispered, then took her to a seat at the table, where people had gathered. She needed to sit. She was still trembling. He introduced her to his friends: Conrad, whom she knew; Carl, who owned the landscaping company; Mickey, the man he shared his cab with; guys he knew from martial arts and others—bringing her into each conversation, making her feel welcome, making her feel a part of things, a part of his life.

The food was delicious, the conversation warm and easy. She felt Mary's gaze on her often, assessing her, measuring the interactions between her and Gabe. The woman had every right to doubt her. Time would tell. For now, Felicity was thrilled to know that Gabe loved her. Maybe they were figuring it out after all.

He blew out his thirty-four candles without pausing to make a wish. That made her sad. She always made wishes, then worked to make them come true. Gabe didn't dare.

After that, the twins insisted he open their card, which contained their gift to him. He read it silently, then looked up. "Salsa lessons?"

Everyone laughed and clapped. Mickey whistled.

"And tonight's your first one."

"Because we need a ride to the club," Shanna threw in.

"Sorry. I need to work."

"Not on your birthday," Trina said.

"But it's not my birthday."

"If you don't come, we'll leave our pepper spray home and let strange men buy us drinks."

"Felicity wants to come," Trina added. "Don't you?"

"I did take ballroom dance in college."

He blew out a breath. "This is ridiculous."

"The best things are," Felicity said. She loved seeing him thrown for a loop—it made her feel as though she wasn't the only one.

Soon, Gabe was driving Felicity and the twins to the club, the van smelling of clashing perfumes and the twins' Juicy Fruit gum. They chatted away and texted their friends.

"You okay?" Gabe asked Felicity, reading the dazed look on her face. He patted her thigh through her skirt—it would be tight for dancing, but at least she had on low heels. She'd taken off her suit jacket and rolled up the sleeves of her silk blouse.

"I'm a little stunned."

"Me, too. Salsa lessons? Damn."

"A lot just happened to us," she said, ignoring his joke. "We had that fight about my uncle and then got hit with the surprise party—"

"And then you blurted—" he glanced at the girls, then whispered "—that thing you blurted."

"And you blurted it right back," she said.

"I did." He sighed, put his arm around her and pulled her against him. "I'm sorry Mom was so harsh."

"She had every right. It will take time, like she said." Though she did feel uneasy. What if she did hurt Gabe? She had no clue how love worked. What if she messed up? Mary would hunt her down and shoot her.

"She'll come around. That'll take time, too."

"I liked your friends. And your family. They're so different from mine."

"That's because you don't have any siblings to annoy the crap out of you."

"I mean how close and loving you are, the way you joke and tease each other. My parents and I hardly talk, and when we do it's always awkward and superficial. My dad's still bitter about his failed company. He lives in this sad singles' complex and works in a bank. My mother only talks about her interior designer or her latest trip. My stepdad's nice, but he works too hard—has to keep up with my mother's spending habits."

Gabe didn't say anything.

She realized how what she'd said might have hit him. "I sound spoiled, huh? You lost your dad and your brother to gangs, had to quit school to support your family and raise your sisters, and I'm whining because my parents didn't love me enough."

He stopped at the light. "It's what you're used to." He whispered in her ear, "Right now, all I care about is getting this over so I can get you naked."

"I'm with you." Forget their differences. They loved each other. Maybe that was all that mattered.

GABE WENT TO HELP FELICITY out of the van. She was right. A lot *had* happened. The biggest was realizing how he felt about her. When he'd come out of the party and found her gone, possibly for good, he couldn't bear it. He loved her, too. That was all there was to it.

He held out his hand to help her down. For better or worse, he'd fallen for this petite blonde with bird-feather hair, starlit eyes and more energy than any one person should be allowed. Forget the insecure girl, the ambitious climber he'd glimpsed in that hotel elevator. This was the Felicity he loved. This was the Felicity who counted.

She gave him her hand. Just the touch of her fingers set him on fire. And when she smiled, he wanted to take her to the back of the van and tear her clothes off. "Ready?" she asked him.

"As I'll ever be." All he had to do was endure a dance lesson, then he could take her home and make love to her, seal the deal…so to speak.

When they got in the club, it turned out the group lessons weren't available that night. "I guess we can take off. You girls are riding home with friends, right?"

"No way you're getting out of dancing," Trina said.

"That's right," Felicity said. "You taught me to fight. I'll teach you to salsa. Fair's fair." He followed her onto the dance floor, where she put one hand on his shoulder, the other in his palm. "The secret is to stay loose," she said, rocking her hips back and forth.

He put his palms there. "I'm liking this already."

She showed him the footwork, an easy two-step move.

"So, let me see if I understand." He grabbed her ass with both hands. "You tighten these muscles." Then he shifted to her hips, sliding them up and down real slow. "And loosen these."

"Two can play that game." She reached both hands to his backside and hauled him closer.

"Keep that up and we might get bounced for indecent behavior."

"Mmm," she said, her eyes glittering at him. "Not with the girls around." She smiled over his shoulder, and he turned to see the twins shooting them thumbs-up signs. They had an uncanny knack for crashing private moments with Felicity.

WHEN THE NEXT SONG BEGAN, Felicity was startled when Gabe abruptly whipped her out and back, then spun her in a confident swing move.

"You know how to dance," Felicity said.

"I learned just enough to get laid." He tugged her close, so her back was against his chest, and rocked her side to side, before spinning her again.

The music had a delicious grinding percussion and she was breathless with the pleasure of moving to it in Gabe's strong arms.

"If the next song's slow, I can't be held responsible for my actions," Gabe growled near her ear.

A leisurely ballad started up. "Damn. I can't get a

break." He hauled her close, his hands clasped low on her back. He leaned in to kiss her neck and her knees nearly gave out. "I got you, girl," he murmured, holding her up.

"You do. You have me." She closed her eyes and let the singer's anguished voice wash over her.

"Listen to those lyrics," Gabe said. "Latinos moan about love like nobody else. 'My heart is broken into a million shards. I walk the lonely streets calling your name. When will this misery end? Never, never, never. You have smashed my soul, left me with this burning agony of my very being.'"

She laughed. "I think it's romantic. So passionate. You're like that. Did you get that from your father?"

"I hate to think what I got from him. His temper, for sure. His fierceness."

"Surely he had good qualities, too."

"He loved us. He was loyal. And he had courage. Though he used it stupidly—in the gang. My mother tried to get him to leave, but he refused."

"Terco," she said, tapping his chest.

"Yeah. I got that from him, too, I guess." His smile was sad.

"Stubborn can be good," she said. "It got you this far. It would take you much farther, too." She took a deep breath, then went for it. "Like to college. To finish your degree."

"Why would I want that?" He went tense, totally resisting the idea. But if she hired him to direct her program, he'd need to work toward a degree.

"To have more options. You're talented and skilled and smart—"

"Stop trying to write me a résumé." He dipped her nearly to the floor. "I've got my hands all over you in public and it's totally legit. Let's make the most of it." He raised her, making her feel light-headed.

Maybe later, then.

The music vibrated through her, harmonizing with the desire she felt for Gabe. She was totally tuned in to him—his voice, his eyes, his touch, his heat, the great way he smelled. It was mutual. She saw it in his eyes, felt it in the pressure of every finger, in how his body rocked against hers, not allowing an inch between them.

"What are you thinking?" he asked.

"That dancing with you is really, really sexy."

"Not nearly as sexy as after." Then Gabe kissed her and the club faded away, leaving only the two of them, moving together, mouths linked, all alone in a world of their own.

When they broke apart, she looked at him, feeling a little unsure. "What happens next? Where do we go from here? This is my first time in love."

"Well, it's not like your futon. There's no instruction book. We do our best, day-to-day, to take care of each other, be there for each other."

"I think I can do that."

"Then we have a deal."

She caught sight of them in the bar mirror. Anyone who saw them would think them an unlikely couple—with her being so blonde and small and sweet-looking, and him so big and dark and dangerous-looking. There were differences that didn't show, too—their backgrounds, their work, their ambitions, their personalities.

But maybe love could overcome all that. If those had been her birthday candles, not Gabe's, that was what she would have wished, then worked like hell to make it come true.

THE MORNING OF THE FESTIVAL, Felicity's alarm went off at 4:00 a.m. She reached for Gabe, as she did each morning. Sometimes he was there, sometimes he was already up and gone.

This morning, he was gone, but he'd left a candy necklace and a note:

Something to nibble on while thinking of me. Take your time. Use lots of tongue. Gone to start setup. Miss you already. You'll rock the house today.
Love, G

Love. The word made her heart sing. Gabe was definitely romantic, whether that came from his Latin roots or his own tender heart. They'd been so busy the past few days, they'd hardly talked. They'd managed to make love, though, finding each other in the dark, missing sleep, but not caring. She'd balanced work and love pretty well so far. She was proud of herself.

She reached Discovery by 5:00 a.m., her nerves tight, her stomach jumping. Today had to go well. For her kids, her teachers, for STRIKE, for Discovery and, possibly, for the United Giving grant. The director, Carson Mellon, had told her he was coming.

She spotted Gabe moving risers around the stage where they would have music, demonstrations and the unveiling of the murals.

The sight of him made her whole body go electric and her heart surge. She felt so close to him, as if they belonged together. Was she getting carried away? A large part of her thought this was too good to be true.

When he saw her, he grinned and started to reach for her until he realized where they were. Instead, they looked at each other, a million connections zipping between them. "You doing okay?" he asked.

"I'm nervous. Today has to work."

"It can't fail. You planned it."

Damn, she loved him.

After that, time flew, with Felicity putting out fires, arranging, advising, helping, not taking a breath until the festival had been going for an hour. She looked around. The place was packed with Discovery students and their families, kids from other schools and people from the neighborhood.

She was so proud of the students, who were running the game booths they'd set up, selling raffle tickets, carrying supplies to the food booths, staffing the science booth, the art booth, the auto-shop station.

Gabe's fighters, wearing black STRIKE T-shirts, were taking tickets. Dave guarded the entrance, watching for troublemakers and checking bags for contraband. He'd gone above and beyond to make the day go well.

Feliz Mercado had donated bottled water, dozens of their mouthwatering tamales and bags of their popular homemade pork rinds, as light and airy as popcorn, as well as day-old baked goods. Beatrice had gotten parent volunteers to staff the table where the items were sold. She had an uncanny knack for fundraising ideas.

Once Felicity had unleashed Beatrice's natural leadership talents, she'd become a champion of the school. It warmed Felicity's heart that the woman had gone from trying to get Felicity fired to singing her praises to all who would listen.

At three o'clock, Los Tres Luchadores performed, entertaining the crowd with Latin-flavored retro rock. When they finished, it would be time to unveil the murals. Felicity said goodbye to Carson Mellon, so excited about what he'd said she wanted to squeal. She looked for Gabe, who was heading her way. It kept surprising her how telepathic they seemed with each other.

He held out a water bottle. "Drink."

She hadn't realized how thirsty she was until the cool liquid rolled down her throat. Gabe watched her tenderly. She couldn't believe how different he seemed to her now—softer, more open, far less angry. Love had changed him.

"Here." He held out a piece of corn-on-the-cob on a stick, smothered in mayo, parmesan and hot sauce. "Mexican street snack. You'll love it."

"How did you know I was starving?"

"I just do."

She took a bite. It was amazing, juicy and tangy and cheesy. "Yum."

"Great turnout." He motioned toward the crowd around the stage.

"I know. Plus, I've got news. I talked to the United Giving director. He practically came right out and said we're the top choice for the grant."

"Wow. That's great," Gabe said.

"Great? It's amazing." It was her fondest hope. She was so happy, she couldn't keep from telling him her plan for him. "If we get it, how would you like to be the director of the After-School Institute? We'd expand what we offer, of course, so there would be plenty of work for a full-time position."

He looked at her. "Thanks for the offer, but it's not for me. I coach STRIKE. That's all I want." He'd completely dismissed the idea.

"But wouldn't you rather work with kids than drive a cab or landscape?"

"I like what I do. I've told you that."

"I know. It's just—" He was stubborn. It would tak some time. "I know you'd love it and you'd be great a Think about it, okay?"

His eyebrows dipped into a glower. "I said I'm not in terested."

She'd offered him a great job and he acted offendec "I want the best for you. I know you feel the same abou me, like when I—"

"Is it time?" Alex stood at her elbow, his eyes mor eager than she'd ever seen them. He wore crisply irone baggy shorts and a new plaid flannel shirt buttoned to th top. His hair had been gelled and his athletic shoes looke new. Behind him were the other three students whose ar had been chosen to grace Discovery's walls.

She looked at her watch. It was ten minutes past tim She'd nearly let an argument with Gabe derail her fror the crowning moment of the entire festival—unveiling th murals. "You're right. Let's get onstage." She glanced a Gabe, who waved her on, the argument clearly set asid For good, if he had his say, she knew, with a pang.

Felicity led the student artists to the stage, motionin for Adelia to join them from where she stood talking t the mayor's PR manager.

Felicity took the microphone and looked out at th crowd, which included city officials, business leader and top district folks. Tom Brown stood next to Carsor wearing a big grin.

She'd sent her uncle a personal invitation, addressin him as Dr. Evers out of respect, but he hadn't come. I didn't matter. This was a triumph, whether he knew abou it or not.

She glanced at the three walls of the courtyard, al draped by tarps. Alex's mural was on the street wall be cause it had gotten the most votes from students an would be the last to be unveiled. They would shift the crowd out to the street, which the police had blocked off.

Media were everywhere, including a stringer from *Newsweek* working on a story on urban school initiatives. She spotted Leonard Lancaster being interviewed by a TV reporter. He was no doubt trying to take credit for the success. The man shamelessly manipulated information to feed his ego and advance his private ambitions.

Gabe had compared her to him. They'd been quarreling, of course, and he'd taken it back, but there was truth behind his blunt remark. He disapproved of her emphasis on image and presentation.

But he was learning, wasn't he? Certainly, today's event was proof that she'd been right. She pushed the niggle of doubt, that sense that Gabe thought less of her, to the back of her mind. She wouldn't let it spoil today's triumph.

She smiled at the crowd and took the microphone in her hand. "Welcome to Discover Discovery Day," she said. "This is our chance to share our school with all of you." She thanked key people, made a few announcements, then handed off to Adelia, who told the audience that the students' talent and dedication had inspired her to start a project to paint murals across the Valley. She'd named it *Building Neighborhoods: Wall by Wall* and already had several artists signed up to participate. Felicity was thrilled that the festival had led to something so wonderful.

After that, Adelia called up the first artist—Emily Jefferson, a shy black girl, her hair in fresh cornrows, her smile peeking from beneath downcast eyes.

"Shall we see Emily's work?" Adelia said. Felicity motioned for the STRIKE fighters on the roof to release the canvas cover. Emily's mural shone from the wall—

a circle of hands of all colors gripping wrists over the background of a glowing sun in a bright blue sky. The crowd gasped, then applauded.

When they'd quieted, Adelia held the mic for Emily, who leaned in and mumbled quickly, "It's about people together creating a sunny future." She dashed away before the applause began, to be hugged by her mother and little brothers in the audience.

The second mural, sketched by sixth-grader Miguel Cervantes, showed children dreaming of themselves in various careers. It was equally well received. Miguel looked as if he was floating on air as he left the stage.

Jeremy Pritchard, a loner who'd made friends during the mural painting, was next. He'd covered the wall with the coats of arms the Institute kids had drawn, overlapping them so images, character traits and slogans angled every which way.

After that, Adelia asked everyone to join her street-side for the final mural—Alex's. He stood beside Adelia, shoulders back, feet in fighter's stance, arms at his side—nervous, but keeping his face stern and serious.

When the tarp dropped, people went nuts and Alex turned bright red. When the crowd quieted, Adelia explained that Alex had coordinated the contest and was a remarkable artist besides. She held out the mic so he could talk into it, as the other kids had done, but he took it out of her hand and went over to the mural.

He pointed to the words at the bottom. "*Mi tierra, mi gente, mi futuro.* For you gringos, that means *my land, my people, my future.*" The mural showed a girl, clearly Carmen, between two boys, her hair flowing in waves surrounding cultural images—the American flag, the Mexican flag, the Virgen de Guadalupe, a girl in a confirmation dress, a field-worker in white, a Mayan head-dress.

"Yeah, so, like, this is street art for the people, like Adelia says. Street art shows we own our neighborhood with beauty, not show-off scribbles. That's all I got." He gave a quick pat to his heart with his fist, kissed two fingers and held them out toward Gabe, who looked as proud as if Alex were his own child—or his little brother. Felicity swore she saw tears in Gabe's eyes.

Suddenly, loud boos broke out, along with hisses and profanity, coming from a group at the edges of the crowd. Felicity recognized them as the gangsters who'd bullied Alex. They threw signs at Alex, who froze, staring out at them.

Dave and Gabe headed for the thugs, but they scattered like leaves. Felicity leaned down to Alex. "They hate you because you succeeded where they failed. Don't let them get to you."

But her words had no impact on him, she could see. His eyes were cold stone, his face hard. He would not let this go, she knew, and her heart sank.

After the ceremony, people spent time walking along the murals, pointing and commenting, and the artists answered questions. Alex disappeared.

Not long after the festival closed and Felicity and Gabe were taking a short break before beginning the cleanup, they heard fierce shouts from out front.

"Sounds like a fight," Gabe said and took off running toward the noise. She ran, too, her heart in her throat.

CHAPTER FIFTEEN

THEY FOUND STRIKE KIDS and Doble gangbangers circled around two boys fighting on the ground, wrestling and punching. *Please, please, don't let it be Alex,* Felicity prayed.

The boy on top was Li'l B from the sidewalk confrontation. When he moved to the side, she saw the boy on the ground was Alex.

Gabe pushed past the watchers and yanked Li'l B to the side to crouch beside Alex. Blood poured down his face from his nose and mouth and a cut on his cheek. He held one fist, scraped and starting to swell.

Gabe checked each injured spot, then looked at the STRIKE fighters gathered around. "You should have stopped this," he snapped. "Get out of my sight."

Reluctantly they backed away, still watching. The gangbangers had faded off as soon as Gabe arrived.

"Let's get you cleaned up," he said to Alex, helping him to his feet.

Felicity unlocked the door to the gym and assisted Gabe, bringing ice bags and wraps. Gabe didn't speak as he worked, but his jaw muscle jumped and he was clearly furious. He packed Alex's nose, bandaged his cheek and wrapped an ice bag over his battered hand.

Felicity brought Alex aspirin and a paper cup of water, which Alex had trouble drinking because of his injured mouth.

"You let that thug get to you again," Gabe snapped.

"He disrespected you," Alex said, wincing. "He called you a narc, said you ratted on Ochoa, that you got him murdered."

"Ochoa got his own ass killed. But that's not the point. The point is you're his bitch. He knows your weak spot. All he has to do is dis Carmen or your coach or your art and he knows you'll foam like a rabid animal. *I trained you better than that.*" He growled the last words.

Alex was breathing hard, listening, but angry, too, Felicity could tell.

"Ms. Spencer cut you slack, helped you, and you shit on it. You risked jail. And for what? Bullshit pride."

"Pride is not bullshit," he yelled. "Just cuz you don't have any, that don't make you right. You're ashamed of your race, your *familia.* That's what's bullshit!" He was clearly near tears and in pain and fearful that he'd back-talked Gabe, but so furious he couldn't help himself.

Gabe held his silence for a long tense moment. "I don't use my race or my history to excuse crime or stupidity. I'm done with you, Gomez. You don't belong in this gym. Don't show your face here again."

Alex stumbled backward, as if he'd taken a punch. His mouth dropped. He clearly hadn't expected that. Neither had Felicity.

It was wrong. They would lose Alex altogether. "We're all angry," she said. "How about making it one week out of STRIKE, with some community service?"

Gabe turned to her, nostrils flared, breathing hard. She'd undercut his authority, but she wanted to keep him from crossing a line she knew he didn't want to cross. Without looking back at Alex, he said, "You heard me. *Véte." Get out.*

Alex left the gym looking desolate.

"What the hell do you think you're doing?" Gabe said to her. "I run STRIKE. Unless you're working up another crappy *deal* on me." He was so angry he scared her.

"I'm sorry, but I know you didn't want that. Alex needs STRIKE. You said so yourself." He'd shut out Robert just as unwisely, but she wouldn't mention that.

"You don't know the first thing about what he needs. You're in way over your head, lady."

"Maybe my experience with urban schools doesn't count as much as your *street cred,* but it counts for something."

He glared at her, his jaw muscle working, his hands curling and uncurling, clearly trying to calm down.

She would focus on the positive. "At least no reporter was around. Think of the headline—Peaceful Festival Defeated by Brutal Gang Battle. That would negate all our work. With my United Giving presentation coming up, we can't afford bad press."

"You care too damn much about how things look. Putting a bow on shit doesn't make it steak."

He looked at her with disdainful superiority, dismissing her. His was not the only way.

"Well, you care too little," she snapped, fired up now. "You let your image lose a job you loved. You could have started taking classes, made an effort."

"You never let up, do you? Fight the good fight, beat the odds, get a college degree. Give it up, for God's sake."

"Sneer at me if you want, but it was me fixing your image with the PTO that saved your gym. You're telling me that didn't matter to you?"

"Not the same thing." She hated the distance in his eyes, the bitterness on his face—the same as the day they'd met. Nothing had changed.

She felt afraid and lost. As though she'd made it all up—the love, the closeness, Gabe becoming softer.

She'd fallen in love with a man who despised her.

Reading her face, Gabe gentled his tone. "I don't want to fight with you. It's Alex who matters here. I want to do right by him."

"He failed a test," she said softly. "What matters is how he fixes it. It's like at your meet—you ask them what they learn after a fight, win or lose. This is a teaching moment. Teach Alex what to do after he's blown it."

He let long seconds pass, while emotions crossed his face—frustration, worry, then finally acceptance. "I swear to God, you could talk a fish out of its gills," he muttered. "I'll think about letting him back in a week, if he earns it doing whatever the hell you cook up."

"That's all I ask," she said, relieved.

"I need to break down the risers. Are we good?" He sounded so weary. They'd gotten through another fight, but the issues had not been resolved. Worse, she was afraid if they talked more about them, they would ruin what they had going.

"We're good," she lied. And that wasn't good at all.

TEN DAYS LATER, Gabe headed for a cab pickup, thinking about the afternoon at the gym. It had been Alex's first day back at STRIKE. He'd seemed humble and had worked damned hard.

As much as Gabe hated to admit it, Felicity had been right. Alex needed STRIKE. Even better, she'd turned his punishment into a chance to start a service program for the school. She'd had him do chores for neighbors and merchants on the block, building more community links.

Felicity was a wonder. Gabe felt bad about the tension between them since the argument over Alex. They'd said harsh things that neither had exactly taken back. Now they were tentative with each other.

Had to be expected with people who were so different. Sex could only do so much to keep you close, though their lovemaking was still going strong, possibly more intense every time.

In fact… He looked at the clock on his dash. Eight o'clock. He hoped she'd be awake when he got off his shift. She'd had some kind of dinner meeting, according to the message she'd left him.

He pulled up to the address dispatch had given him—an office complex. Out of the dark, his passenger bounded up and leaned into the passenger window. It was Felicity. He smiled.

"Surprise!" She jumped into the seat. "We got it!" she said, her eyes bright and wide. "We got the grant! I can't believe it!"

"That was your meeting? United Giving? Congratulations!"

"I'm so excited I feel like my mind's about to explode." She bounced in the seat. "I've been coming up with so many ideas for *if* I get the grant. Now it's *when* I get it. I'm in heaven."

"I can see that. You're bruising your skull on the roof."

"Do you have time to swing me by the school so I can leave a couple of notes? I need the janitors to set up for an assembly."

"I'll make time." He liked seeing her so happy.

"You should have heard Carson Mellon. He said Discovery will be a lighthouse school. That means educators from all over will visit us. Talk about getting a head start on getting back to consulting! Ooh, yeah. I need to print up more curriculum guides." She sighed. "I am so stoked. This means everything."

"I can tell," he said, but his gut tightened. She was on that ladder, leaping madly up the rungs. She would never be content. She'd warned him on the Buttes, looking out at the city, the spring breeze lifting her hair, that she was always thinking and planning, never stopping.

"I can seriously offer you that job now. Have you thought about it?" Her voice rose eagerly.

She'd never be content with him, either. His gut twisted another notch.

"I'm just happy that STRIKE gets to stick around. Maybe you can hire me an assistant coach and buy more equipment. That'd be plenty."

"Sure," she said, but her energy sank like a stone.

He shifted uneasily in his seat and they drove in an awkward silence that he finally broke. "So, Alex did great today. It was his first day back. He said you made him a Discovery *Ambassador?*"

"Yeah. That's what I'm calling the service club—Discovery Ambassadors."

"He was real proud of the title."

"He should be. An elderly woman he got groceries for called to thank me for sending her such a polite young man who wouldn't even take a tip."

"That's good to hear," he said, feeling a stab of pride.

"After he hosed down the loading dock for Feliz Mercado, the ladies made him fresh sopaipillas and fussed over him."

He smiled at that. He rounded the corner toward the school, planning to light up Alex's mural with his headlights. Damn, he loved that kid.

But when his lights splashed the wall, all he saw were ugly black spray-paint scrawls covering every inch of Alex's art. There were crude gang tags among the scribbles and shapes.

Felicity gasped. "Why? Murals get respect. Who di
this? Is this part of the fight with Alex?"

"Could be." Leaving the headlights on, he got out t
study the marks, his heart heavy.

Felicity joined him.

"This is clumsy work. It doesn't have the sharp angl
or the shading taggers practice. Tons of drips, too. Eve
toys practice their signs." He ran his fingers over a gan
name. "That's *Fourteen Ave,* but this block's not in di
pute. It's suicide to declare war here. Makes no sens
Coop needs to see this."

"You're saying aimless vandals did this?"

"Not aimless. They covered every inch. This is delib
erate. Who and why I have no idea."

"Alex will be devastated." She turned to him. Th
shadows didn't hide how pale she'd become. "He'll wa
to retaliate, won't he?"

"If I have to handcuff him to a chair bolted to the flo
I won't let him."

She nodded. "This is…terrible. The students will b
so upset. I was going to announce the grant in the mor
ing. Now I'll have to explain this."

"I'm sorry," he said, putting his arm around her, fe
ing pretty devastated himself. He had to intercept Al
before he saw this. Get Coop here to analyze the mark
Rattle some cages to figure out what was going on.

"This won't stop us," Felicity said firmly, interru
ing his thoughts. "We'll paint the mural again, damn
Involve more kids this time. Adelia says there's a pai
on the market with a plastic coating so graffiti wash
right off. It's pricey, but maybe the company would don
some for the publicity. I'll call them."

"You never give up, do you?" The woman was indom
table. His heart surged with love for her.

"I can't afford to. Will you help me drop a tarp over this so the kids don't see it first thing?"

Focus, concentrate, do what needs doing, Felicity told herself, her fingers trembling as she looked for the gym key among her wad of school keys.

Gabe reached around her and unlocked the door for her. She was grateful for his calm strength. He held the door and she flipped on the light.

What she saw made her gasp. Gabe swore harshly.

The gym had been wrecked. Spray paint covered the walls with ugly threats. Mounds of sand lay beneath sliced punching bags on mats that had been sprayed and torn. Beer cans and liquor bottles littered the room.

Her room dividers had been tipped over, chairs thrown into the walls, the computer monitors smashed, the towers knocked over.

"The lock wasn't jammed," he said through gritted teeth. "Someone let them in here."

"Who has keys besides us? Dave…the janitors… Conrad. Who else?"

Before Gabe could answer, his phone rang, the boxing bell echoing in the ruined gym, as if signaling the end of a terrible fight.

"Yeah?" Gabe said into the phone. The caller spoke and he stiffened. "How bad?…How many?…Damn. I'll come to the station after the hospital."

"The hospital?"

He put his phone in his pocket and looked at her, his eyes troubled, his jaw tight. "Alex is at county hospital. Minor injuries. They got into it with a crew from Doble. Ten of my guys are being held at the jail. Let's go."

Felicity felt as though someone had poured ice down

her body. The gym had been wrecked. Alex and his friends had retaliated and been arrested. Could it get much worse?

GABE DROVE TOO FAST to the hospital, adrenaline rushing through him as if someone had stabbed his chest with a needle of it. Felicity sat stiffly, twisting her fingers, as scared and worried as he was.

He was also angry. *Your boys are in big trouble,* Coop had said. *I can't protect them. Don't even want to.* He had to hear what had happened from them. It couldn't be as bad as Coop made it sound.

A patrol officer stood outside the curtained-off bed where Alex lay handcuffed to the bed rail. He looked so small and broken, one eye swollen shut, the lip that had barely healed split again, his chest crosshatched with bloody stitches.

For a second, Gabe couldn't breathe. His mind flashed to Robert unconscious on the sidewalk, dying. He shook himself to the present, to Alex, who opened his eyes.

Seeing them, he winced with shame. "It was jus' s'posed to be a fight in the ring. Li'l B and me," he said, the words muddied as he talked around the hamburger the inside of his mouth must be.

"Over the tags on the mural?" Gabe's voice cracked. He felt as if a tiger had clawed his insides. He wanted to shake Alex so hard his teeth rattled.

"That was *mi alma* on the wall. I *had* to step up. For *pride.* Don't say that's bullshit." He lifted himself from the pillow, rattling the handcuff against the bar, his eyes on fire. "Li'l B said my mural was whitey kiss-ass shit, not worth Doble time, but that the markup was righteous." He swallowed and his lips stuck together, as if they were dry.

"Doble didn't do it?"

"So I told him, back off or fight straight—in the ring, by the book, to settle it for good. Controlled, like you always say."

"Controlled means official, with a ref, not some vendetta. You let them into my gym? I trusted you with a key."

"His crew stepped in to watch. That was cool—more to tell the story, I thought." Alex lifted his gaze to the ceiling. "But they held me down and beat me, while they trashed the gym." He screwed up his face, trying not to cry.

"So you sent STRIKE after them?" he snapped, refusing to succumb to his sadness, to his desire to hug this boy, tell him it would be okay. It wouldn't be, and Gabe couldn't pretend otherwise.

"I called Victor. He brought the rest. We had to defend our gym." He swallowed. "You would do the same."

"After the breaks you got, you do this, then drag the guys with you. They've been arrested. You're going to jail, Alex. You put yourself there."

"My mom can't post bail," Alex said quickly.

"You think I can? If I could, I wouldn't. I'm done with you."

"We haven't talked to the police," Felicity said. "Maybe we can work this out."

"What's to work out? You think Alex sweeping sidewalks and carrying groceries will fix this? No. This is gang activity. They'll throw the book at him."

"Let's talk to Detective Carter, okay? Check on the other boys." She thought she could talk her way into a deal, he could tell. Just like she'd done with Robert—she'd escaped, while he took the fall. She didn't get it.

Alex had proved what Gabe knew and hated—that

kids like him couldn't escape their lot, not unless they were superhuman or insanely lucky. Alex Gomez was neither one.

At the jail, they found STRIKE parents milling around the lobby, mothers crying, fathers angry. Gabe had let all these people down. He wanted to punch a wall.

Victor's father saw him and approached. "How did this happen? This ain't how he was taught at home, or how you coached him."

"The bangers provoked the boys," Gabe said, hating the puzzled disappointment on the man's face. "They saw their gym trashed, their friend bloody, and they reacted."

"Victor's never been in trouble with police."

"That's good. He should get probation at the worst."

"Detective Carter's here," Felicity said, nodding to where they could see Coop through the window in the security door. The receptionist clicked the release and they joined the detective.

They'll be charged with gang activity," Coop said. "There was property damage—a couple cars got dented during the fight."

"Okay," Gabe said.

"It's worse than that. Feliz Mercado got hit with Molotov cocktails. We've got cell-phone video of two of your boys throwing flaming bottles, then fleeing."

Gabe could hardly take Coop's words in. He felt as though someone had tipped the world upside down and shaken it. "Not my guys. No way. They fought, sure. They were defending Alex and the gym. But they would never start a fire. Feliz is a friend. He's always giving them free food."

"The faces are blurred, but they're wearing STRIKE T-shirts."

"Then someone stole the shirts."

"No one's been charged yet on the arson. We're investigating. That's all I can tell you."

He felt sick inside. "How bad will it be on the fight?"

"This is a first offense for most of them. Once it's clear they're not gangbangers, it shouldn't go too bad. For the ones with records, depends on what deals get worked out."

"What about Alex Gomez?"

"He resisted arrest. Hit a cop. Juvenile hall for sure."

"Damn it to hell." His insides turned to water.

"You did what you could. Better hope they don't get charged with arson."

"What happens now?" Felicity asked, her face pale as milk. "Tonight, I mean."

"Parents who can will put up bail and they go home until they're due in court."

"But what if they can't afford it?"

"Then they stay in jail."

"I'll post bail for the ones who need it," she said.

"Are you crazy?" Gabe said. "You can't afford a car. How the hell can you pay bail? It's probably two to five K per kid, right, Coop?"

"Yeah."

"Could we talk about this outside?" she said, glancing at Coop, clearly embarrassed to be arguing in front of him. Promising to keep them posted, Coop held the door so they could leave.

FELICITY HAD BEEN SUBMERGED in Arctic waters. She couldn't feel her arms or legs. She could hardly breathe. All she knew was she had to rescue these boys. The blows had come fast and hard—the vandalized mural, the wrecked gym, Alex beaten and in handcuffs, the STRIKE kids in jail and now suspected of *arson.*

Gabe had taken this badly. His face had turned to stone, all except for his eyes, which burned with anguish.

"I'll have my stepdad wire me the money. As a loan."

He eyed her, letting her words sink in. "You're not paying bail for Alex. He stays in jail. This is all on him." She hated how cold he sounded.

"He's suffered enough already."

"You can't buy his way out of this. He needs to feel what he's done. He knew what would happen if he screwed up again."

"I can't believe you're saying this. You know how much his mural meant to him. He was trying to set up a fair fight in the ring, but they ambushed him. He's only human, Gabe. And he's young."

"He knows better. So do you."

"You're not punishing him for his own good. You're punishing him for disappointing you. Like you did with Robert." The words flew out before she could stop them.

Gabe recoiled as if from a punch.

"That wasn't fair. We're both upset."

"It's what you feel," he snapped. "Blunt, for a change. I like it. So let me return the favor. You think if you buy Alex out of this, you'll make up for letting Robert go to jail for you. It doesn't work that way."

She was horrified that he would bring that up. And hurt, terribly hurt. "Even if that were true—and maybe subconsciously it is—so what? Alex still needs help and I'm willing to give it to him. Unlike you."

"You don't get it."

"I'm sick to death of you saying I don't understand being poor or disadvantaged. This isn't charity. This isn't to assuage my white guilt. This is what money is for. You said it yourself. If you had it, you'd spend it." She was furious now, too, and they glared at each other.

"I'm going to see who needs help, call my stepdad and pay the bail as fast as I can. You can leave. I'll call a cab to get home."

"I have a cab. I'll wait out front."

In minutes, her stepdad had wired the cash, no questions asked, to the nearest Western Union office. Gabe drove her there in stony silence, the tension between them as thick as the darkness outside. An hour later, she'd bailed out the boys who needed it, including Alex, who would spend the night in the hospital.

Finished, they headed home.

Felicity had to break the silence. "I know you're angry, but we have to figure out how to position this with the media. They'll start calling soon."

"The media? My boys were arrested for street fighting and face possible arson charges. I don't give a shit about the media."

"Well, I have to. A number of my students, trained in a martial-arts program I sanctioned, were involved in a gang fight that put one boy in the hospital and burned down a beloved neighborhood market." Her voice was shaking so hard she had to stop talking.

Gabe took that in and seemed to make a decision. "I can fix that. I'm shutting down STRIKE."

"What are you talking about?"

"STRIKE caused this. It's on me. I trusted Alex with the key to the gym. I trusted my guys not to fight. I failed on both counts. So you can wash your hands of us. Problem solved."

"Blame is useless. You said so yourself. Here's the approach I suggest we take. We'll stress that this regrettable incident came about because the mural was vandalized, the boys were upset by the unwarranted assault on their friend." She paused for a breath. "This incident doesn't take away from all we've achieved at Discovery. We'll repaint the mural and keep up our efforts to transform the school. We hope the police quickly find and arrest the vandals who defaced the school and the arsonists who destroyed the grocery market."

"Except STRIKE kids are the suspects."

"And we know they're innocent. We should stress that the United Giving grant is a vote of confidence in what we're doing, including STRIKE." She stopped. "I'd better give Carson a heads-up in case he gets called."

"And what if he gets cold feet about the grant? Hell, we just proved the PTO lady was right in the first place. You have to take a strong stand. Tell them all you're shutting down STRIKE."

"STRIKE is part of the Institute now. Your boys count on STRIKE. It keeps them in school. You can't quit."

"All I did was teach them to be better street fighters."

"Gabe. That's not what you want."

"Don't tell me what I want," he snapped. "STRIKE is done. You're right again. STRIKE has no place in a school. I'm not sure it has a place anywhere."

He was so damn stubborn. And so damn wrong. He was overreacting again. "You fought like hell to keep STRIKE and just like that, you shut it down?"

"STRIKE did more harm than good. I can see that."

"Not true. This was an extreme incident. And what about your boys? They need you in their lives."

"I'll still be there. I just won't train them."

She was so angry, so frustrated. "You're selling your boys short—and yourself. That's what you do, isn't it? You hit a wall and you say, 'Oh, well, can't fight city hall.' That's crap. It's an excuse to give up."

"Careful," Gabe warned, but she couldn't stop. She'd

had it with his attitude and all the ways it had limited his life.

"It's true. You did it with the rec job. And I offered you a great job and you dismissed it without even a thought. Sure, you got a raw deal growing up, but that's no excuse to crawl into a hole and pull the dirt over you."

They'd reached her apartment and Gabe stopped the van. "As long as we're being *honest* here, you offered me that job to make yourself feel better. You need to polish up the homeboy, get him a college degree, make him respectable."

"That's not true."

"I don't blame you. You need to socialize with politicos and bigwigs. Right now, I'm a gangbanger poster boy, good for show-and-tell. But if I'm going to be your *boyfriend,* I need a serious upgrade."

"That's not fair."

"Sure it is. I've heard your spiel. Truth doesn't count, only perception. That goes for people as well as schools, right?"

"Because I want to give you a chance to do more of what you love, I'm bad? I want the best for you. That's what people do when they love each other." It hurt to say the word *love* when they were fighting this way.

"Yeah? Well, I want the best for you, too. So stop clawing your way to the top of some bullshit heap and enjoy what you already love—working at Discovery."

"You're so wrong."

"Come on. Admit it. Discovery's not big enough for you. You want to help more kids, thousands of kids, the whole damn world of kids." He waved his arms in exaggerated motions.

She stared at him, unable to hide from the truth this time. "You despise me. You have from the start. You think

I'm a grasping megalomaniac with an insatiable need to achieve."

"Hmm. Not sure a guy with no college *ejication* can grasp those big words, but that seems to nail it, yeah. And you think I'm a low-life, lazy bum wasting my brilliance on cab rides and koi ponds."

His sarcasm was so ugly. This was the Gabe who'd glared at her at Robert's funeral, the one who'd sneered at her when she first came to Discovery. How had she ever believed he'd changed?

"Why are you with me, if you feel that way?" she asked, her throat tight.

"Right back at you, babe."

They stared at each other for a long moment. She no longer felt numb. She felt hot, scalded and empty, except for the tears that brimmed in her eyes. She would not cry in front of him. No way.

Gabe looked sad, but resigned. "I don't want us to hurt each other. It's not worth it. We knew there were limits to being together. I think we've reached them."

"We're breaking up?" She didn't mean to sound surprised, because she agreed with every word he'd said, but it seemed so final, so terrible.

"Why drag it out? Even if this mess at Discovery cools out, you'll be gone soon enough. You're destined for bigger things. I mean that. You're a remarkable person, with a lot of talent. I'd only drag you down. And you'd piss the hell out of me. I don't want it to come to that."

The truth of his words sank in. He was right. Their relationship seemed as wrecked as the gym, as scribbled-on as the mural.

As if on cue, both of their cell phones sounded—her "Flight of the Bumblebee" and his shrill boxing bell perfect proof of how different they were.

Felicity checked her screen. “It’s a reporter.”

“Here, too,” he said. “This is our position—I’m taking responsibility for what happened and closing STRIKE. You’ll repaint the mural and keep up the good work you’re doing at Discovery, blah, blah, the rest of your pitch.”

“Gabe, I—”

“I mean it, Felicity. You’re not going to lose your job because of me. I couldn’t live with that.”

Felicity was too upset, too scared and too heartbroken to argue.

CHAPTER SIXTEEN

In the morning, after barely any sleep, Felicity ran the assembly, a frozen smile on her face. Her triumph over the Adopt-a-School grant was subdued by the previous night's disaster. She stayed positive, promising the mural would be repainted, and they would keep doing good things, but she saw the real story in the stunned, angry and discouraged faces of her students and staff.

The rest of the day, she handled media interviews, coordinating her comments with district officials, who told her in no uncertain terms how disastrous this kind of publicity was for Jefferson schools.

That evening, she watched TV news and read the internet coverage on her laptop, her hands clammy, her brain swirling.

It was terrible. The theme was that gangs had a chokehold on the inner city and fledging efforts like Discovery's were doomed. As proof, they showed the ruined mural, the wrecked gym, the burned-down market. Thankfully, the boys who'd been in the fight were underage so their names and pictures weren't released, but that was small satisfaction.

Leonard was quoted hitting the usual notes: dangerous neighborhood, children of violence, failing schools.

Gabe handled himself with dignity, taking the blame, defending his fighters, making supportive comments about her and Discovery.

Gabe. All she wanted was to fall into his arms, feel the comforting thud of his heart against her chest, his hands on her back, but she forced herself to stay strong.

It had barely been a month since she'd told Gabe she loved him and now her heart had been smashed to bits. She hurt so much it was hard to even concentrate on the mess she faced at school. She wasn't sure she was strong enough. She knew now that she'd been smart to stay superficial with the men she dated. She didn't have the stamina for a serious commitment.

Did Gabe miss her, ache for her? She didn't know. He'd called her early this morning, but only to thank her for bailing out the boys, especially Alex. "Thanks for being the kind of safety net I could never be," he'd said.

"I just backed your play," she'd replied, fighting to hide how choked up she felt. "Like you've always backed mine."

And that was that. So maybe he'd shut off his feelings for her as he'd done with his boys the night before. She'd hated how harsh he'd been, how hard. His standards were too high—for the people he cared about and for himself.

He was right. If they'd stayed together, they would only have hurt each other more. She had to wonder, though, how much more could it hurt than this?

TWO DAYS AFTER the street fight, Gabe watched his boys trail into the ruined gym. He would supervise them while they cleared out the space, patched and painted, leaving it better than he'd found it two years ago.

The boys looked around at all the destruction, their faces tight with anger, with disgust.

The ones who hadn't been in the fight had given the others holy hell over losing STRIKE, which Gabe considered a good start to their punishment. They'd been fined for the destruction of property, but given probation for the other charges, once Coop spoke in their defense, since they weren't in gangs.

All except Alex, who faced a hearing.

No arrests had been made on the arson charges, so they were still in a terrible limbo, their futures at stake.

The school-side door opened and Felicity entered, joining them, sitting on the weight bench beside where Gabe stood, her face full of sadness.

Whenever he saw her he wanted to hold her again. He missed her like his own breath. In fact, the past two mornings, he'd woken up gasping for air, from dreams where he tried to save her, but failed.

The breakup was rough. Holding back his emotions had worn him clean out, exhausted him beyond belief.

"Before you start cleaning up this mess, you got anything to say to us?" he asked the boys who'd fought.

Alex stood, wincing, his face a mass of bruises, but he looked Gabe dead-on. "This is on me. I got puffed up about my art. I let anger rule me. I deserve to be kicked out, but don't take STRIKE away from the rest, Coach."

In the end, Gabe had been glad Felicity had bailed Alex out. A stint in Adobe Mountain would be plenty punishment for the boy. Gabe had let Ochoa anger take over and he felt ashamed.

"They made choices," he said now. "They have to answer for them."

Victor stood beside Alex. "We fought for the gym and for Alex. At the time, that felt solid. But you taught us better. Give us a chance to show you."

"The decision's made," Gabe said, the pain on Victor's face a stab in Gabe's gut. He couldn't go back on his word. That would be the easy road. He had to stay strong. "You knew the rules when you broke them. Anyone else?"

One by one, the rest apologized to him, to the other boys and to Felicity. Three read from crumpled notes, their hands and voices shaking. Afterward, Gabe let the silence hang for a bit, let the words settle in, the forgiveness rise to the surface if the other boys felt it.

"You guys want to say anything?" he asked the ones who hadn't fought, though he suspected if they'd been called, they'd have been in the thick of it. His training had failed and that sank his spirits every time the thought came to him—and it came often, almost as often as the loss of Felicity did.

Tyrell stood. "You suck for what you did," he said to the brawlers, then he turned to Gabe. "STRIKE's the best gym around."

"It's the only gym around," he said, trying for a joke, his throat tight.

"It's still the best. STRIKE's why I go to school most days." He held out a wad of bills. "Here's my next month's fee so you can find a place for us."

The others were fishing cash from pockets and backpacks, too.

Gabe's eyes stung and his lungs hurt like crazy. "Save your money. You've got my number. You have trouble or you need help—" He cleared his throat. "You need *anything,* you call me."

There was a moment of silence. He glanced at Felicity, who had tears in her eyes. She had a big heart…too big a heart.

"Let's get started. Anything usable goes in the truck, the rest in the Dumpster." Adelia had storage space in the warehouse where she was setting up her gallery. He'd keep his equipment there until he sold or donated it.

The boys moved out to work, including the nonbrawlers. "You guys don't have to do this," he said to Tyrell.

"It's our gym. We keep it squared up."

Gabe couldn't stand much more of this, so he headed into the hallway for a private moment to calm down. Except Felicity followed him. She was the last person he wanted in his face now.

"You okay?" she asked gently.

Do I look okay? he wanted to snap just to scare her off. But he'd already hurt her enough being who he was. "Getting by. You?"

"Coping. There's a rumor they're closing Discovery. I have a meeting with Tom Brown tomorrow. I hope it's about the United Giving grant."

"If it's not?"

She sighed. "I put a dozen résumés in the mail."

"You'll leave?"

"What else can I do? There's a strong possibility at my old district in Fresno. The curriculum director is retiring." She looked as weary as he felt. "With all that's happened, at least I look good on paper."

"You did good work. Never forget that. I'm sorry I put you in this spot. I should have left when you asked me." It ate him up, his role in this mess.

"I don't regret that one bit." Her eyes flared, then softened. "What I regret is what happened with us. That we didn't make it work."

"We couldn't. Not and be who we are."

"I'm certainly not your soul mate."

"I'm not sure there is such a thing."

"It was smart to end it while we can still be friends." Her faint smile went nowhere near her eyes—their silver stars now two gray blurs.

Screw smart. He wanted to crush her against him, take

it all back and go to bed, where they made all the sense in the world.

But that was pointless. She would never stop pushing him—or herself—and he would never stop resenting her. Worse than that, *she would leave.* She already had one foot out the door, résumés all over the place.

She'd left Robert and she would leave Gabe, too. He wasn't about to lose one more person, not after he'd lost his dad, his brother, Adelia, even his mother for a while. He was done losing people he loved.

"I'd better get back to it," she said. "See you later?"

"I'll be around."

She walked backward a few yards, holding his gaze, then turned and left, disappearing into the dimness, as she would soon disappear from his life.

Back in the gym, Alex ran up to him, holding out a crumpled STRIKE T-shirt. "All the shirts are gone but this one. The Dobles swiped them when they trashed the gym—to frame us for Feliz Mercado."

"That's possible, certainly. I'll let the detectives know," Gabe said.

Alex grinned, as if he'd solved the crime and justice would be done. Gabe doubted the shirt would change a thing. And justice was elusive at best.

Somebody had set his boys up. Who? And why? Who would want the market torched? Surely Feliz Gallegos would have some ideas. Gabe would talk to him when he took the boys there to offer help with the cleanup.

FELICITY STEPPED INTO the small conference room for her meeting with Tom about the grant, her stomach full of butterflies. She had hope. Carson had told her he understood how media frenzies distorted reality, so she knew he hadn't gotten cold feet. At least not yet.

In case, she'd planned a rebuttal for every possible charge. She studied the sweat-softened index card in her hand:

Formed new community bonds
School is a safe haven
Last chance for at-risk students
Isolated incident
Grant will quadruple our success
Parents united in support

After a bit, she looked at the clock. Ten minutes late. What did that mean?

She had to focus. Not easy since the breakup. She couldn't stop thinking about Gabe, missing him, wishing they could try again. Standing with him yesterday, she'd been dying to throw her arms around his neck to stop the pain. The pain was *so* much worse than she expected. Love was not for sissies. She knew that cold.

She looked at the clock, then at her note cards, then out the window, the clock again. She finally got up and paced the room.

Eventually, forty-five minutes late, Tom appeared. "I'm sorry, Felicity. I was making one last plea."

"A plea?" A chill went down her spine. She dropped into the nearest chair.

He sat across the table from her and gave her a pasted-on, official-looking smile. Uh-oh. "I want you to know how much we appreciate all you've done at Discovery in such a short time. We commend you for your remarkable efforts."

However. She'd heard the word as if he'd said it.

"Unfortunately," he continued, "we will no longer be offering instruction at that location."

"What are you saying? You're closing the school?"

"This is not about you or the quality of your work or—"

"But we got the grant. Next year it will all come together."

Tom raised his hands. "For some time, the board has questioned the value of our alternative schools, especially as state funding cuts went deeper. I'm afraid the recent incidents sealed the school's fate."

"But you know the news coverage distorted what happened."

"I do. And, believe me, I fought for you. But there's nothing to be done."

Her heart plummeted. "What about the grant?"

"We've suggested they redirect the award to another finalist from our district, but it's up to them to choose."

"I don't believe this." Her mind swirled, as if her thoughts were going down some drain and she couldn't catch a single one.

"The good news is you'll still have a job in the Jefferson district. We'd like you to become the new Curriculum Development Associate, working with Dr. Owen Mackey, Assistant Superintendent of Curriculum."

The man was totally out of touch with current curriculum research. Teachers prayed for him to retire. "He wants to hire me? Why? He's never said a word about my system."

"You'll have to discuss that with Owen." His eyes flitted away and she had a terrible thought.

"Wait a minute. You said *new associate.* Was this job *created* for me?"

He cleared his throat. "It's my understanding we needed to expand teacher outreach and since you're now available—"

"Did my uncle tell you to make up a job for me?" Before he could answer, another truth slammed her. "Wait. Did he tell you to hire me in the first place—as principal?"

When he hesitated before answering, she knew she'd guessed right. "I specifically asked you about him and you said he had no role in hiring."

"That was true. Phil asked me to consider you, but once I saw your résumé, I was sold."

"So, you lied? It was all a sham. I got the job because of my uncle?"

"Does it matter? You did great work at Discovery, despite all odds. The important thing is you'll have a job next year."

"Where I'll make copies and count paper clips?"

"That will be between you and Owen."

She felt like a complete fool. The rumors had been correct. She'd gotten the job because of her uncle, not her credentials. She had been a naive cheerleader waving her pom-poms ragged. "Thank you for your time. I have to go." She pushed to her feet, fighting emotion.

He stood and held out a hand. "Now, don't get down on yourself. You did a remarkable job out there."

She struggled to sound professional or at least to *not cry.* "I know you've been my advocate, Tom. Thank you. I'll think about your offer and let you know." On numb legs, she made her way past secretaries and administrators, her shoulders back, her head high, a smile on her face. She would not let them see her sweat…or sob.

WHEN GABE STEPPED from his van, water jug in hand, he could hear someone pummeling the hell out of his punching bag. One of his boys, of course. He was glad. He'd missed the hell out of them since he'd closed STRIKE.

But when he stepped through the gate, he saw it was Felicity, barefoot, but dressed in one of her classy business suits, slugging the bag as though she intended to pulverize it.

God, she looked good to him. The sight of her was like a flipped-on light in a dead-black room, a sip of water after a marathon, a warm coat in a cold rain. "You're really wailing on that bag," he said.

She looked up, startled, her face red, trails of sweat and what he'd bet were tears running down her cheeks. "Yeah…I thought you'd shower before your shift. So we could talk." She fought for breath. Her hair clung to her skull. She looked fragile and exhausted and very hurt.

"Sit before you fall," he said, helping her to the bench. He handed her his jug and she gulped down the contents, handing it back empty.

"They're closing Discovery," she said.

"Damn. I'm sorry."

"The board's been pushing for it and the gang attack gave them the excuse they needed. The grant's gone and the school's closed. I feel so bad for the kids and their parents and my staff. I let them all down." Her mouth twisted as she fought not to cry.

"No, you didn't and they know it. You've turned the school around."

She shook her head, then looked at him, her eyes lost. "You don't know the whole story. My job was a scam from the start. Uncle Phil made Tom hire me. Tom lied to me." Her shoulders heaved as she fought a sob.

"Are you sure about that?"

She nodded. "I've been a fool. Waving my pom-poms while the school….crumbled…all…around…me."

"Your pom-poms?" What was she talking about? He pulled her into his arms and her shoulders shook as she finally let herself cry. When she'd calmed a little he said, "Closing the school is bullshit. The tags weren't done by gangs. And the gym attack was staged, Felicity. I think I've figured it out. I wanted to tell you about it. I think I can explain the arson, too."

"You can?"

"Yeah. But how can they shut down the school? You won the grant. You've got the money. When the truth gets out about the attacks, they won't have an excuse anymore. You have to fight this." He wanted to kick her uncle's ass for using her as a pawn.

She shook her head. "I can't afford to. I need good references for my next job." She heaved the saddest sigh he'd ever heard. "You were right. Sometimes you can't fight city hall."

It burned him up to see her so defeated.

Abruptly, she sat straighter. "Anyway, thanks for listening to me. And for letting me punch the bag. You can guess whose face I pictured, too."

"I think I can."

"It's time to move on, I get that, but it's just... The teachers were so excited." She puddled up again. "I can't stand thinking about the kids. This is so unfair to them."

"They'll survive. We grow up tough in the barrio, remember?"

She tried to smile, but failed. "Tell me about what you figured out."

"Like I said, Coop verified the tags were done by amateurs, not by a gang graf crew. Then, while we were cleaning up the gym, I overheard the guys saying they'd heard that Mad Dog ordered a beat-down for Li'l B over some unsanctioned riff. I figured it was the arson."

"Li'l B burned down the store on his own?"

"Exactly. Very risky. Gangs run like the military—

strict hierarchy and unquestioning obedience. A gang chief needs total control over any gang actions."

"Why would Li'l B do that?"

"Good question. So Tyrell heard from his cousin that Li'l B and his family were moving out of their crappy apartment into a bigger place in a nicer building—Park View Apartments, which happens to be owned by Leonard Lancaster."

"Yeah?" she said, frowning. "And?"

"Why would Lancaster rent a nice place to dead-broke tenants?"

"As payment for the arson?"

"That's what I'm thinking."

"Why would Lancaster want Feliz Mercado destroyed?"

"I asked Feliz Gallegos the same question. Turns out there's a developer putting together an assemblage to build a big office complex. Feliz was the last holdout on the block. And he's behind on his insurance."

"So is Lancaster part of the assemblage?"

"No. And that puzzled me. Then I talked with Dave, your moonlighting vice principal. A while back, he was trying to sell one of his properties to the same developers for their base of operations, but they only wanted to rent and, in passing, mentioned Lancaster's strip mall."

"Exactly. And it's tied up by Discovery with a seven-year lease."

"Which means the only way to get rid of the school is to convince the district it's too dangerous, so the district breaks the lease."

"So that's why Lancaster's always going on in the press about the neighborhood being overrun by gangs."

"You got it. So he gets Li'l B to use toys to mess up the mural—or maybe that was Li'l B's idea. They trash the gym—more gang activity—and steal the shirts to set up my guys for the arson."

"With the store gone, the developers get their assemblage."

"Discovery moves out, using the destruction as an excuse, and Lancaster can lease to the developers for lots more cash. They'll improve the property, so Lancaster can make a killing when he sells it, once the area gets upgraded."

"I never trusted that man."

"He's just a forward-thinking businessman."

"And an arsonist. But how can we prove it? You know he's covered his tracks."

"We need the culprits to confess."

"Li'l B? Why would he do that?"

"Because he'd rather be in jail than dead in the ground. Li'l B got a beat-down for the unsanctioned job, but it would have been much worse if Mad Dog knew Li'l B got paid and didn't cut Mad Dog in. Robbing the *jefe?* That's a death sentence."

"Really?"

"If I'm right, Li'l B will beg for jail to keep me from talking to Mad Dog. So Li'l B rolls on Lancaster and justice is served. Our boys are free of all charges."

"But you have to convince Li'l B to confess."

"That's the plan. Wish me luck."

"You don't need luck. You know how kids think. You know how to reach them. You'll make it happen. I know you will."

"My boys are innocent. I have to prove it."

They looked at each other for a few seconds. "I'm sorry about your job," he said finally.

"Me, too." She seemed on the verge of crumpling again.

"Ah, Cici," he said, pulling her into his arms. He breathed in the orange scent of her hair, her candy smell, wanting with everything in him to make this right for her. But how?

He was watching her walk away when it hit him.

She couldn't fight city hall, but *he* could. And get the parents, teachers and neighbors Felicity had gotten to care about Discovery to fight right beside him.

CHAPTER SEVENTEEN

AT THE PODIUM, Felicity looked out at the enormous crowd and wall of media that had appeared for the unveiling of Alex's repainted mural. She was puzzled by the turnout, especially all the cameras and reporters. She'd emailed a news release about the new graffiti-resistant paint, but that would hardly draw a crowd. Besides, it was the middle of May, so the late afternoon was hot as blazes, even in the shade.

She would keep it brief, which would keep her emotions in check, too.

Near the stage Gabe shot her a thumbs-up. What was he so delighted about? He'd been acting cheerful all week, actually grinning half the time. She still missed him like crazy. Had he gotten over her that easily?

He had to be happy about Alex, who stood beside her now, looking solemn and proud, waiting for his mural to be unveiled.

As Gabe had predicted, Li'l B had confessed to the police about the arson, and they expected Lancaster to be taken into custody any day. Coop had convinced the officer Alex had assaulted to drop the charges against him, and due to mitigating circumstances, he'd gotten probation and community service, no jail time.

Alex had shown new maturity since his arrest. He'd helped Feliz Gallegos set up his shop in a small rented space and worked for free there.

"You ready?" she asked him now. When he nodded, she faced the crowd.

"Welcome," she said into the microphone. "Thank you all for coming. Your support means a great deal. Our school will soon close its doors, but we hope this mural will bring beauty to the neighborhood for years to come."

She swallowed hard, steeling herself against the emotions that rushed through her. She would miss the school and everyone involved with it so very much. The week had been torture, as people expressed their regrets and thanked her for what she'd done. She'd been especially touched by Dave, who'd told her she'd taught him about leadership, even getting choked up.

"I want to thank the students who volunteered their time to repaint the mural, and especially Alex, for creating it in the first place. Thank you." She looked down at him and he gave her a quick smile.

She turned back to the audience. "I want to tell you that I've loved working with you and for you...even for such a short time...and I..."

The urge to cry hit so hard, she turned away to cough, as if she had a tickle in her throat. She forced herself to focus on the positives, on moving on. She had an interview next week in Fresno and a good chance at the job. She'd be implementing her system in a school district, which was what she wanted to do, so it was all to the good. Moving on, making progress.

Still, her heart was so heavy about Discovery. It was wrong to close the school. Should she have fought harder? Done more?

It was too late for regrets. She forced a smile on her face and returned to the microphone. "Enough from me. A picture is worth a thousand words," she said. She raised her arm, signaling Dave and the custodian on the roof behind her to release the tarp.

She heard the thump of the tarp landing, then a huge gasp from the crowd. They looked surprised. Then they cheered loudly.

She turned to look at the wall. It was changed. She hadn't gotten a glimpse of it, since the students had covered it every day.

"I added shit," Alex said to her, grinning. "It's your surprise." He took the microphone from her. "I'm gonna run down the new stuff," he said into it and strutted to the wall. "Stuff about this school had to be told." He motioned at a new section. It was a man and a woman slugging a punching bag covered with words—*greed, gangs, violence, hate, bigotry, ignorance, anger.* They looked a lot like Felicity and Gabe. Beneath it, Alex had written KO the Ugly so the Beauty Can Win.

"Good people make a school good," Alex said.

She saw that he'd also added Gabe's tattoo of the thorn-stemmed rose, with the words *De la espina, crece la flor,* which was pretty much what she would say about Alex himself.

The slogan was different, too. Instead of *my land, my people, my future* in Spanish it said, *my people, my school, my future* and he'd included the English translation, as well.

"So, what I'm puttin' out is that this school is our future...and that's no bullshit." His voice got loud at the end, with an edge of excitement. She felt movement through the crowd. Gabe sprinted around the side of the building.

"So we can't let it go down in flames," Alex said loudly. "It's our lives here on the line. Our futures, man. We only get one future."

"Save our school…save our school…save our school." The chant came from the side of the school, where a line of kids and adults with picket signs emerged—STRIKE fighters in their T-shirts, along with their parents, all yelling the words.

What was going on? She reached for the microphone, but Alex fended her off. "Sorry, Ms. Spencer, but you gotta step back."

People were lining up to get onto the stage—Beatrice first, carrying a stack of papers. "We kept it a secret," she whispered to Felicity, "so the district couldn't blame you."

Alex handed Beatrice the microphone, then jumped off the stage to join his friends. Meanwhile, people crowded the stage—Detective Carter, Feliz Gallegos, Adelia Flor, even Mrs. Snyder, the woman Alex had delivered groceries to. Gabe came last.

"Was this your idea?" she asked him.

"I just stoked the fire you lit." He nodded out at the crowd. "It was easy."

Felicity squeezed his arm, unable to not touch him. She noticed at the edge of the crowd, people held bouquets of helium balloons in Discovery's colors of purple and gold. "Wow." It was all she could say. "Wow."

Beatrice spoke into the microphone. "About two months ago, I would have been happy to have Ms. Spencer fired and this school shut down. Today, I want with all my heart to keep them both. These two showed me the light." She motioned at Gabe and Felicity. "Ms. Spencer brought new energy, new hope and new ideas to this school. We need her. Desperately."

Applause rolled through the crowd and there were shouts of agreement.

"And we need Discovery. Certain interests have lied about our neighborhood, made our kids out to be thugs, for their own gain, for under-the-table deals. Today that ends."

The crowd roared.

"Discovery parents raise a united voice to demand the Jefferson district keep Discovery open next year and for many years to come." She lifted up the stack of papers. "These petitions have been signed by ninety-five percent of Discovery parents. I will take them to the school board, along with the balloons you're being handed. On the card tied to the string, jot down what Discovery has meant to you and your children and our community. We will fill the boardroom with our petitions and our hope-filled balloons."

Applause and whistles filled the air.

Felicity's heart lifted like the balloons bobbing among the crowd now. No matter what happened, no matter what the district, or her uncle, said, she knew she'd done something good here—no, something *great.* That was what mattered, perception be damned.

One by one, the speakers took the microphone to thank her and Gabe and Discovery. Coop talked about the school being a safe place from gangs, about Gabe keeping STRIKE fighters on the straight and narrow. He even said that Mad Dog had been angry about the mural tags and promised to protect the new one from harm. That could have been total BS, but the crowd loved it and reporters scribbled it down.

Adelia spoke about her mural project. Mrs. Snyder said how much she and her neighbors had come to depend on the Discovery Ambassadors. Felicity could hardly see for the tears in her eyes.

"And finally, you need to hear from Coach Cassidy," Beatrice said. "Let me clear up an ugly rumor going around. Gabriel Cassidy is not a gangster and he does not teach kids to street fight. Sure, he's scary-looking with the tattoos and muscles and all, but looks can be deceiving." She turned to Gabe. "We know you're just a big brown teddy bear...with a really sexy earring."

She turned back to the laughing crowd. "Coach Cassidy teaches our kids to be strong, to know what they stand for and to stand up for it."

The crowd called out supportive words.

"Because of STRIKE, my daughter treats her teachers and me with more respect. She tries harder in school. And she can deliver a mean snap kick, too."

Everyone laughed. In the front row, Bethany beamed.

Gabe took Beatrice's place at the microphone, so strong and tall and imposing. Gabe hated politics, but he'd set this up for Felicity. She loved him so much. How could she give him up?

"My father, Xavier Ochoa, was a gangbanger, shot dead when I was ten, my brother seven, my baby sisters just infants. Because of him, because of what I saw, I hated gangs with all my heart. I stayed clear, studied hard, tried to set an example for my little brother, Robert. I lectured him, I yelled at him, I watched over him as best I could. But it wasn't enough to keep him from being killed in a gang fight when he was sixteen."

There was a quiet wave of sympathy from the crowd.

"I didn't tell you that for your pity, but to show you how tough it is for our kids. It feels like a fixed fight—no way out but down for the count." He looked out at the crowd. He had them in the palm of his hand.

"I wanted to do something for kids like Robert, so I created STRIKE. To give them a way to become so strong in themselves they didn't need a gang to get respect. They work hard, my boys. They stay in school and out of trouble. I'm damned proud of them." He looked out at where they all stood, hands down, signs braced on the ground, listening to him, eyes burning with devotion.

"I'm proud of the Discovery kids who took my classes. They've put their all into the workouts, the girls as much as the boys, often more. Don't let anyone tell you that girls can't punch as hard or kick as high as any boy, right, Kadisha?" He smiled at where she stood with her crew of fighter girls.

"You've all read that some of my fighters were in a street brawl. Yeah. They were. But they were set up, goaded into fighting by an unsavory individual who wanted to frame them for a crime they would never have committed—the arson of Feliz Mercado." He paused, while the crowd murmured. "Read tomorrow's paper. It will answer all your questions."

Leonard must have been arrested. She was so glad.

"So I shut down STRIKE, thinking I'd failed, that my training hadn't helped, that it was a joke and a sham." He swallowed hard. Then he turned and looked straight at Felicity. "This woman tried to tell me I was wrong, that I shouldn't give up on myself or my boys. She was right." More quietly and just to her, he said, "You were right about a lot of things."

She smiled, her heart full and spilling over.

"So I'm going to open up STRIKE gym again," he said to the crowd. "As soon as I can find a space I can afford. If you have a spare garage, let me know." He gave a soft chuckle. "And when I find it, I hope you'll trust me enough to let me train your kids."

"I've got space!" Adelia yelled from behind Gabe. "Clear out the junk in the storage area in the gallery and you can rent it cheap."

Gabe grinned. "Then I guess STRIKE is back."

The STRIKE fighters went nuts and the crowd cheered

The protest ended and Beatrice and her PTO friends took the balloons and the petitions off to the district office.

It was a grand gesture, for sure, but Felicity knew the district would simply wait out the furor and keep with the plan. But for this moment, surrounded by all these people who supported her, she was willing to hope right along with them. "Thank you, Gabe," she said to him. "For believing in me. For fighting for me."

"You've fought for me from the beginning… It was the least I could do for you."

They held each other's gaze, a million hopes and regrets flying between them, the connection still there, stronger than ever, it seemed. They hadn't given up on Discovery. How had they given up on each other?

She started to speak and so did Gabe, but reporters descended on them with a million questions, so they had no choice but to break apart once more.

TEN DAYS AFTER THE RALLY, and a week before the end of school, Felicity held her office phone to her ear, stunned to her core. If only she hadn't boxed up her desk toys. She needed something to do with her hands.

Tom had just told her that the school board had decided to keep Discovery open. Even better, United Giving was still giving Discovery the grant.

"Felicity? You still there?" Tom asked.

"I'm here. Yes. Stunned, but here." She was thrilled… except she'd accepted the Fresno job yesterday.

"There's one problem," he said, clearing his throat. "We can't have you as principal."

"Oh." That was a slap in the face, after all she'd done.

"Between you and me, the board wants payback for the public humiliation. No matter what I say, they insist on blaming you for 'bullying, blackmail and pedagogical extortion'—yes, the school-board president really said that, the pompous ass. So that's the price of Discovery's survival. I'm sorry."

"It's all right. Just as well, I guess, since I took the Fresno job." It was the next step in her career plan, but still…

"You can be proud that you laid a solid foundation for Dave Scott to build on."

"Dave's taking over?"

"He seemed the wisest choice. He's been working with you on the changes and I hate to throw a new person in after so much turmoil."

"He'll do fine," she said. But what about the grant? Would he know how to maximize it? Had he fully committed to the school? Her stomach churned.

"If it matters, Phil said he was damned impressed with you. He called you a *fireball.* He likes fireballs. It's his favorite compliment."

"That's something." When she'd called to thank her stepdad for the bail loan, she'd learned the sorry details that had led to her uncle giving her the job. When she'd had to close her business, her stepdad had offered her money to hold her over for a while. To reassure him that she would find work, she'd emailed him the list of places where she'd applied. Her mother had noticed Jefferson district on the list and broke decades of bitter silence to beg her brother to give her "poor, unemployed daughter a job so she could sleep at night."

Frustrating, but her mother had meant well, so Felicity had kept her cool about it.

She finished her call with Tom and looked around her office. She'd been emptying it out, picturing it razed to the ground after she left, but now she realized Dave would be sitting right here next year instead of her.

There was a tap on her door and Dave stuck his head in. "Is it safe?" he asked. "Tom told you the news?"

She smiled. "It's safe. I packed up all my desk toys so I have nothing to throw at your head."

"I'm sorry, Felicity," he said, looking sheepish. "It was Tom's idea."

"I'm happy for you. You'll do a good job."

"I intend to. Though I've been reading through the grant you wrote. It's pretty intimidating." He shifted his weight, foot to foot. "All eyes will be on me."

"I'm a phone call away."

"Yeah. About that. I'd like to pay you as a consultant to work on the plans this summer with me. Whatever time you can spare." He looked so eager, so different from the smug jerk she'd first met.

"If I can work around my new job, I'd like to help."

"Good." He looked relieved. "I didn't much appreciate that trip to the woodshed you took me on, but you made me see I'd let my priorities slip. So thanks, chief. And I mean *chief* in the respectful sense."

"That's how I heard it."

He left and she sat there, thinking about the news. Discovery was back, thanks to Gabe's efforts on her behalf. He'd fought for her when she'd given up. She had to thank him for that.

She noticed the boxing poster sticking up from the trash can she'd been filling. She unrolled it and read the quote:

Champions are built, not born.

The drive comes from inside, fed by dreams, fueled by desire.

Champions fight harder, longer, faster than all the rest.

They have the moves, yeah, but what counts is the heart.

A champion's heart beats a rhythm only he hears.

El corazón es todo—the heart is all.

That was Gabe to a T. He was a champion. Sure, he'd stalled a couple times, but he kept fighting for what he believed in—his family, his fighters and her.

She'd accused him of giving up, of limiting himself, settling for less. But that hadn't been fair of her. Gabe had fought against tough odds and he'd made a life for himself that worked.

Who was she to judge him?

Gabe believed love wasn't enough to outweigh their differences. But what if their differences made them stronger? Hadn't they saved Discovery together? With Gabe's street smarts and her political finesse, his practicality and her energy? Together they were stronger.

So what if they were different? Differences enhanced you. They didn't have to divide you. It was all in how you saw it, right?

Gabe thought she was too ambitious, that she'd never be content. She'd *had* to be driven to get here. But that didn't mean she would let ambition interfere with happiness when she found it. He hadn't been fair, either.

Her job in Fresno would be the next step on her path, but was there another route? A way that would allow her to be with the man she loved?

If he would have her…

Her heart began to race and she sucked in air, almost dizzy with excitement. She had the beginnings of a plan. Then she would have to convince Gabe she was right.

She didn't intend to take no for an answer. She could be pretty *terco* herself, after all.

GABE PUSHED THE WEIGHT BENCH into place in the half-cleared gym. A noise made him turn. Alex stood in the doorway. "We got Discovery back, Coach. We won."

"Yeah? You're kidding! How'd you hear?"

"Bethany's mom found out."

"That's great." His heart lifted. "Yeah. Damn." The effort had paid off. They'd fought city hall and won. Felicity would have her job.

And would she have him? Electricity flew through him. This was it. A second chance. He would not blow it this time. He gave Alex a high five, then noticed his face. "What's up? You don't look that happy."

"They fired Ms. Spencer for being a troublemaker. It was because she defended STRIKE. That's on me, why she lost her job." He looked so anguished.

Gabe wiped the bench with a rag. "Sit." Alex sat. Working with Felicity these weeks, he'd learned a thing or two about how school politics worked. He could pretty much guess what had happened.

"They fired her to save face, Alex. Not because of you or me or STRIKE. They had to give us the school because of the public pressure, so they fired her to flex their muscle. It's bullshit, but that's how the world rolls."

"Yeah?" Alex looked puzzled.

"Think of it like this. We fought them and won, but they can't let us have a KO, so they're taking a round on technical."

He nodded. "I guess." He looked up at Gabe. "Bethany's mom called Ms. Spencer to do another protest, but she said no, that she had a better job already. Can you believe she said that? Why doesn't she want to stay?"

"That's complicated, Alex. Ms. Spencer did a lot for Discovery. She set the school on the right path, but there are other schools that need her ideas. It's like she graduated. Like you'll graduate from Discovery next year and move on to high school—to a bigger challenge."

Alex studied him, absorbing the idea, not happy, but feeling less abandoned, Gabe could tell.

He thought about what he'd said. It was true. Felicity did have a lot to offer schools. Who was he to tell her to slow down, stay put, limit herself? He'd been an ass.

"What about you, Coach? Can you bring STRIKE back to Discovery?"

"Depends on what happens with the loan I applied for. I want this to be a full gym with a solid program. If I can work it, I'd like to offer classes at schools, but that'll take time." He'd put together a business proposal he was pretty proud of. Felicity had pushed him out of his rut for good.

"Yeah," Alex said, drooping.

"You've always got a spot in my gym, Alex. That won't change. I gotta stick around, see the decent man you're gonna become." Gabe squeezed the kid's shoulder and Alex managed a grin. "Now make yourself useful and scrub down these mats. Then take ten minutes on the speed bag."

Left to his own thoughts, disappointment hit Gabe hard. For that moment when he thought she'd be staying, he'd felt alive again. Damn. He loved Felicity more than ever. He wanted her in his arms, in his bed, wanted to hear her relentless talk, like a stream bubbling by, from which he snatched smiles and surprises.

She'd made him walk lighter, made him forget the sad past, given him the drive to go for more. She'd changed him.

Even his mother had seen it.

The night of the rally, his family had crowded around the TV watching the news stories with him. His mother had followed the coverage since the festival and then the mural destruction. She'd seemed impressed by how much Felicity cared about the school in the sound bites that appeared on the news. *Maybe she learned her lesson,* his mom had mused.

After the rally story ended, his mother had studied him. "I've never seen you stand so tall or sound, so strong and sure. They loved you. You could run for mayor or governor. Whatever you wanted. You're so different now. What happened to you?"

"Cici, Mom. Cici happened to me. She made me want more." His throat went tight and he saw Giorgio was looking at him with sympathy.

For once his sisters were quiet, watching and listening closely.

His mother narrowed those sharp blue eyes of hers and snapped, "And you let her go? Just like that?"

It was almost funny, except it hurt too much.

You let her go?

What the hell was wrong with him? So what if she moved to California? He could drive. He could fly. Maybe he'd be ready to move in a year or two. Or, hell, maybe she'd get some world-changing job in Arizona.

In the meantime, he'd do all he could to make her happy, do every ridiculous thing on her ridiculous list—eat candy jewelry, ride roller coasters, go salsa dancing. He still had those stupid lessons hanging over his head.

He'd see her tonight, tell her how he felt, dish out all the romantic drivel he could scrape from the bottom of his Latin soul. He'd fought for her school and for her job and now he'd fight for her heart.

"Coach? You okay?" Alex asked, looking at him standing there as if he was about to take down an opponent.

"Not yet, but I will be soon."

HE WAS ON HIS WAY to Felicity's place that night when dispatch came through with a fare. "I've got somewhere to be," he said.

"You're it on this one." The dispatcher gave him the address. It was a tough neighborhood on west McDowell most drivers avoided.

"After that, I'm off the clock." He pulled up to the address and saw it was a flower shop. Then he saw Felicity dash out the door, her arms full of snapdragons, a grocery sack hanging from a wrist thick with candy bracelets.

"Did I surprise you?" she said, jumping in beside him, totally swamping him in the smell of candy and flowers.

"You did. You always do." And he loved it. He grinned so big he thought his cheeks might split right open. "I heard about Discovery. Congratulations."

"You already know? That's what I wanted to tell you. Except the bad news is—"

"That you're not principal. I'm sorry about that, but you do know it's only bullshit politics, right?"

"I'm fine with it. Like you said, I know what I did and that's the most important thing. Who cares what they think?"

"Exactly."

"So I want to celebrate. And we need to talk."

"Uh-oh," he said, still grinning. "Should I be nervous?"

"No more than I am," she said, her eyes lit with excitement. "I can't decide where to go. The Buttes? Your gym? I'd love to see it."

"I know the perfect place." He drove her to Encanto

Park and parked near the Enchanted Island, where the carnival rides lit the sky. He led her to a picnic table. There was a warm breeze, and the smell of grass and cotton candy came to them. In the background, the merry-go-round's calliope jingled.

"This is perfect," she said, smiling at him. "Another place I forgot about."

She put the vase of flowers on the table and handed him a soda and a small bag of chips.

"So what are we celebrating?" he asked, tapping his can against hers.

"Discovery, of course, but also my new job. I start as soon as school's out."

"That's quick." His heart sank at how happy she seemed to be leaving him. Maybe she'd moved on. Maybe the long-distance idea was lame. "You need help taking apart that futon?" he asked.

"No need. I won't be moving." She gulped soda, then beamed at him, her lips wet with bubbles. "I'm taking the fake job."

"You're what?"

"Yep. Uncle Phil made Tom create a curriculum job for me. It's bogus, but so was me being principal at Discovery and look what I did with that."

"You're staying?" He couldn't wrap his mind around that. He kept watching her hair float and her eyes shine.

"I'll make the job what I want it to be. I got the idea when Dave asked me to consult on the grant—he's the new principal. Other principals have asked me about my system already. So I'll work with them."

"Will that be enough for you?"

"It's a challenge. It's reaching more kids. My boss might give me trouble."

"Only if he underestimates you. Make him one of your deals and he won't be able to resist."

She laughed.

"The Fresno job was more what you had in mind, wasn't it?"

"Sure, but I'm not just a megalomaniac with an insatiable need to achieve." She paused. "I'm also a woman in love. I want to be with you, Gabe. I want to try harder and make it work." Her eyes searched his, hopeful and fearful at once.

"Yeah. That's what I want, too." Damn, he was happy. "I have to say I'm glad you're staying here. Round-trip economy to Fresno is six hundred a pop."

"You checked out flights?"

"I need you in my life, Cici. Whatever I have to do to make that happen."

"I feel the same way. I was wrong to push you. If you're happy mowing lawns, then mow lawns."

"I needed a shove. I'm applying for a loan for my gym. If you check the backseat, you'll see a college catalogue. I might take a business class if there's not too much bullshit involved."

"It's your life. Your decision. I had no right to judge."

"You wanted the best for me. I see that now. I figure that having to stay strong for my family after Robert died got me into the habit of keeping up barriers. Fighting stance, you know? Fists up, elbows in, chin down. All the damn time, even when I didn't need it anymore."

He touched her cheek, ran his fingers through her hair, so glad to have her warm gaze on his face. "You got through to me. You showed me tough's not the only way to be, that there's room to be tender. Look at Alex. Between the two of us we've got him straightened out."

"For now," she said. "Who knows with teenagers?"

"Damn I've missed you. My chest felt like an open, sucking wound."

"And you claim you're not a sentimental Latino."

"I want you in my life—with your candy smell and your flyaway hair and your chirpy voice and all that damn *hope.* You're right. You have to be tough to hope." His voice shook with intensity. "When Robert died, I think I lost that. You made me remember all I'd wanted, all I'd once believed in, all the doors I'd shut."

He got off the bench and pulled her into his arms.

GABE'S WORDS WASHED THROUGH Felicity like warm honey. "I still wish I had an instruction manual. I don't know how this is supposed to work. And I know I'm not your soul mate, but—"

"People aren't born soul mates. Maybe they *become* soul mates. Grow into it, you know?"

"Yeah?"

"You have to accept the differences, learn from them. I figure when you trust each other, you don't have to tag every inch of your neighborhood."

"Interesting way to put it."

"Hey, you can take the homeboy out of the barrio, but you can't take the barrio out of the homeboy."

"I wouldn't have it any other way." Her heart was filled to overflowing. She put her hand on his chest, so happy to be in his arms again.

Gabe ran a thumb across the candy bracelets she'd twined there. "You've got quite a wad here."

"I got carried away," she said.

"You always do. That's one of your charms." He smiled, then looked at the flowers on the table. "Do you want to take those to the cemetery?"

"These are for us tonight," she said. "Do you think Robert's happy for us?"

"Absolutely. He brought us together. Gave us this gift."

"I think so, too." She kissed him, soft and slow, relishing this moment. She knew enough about love to know she was in it. "What should we do now?"

"You know you've racked up one hell of a cab bill. I have some ideas for how you can start paying me back. They all involve you naked."

"I can't wait," she said as his lips met hers, the taste of candy on her tongue, the feel of forever in her heart.

* * * * *

HEART & HOME

Heartwarming romances where love can happen right when you least expect it.

COMING NEXT MONTH

AVAILABLE FEBRUARY 14, 2012

#1758 BETWEEN LOVE AND DUTY
A Brother's Word
Janice Kay Johnson

#1759 MARRY ME, MARINE
In Uniform
Rogenna Brewer

#1760 FROM THE BEGINNING
Tracy Wolff

#1761 JUST DESSERTS
Too Many Cooks?
Jeannie Watt

#1762 ON COMMON GROUND
School Ties
Tracy Kelleher

#1763 A TEXAS CHANCE
The MacAllisters
Jean Brashear

New York Times and *USA TODAY* bestselling author Maya Banks presents book three in her miniseries PREGNANCY & PASSION.

TEMPTED BY HER INNOCENT KISS

Available March 2012 from Harlequin Desire!

There came a time in a man's life when he knew he was well and truly caught. Devon Carter stared down at the diamond ring nestled in velvet and acknowledged that this was one such time. He snapped the lid closed and shoved the box into the breast pocket of his suit.

He had two choices. He could marry Ashley Copeland and fulfill his goal of merging his company with Copeland Hotels, thus creating the largest, most exclusive line of resorts in the world, or he could refuse and lose it all.

Put in that light, there wasn't much he could do except pop the question.

The doorman to his Manhattan high-rise apartment hurried to open the door as Devon strode toward the street. He took a deep breath before ducking into his car, and the driver pulled into traffic.

Tonight was the night. All of his careful wooing, the countless dinners, kisses that started brief and casual and became more breathless—all a lead-up to tonight. Tonight his seduction of Ashley Copeland would be complete, and then he'd ask her to marry him.

He shook his head as the absurdity of the situation hit him for the hundredth time. Personally, he thought William Copeland was crazy for forcing his daughter down Devon's throat.

Ashley was a sweet enough girl, but Devon had no desire

to marry anyone.

William had other plans. He'd told Devon that Ashley had no head for the family business. She was too softhearted, too naive. So he'd made Ashley part of the deal. The catch? Ashley wasn't to know of it. Which meant Devon was stuck playing stupid games.

Ashley was supposed to think this was a grand love match. She was a starry-eyed woman who preferred her animal-rescue foundation over board meetings, charts and financials for Copeland Hotels.

If she ever found out the truth, she wouldn't take it well.

And hell, he couldn't blame her.

But no matter the reason for his proposal, before the night was over, she'd have no doubts that she belonged to him.

What will happen when Devon marries Ashley?
Find out in Maya Banks's passionate new novel
TEMPTED BY HER INNOCENT KISS
Available March 2012 from Harlequin Desire!

HDEXP0312

Harlequin
Presents